Shaken deeply, Pete backed away.

The look of love on Tess Ramsey's face as she tended the helpless Vietnamese child had suddenly gripped him, held him, as nothing in his entire life ever had.

He scowled, experiencing a mixture of pain, hope, anger and need. It was a stupid array of feelings churning within him, but he wanted to be in Tess's arms, being stroked by her caring hands, seeing that look in her eyes for him.

Muttering a curse under his breath, he stalked to the door of the hut and stared out blindly, unable to sort through what was going on inside him.

Why should this particular scene get to him?

Why now?

Dear Reader,

Welcome to Silhouette **Special Edition** . . . welcome to romance. Each month, Silhouette **Special Edition** publishes six novels with you in mind—stories of love and life, tales that you can identify with—romance with that little "something special" added in.

And this month has some wonderful stories in store for you. Lindsay McKenna's *One Man's War* continues her saga that is set in Vietnam during the sixties—MOMENTS OF GLORY. These powerful tales will capture you from the first page until the last! And we have an exciting debut this month—Debbie Macomber begins her new series, THOSE MANNING MEN. Don't miss the first book—*Marriage of Inconvenience*—Rich and Jamie's story.

Rounding out March are more stories by some of your favorite authors: Mary Curtis, Erica Spindler, Pamela Toth and Pat Warren. It's a wonderful month for love!

In each Silhouette **Special Edition** novel, we're dedicated to bringing you the romances that you dream about—stories that will delight as well as bring a tear to the eye. And that's what Silhouette **Special Edition** is all about—special books by special authors for special readers!

I hope you enjoy this book and all of the stories to come!

Sincerely,

Tara Gavin
Senior Editor
Silhouette Books

LINDSAY McKENNA
One Man's War

Silhouette Special Edition

Published by Silhouette Books New York

America's Publisher of Contemporary Romance

Dedicated to the POWs and MIAs
of the Vietnam War—those who did return
and those who have yet to return

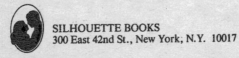

SILHOUETTE BOOKS
300 East 42nd St., New York, N.Y. 10017

ONE MAN'S WAR

Copyright © 1992 by Lindsay McKenna

ISBN: 0-373-09727-1

First Silhouette Books printing March 1992

Printed in the U.S.A.

Books by Lindsay McKenna

Silhouette Special Edition

Captive of Fate #82
*Heart of the Eagle #338
*A Measure of Love #377
*Solitaire #397
Heart of the Tiger #434
+ A Question of Honor #529
+ No Surrender #535
+ Return of a Hero #541
Come Gentle the Dawn #568
+ Dawn of Valor #649
°No Quarter Given #667
°The Gauntlet #673
°Under Fire #679
‡Ride the Tiger #721
‡One Man's War #727

Silhouette Desire

Chase the Clouds #75
Wilderness Passion #134
Too Near the Fire #165
Texas Wildcat #184
Red Tail #208

Silhouette Intimate Moments

Love Me Before Dawn #44

Silhouette Books

Silhouette Christmas Stories 1990
"Always and Forever"

*Kincaid Trilogy
+ Love and Glory Series
°Women of Glory Series
‡Moments of Glory Series

LINDSAY McKENNA

spent three years serving her country as a meteorologist in the U.S. Navy, so much of her knowledge about the military people and practices featured in her novels comes from direct experience. In addition, she spends a great deal of time researching each book, whether it be at the Pentagon or at military bases, extensively interviewing key personnel. She views the military as her second family and hopes that her novels will help dispel the "unfeeling machine" image that haunts it, allowing readers glimpses of the flesh-and-blood people who comprise the services.

Chapter One

Da Nang, Vietnam
April 1, 1965

Hunting time! Captain Pete Mallory savored the thought as he drove the Marine Corps jeep down the heavily potholed red dirt road. Mentally, he rubbed his hands together as he savored his next target: Tess Ramsey, the younger sister of his commanding officer, Major Gib Ramsey.

The village of Le My drew into view as the jeep bumped along. A huge patchwork quilt of rice paddies and dikes paralleled the road, with the village spreading out to his right. Pete ignored the hundred or so thatched huts and the Vietnamese families who lived in them. He was on a mission, his target a woman he'd never even seen. Of course, he had to remind himself, she *was* the sister of his CO, so he'd have to watch his step.

He grinned. Hell, with a little fancy footwork, his famous smile and a few clever lines, he'd have Tess Ramsey in his arms—and bed—in no time. And that's exactly where he wanted this mysterious woman whom he'd been hearing about off and on since he'd been assigned to Da Nang six months ago.

He'd already tired of chasing the local Vietnamese women, who, in Pete's opinion, were lovely but offered no satisfaction to his hunter's instincts. He hungered for a challenge—a woman who was less willing, more of a moving target. And from what he'd heard about the independent Tess, who worked in the field as an agricultural advisor, she might be just what he was looking for. Pete braked the jeep in a cloud of reddish dust and got out. His black flight boots were covered with dirt, he noticed, scowling momentarily. When he got back to his barracks in Marble Mountain, he'd have to have the Vietnamese boy spit shine them all over again.

Then, remembering his mission, he began to hum to himself. Thrusting his hands into the pockets of his one-piece green flight suit, his utility cap drawn so low that the bill nearly touched his nose, Pete sauntered into the village. He had the perfect excuse: Gib Ramsey had sent him to find Tess and bring her back to a small officers' party at the Marine Air Group squadron's headquarters, Marble Mountain, tonight.

Pete had made it a point to learn enough Vietnamese to be able to swap and haggle with the natives. He entered the village, situated on a flat piece of real estate surrounded by trees and lush jungle growth that created a sort of protective wall. He stopped and scratched his head. Who to ask?

Children, naked or wearing only tattered shorts, played throughout the village. Cooking pots hung over small, smoky fires here and there with *mamasans*, clothed in black and wearing pointed bamboo hats, laboring at them. The men were out in the rice paddies plowing behind their harnessed water buffalo. He didn't see many young or middle-aged women. They must be in the rice paddies, too, he surmised.

An old man, his face pinched and weathered, hobbled up to Pete and gazed at him with assessing brown eyes.

Pete hadn't gotten over the fact that the Vietnamese were such a small, slender people. The old man, his chest sunken, his ribs showing clearly beneath several shell necklaces, tilted his head in birdlike fashion. A bright red cotton skirt covered him to his knees, and his large, callused feet stuck out below. The whole pictured seemed comical, and Pete grinned. The old man would never know he was laughing at him, he thought.

"Hey, *papa san,* where's Tess Ramsey? I'm looking for Tess. Where's she at?"

The man blinked.

Pete rolled his eyes and threw his hands on his hips. "You don't understand a damned word I'm saying, do you? Why can't you people learn English as a second language like the rest of the world?"

"Tess?"

Pete opened his mouth, wanting to take back what he'd just said. Obviously the old codger did understand him. Heat nettled Pete's cheeks. Then he shrugged off his guilty conscience. "Yeah, *papa san.* Tess Ramsey. I'm looking for her."

Lifting his branchlike arm, his flesh dark from decades under the tropical sun, the old man pointed toward a rice paddy in the distance. "Missy Tess is with our women out there. You go find her. She like a tall bamboo reed. You will know which one she is."

"Yeah . . . I will." Inwardly fuming because the old man hadn't seemed to take offense at his insulting words, Pete turned on his heel and aimed himself toward the paddies. If anything, he'd seen laughter in the old man's eyes. Pete couldn't bear to be caught off guard by anyone or anything. Irritated, he lengthened his long stride. Then he forced himself to focus on his hunting instincts, pushing away the incident with the Vietnamese man. He couldn't waste his time worrying about some peasant's opinion—now was the time to make a damn good impression on Tess Ramsey.

Tess smiled warmly at the four Vietnamese women standing respectfully around her.

She stood four feet from a huge dry dirt dike, up to her ankles in murky brown water, as she talked to them, slender rice shots surrounding her.

The overhead sun was bright, as always, but Tess's bamboo hat effectively shaded not only her face, but her shoulders and upper back as well. It was, in her opinion, one of the most brilliant designs the people of the Far East had created.

She'd just finished explaining some rice fertilization techniques when she heard her name being called from a distance. Tess looked in the direction of the sound. The four women also lifted their heads.

Coming along the paddy complex's western dike wall was a marine in a dark green flight suit. Tess knew from the uniform that he was a pilot. But she could tell, even at a distance, that it wasn't her brother, Gib. Tess heard a noise behind her and looked over her shoulder. A ten-man squad of marines, heavily ladened with packs, M-14 rifles and protective helmets, was slowly making its way across the southern dike. She frowned. If only the marines didn't have to run patrols around her village of Le My. If only... Tess gave a whispered sound of frustration. The marines had landed in force at Da Nang a month ago, and already their presence was being felt and dreaded. It could only escalate the conflict, she feared.

She excused herself from the women and walked forward through the muddy water toward the approaching pilot. Tess vaguely recognized him. Most of the men in Gib's helicopter squadron were stationed at Marble Mountain, and she had met some of them on various visits to her brother. Although she was sure she'd seen him around, she knew she'd never met this officer. Almost against her will, she noted how handsome he was.

Pete Mallory's heart was doing funny things in his chest. Unconsciously, he rubbed that area as he approached the woman who obviously was Tess Ramsey. He ignored the fact that her dark green cotton slacks, resembling baggy pajamas, were haphazardly rolled above her nicely shaped knees, and the fact that she stood in rank, murky brown water. Her heart-shaped face, wide, intelligent green eyes and full mouth held his fascination. Lord, what a mouth she had. The urge to taste her exquisite lips was nearly overwhelming.

Just as Pete raised a hand, mustering his charm to casually introduce himself, sporadic rifle fire sounded nearby. His gaze snapped to the south, where a marine squad had been slowly making its way across the dike. The men all dived for the earth, flat on their bellies. At a sharp order from the officer they prepared to return fire.

Damn it! Pete's gaze snapped back to Tess and her group of women. They were standing there as if nothing were happening! The idiots! Didn't they hear the sniper fire? The shots probably were aimed at the marine squad, but the women could be in the line of fire!

"Get down!" Pete shouted. He made a sharp gesture for Tess to hit the deck—or, in this case, the flooded rice paddy. "I said, get down!" he roared, beginning to run toward her. How stupid could she be? All five women had curious looks on their faces as he yelled at them. Typical women, Pete decided.

More shots sounded, and the squad of marines began returning fire at a jungle wall half a mile away.

The paddy dike sloped steeply down into the water. Pete didn't give a damn about the four Vietnamese women standing around looking nonplussed as he hurtled toward them. But he did care about Tess Ramsey. She was an American and she could be killed. Pete leaped off the dike and made a lunge for her.

Tess gasped as the pilot jumped directly at her. What was the fool doing? But even as the thought formed, his hands connected with her shoulders and Tess was flung backward. They both landed in the rice paddy with a tremendous splash, sheets of chocolate-colored water flying up in veils around them.

Water flowed up into her nose and choked her as Tess fought the pilot's grip, knocking his hand away so she could struggle out of the two feet of water.

"Let go!" she sputtered as she staggered to her knees, and then her feet. She glowered at the pilot, who was still on his hands and knees in the paddy, sopping wet. "What do you think you're doing?" Tess croaked. She coughed violently, her fingers pressed against her throat.

Scrambling to his feet, Pete could still hear the marines returning fire. He charged Tess. "Get down!"

Dodging his flailing attack, Tess leaped backward out of reach. "What for?" she yelled angrily.

Water streamed from Pete as his jaw dropped in utter disbelief. "What for?" he bellowed. "Lady, there's sniper fire right over there." He jabbed his finger angrily toward the trees. "Now get your butt down in this paddy and stop fighting me! You want to get killed?"

Tess burst out laughing. She couldn't help herself. The marine pilot looked like a drowned rat, his military short black hair plastered to his skull, the flight suit clinging to his lean frame, his intense blue eyes flashing with anger and frustration.

"Captain, it's okay. Really it is. That isn't sniper fire!"

Disgruntled, Pete turned toward the marines hunkered against the southern paddy dike. They'd stopped firing their M-14s and no further gunshots were heard from the jungle.

"What the hell are you talking about?" he snarled, returning his attention to Tess.

The four Vietnamese women covered their mouths with their hands and began giggling. Tess grinned as she pushed her wet hair off her face.

Pete glared at the women. "What the hell's so funny?" He couldn't help but notice that Tess was indeed like a tall piece of bamboo next to the four tiny Vietnamese women. She must be at least five foot eight or nine, Pete guessed, but she was dressed like the other women in every respect. Why? he wondered, when she could have worn her khaki US AID uniform, instead.

Tess ruefully rescued her bamboo hat from the water and tipped it to empty out the contents. "That firing you heard, Captain, was Nguyen Oanh, this woman's son. They own an old rifle—about thirty years old. He was going into the jungle just now to hunt for wild pig." With a shrug, Tess placed the bamboo hat back on her head, her smile widening. "Oanh is only ten years old, and we all know he can't hit the broad side of a barn, but his father's with him to teach him how to shoot properly." Then she added, "I just hope they're okay."

Chastened, Pete looked down at himself. He'd paid the Vietnamese maid extra piasters to starch his flight suit so he'd look good for Tess. The odor drifting upward stung his nostrils, and his lips drew away from his gritted teeth.

"What the hell is this smell?"

Giggling, Tess said, "Water buffalo dung, Captain. It's a great fertilizer, didn't you know?" She looked down at herself and then over at her women friends whose faces were wreathed with shy smiles of amusement. Tess loved the Vietnamese earthy sense of humor because it matched hers. "I'm afraid we both look like drowned sewer rats," she said, laughing. "Would you like to follow me to a nearby stream and wash off some of that fertilizer you're wearing?"

Disgustedly, Pete flipped off several chunks that had lodged in the folds of his flight suit. "I hate this place," he muttered. "Yeah, let's get the hell out of this sewage pit."

Laughing fully, Tess ignored the pilot's angry statement. She told the women in Vietnamese to tell the marines on the dike about Oanh and his father, and to make sure they were allowed to return safely from the jungle where they'd been practicing their marksmanship. She didn't want the marines to injure one of the villagers by mistake. The women realized the seriousness of the situation and quickly made their way toward the confused marines still kneeling on the south dike. Tess gazed after them for a moment. She could tell when the marines understood what had taken place, and she watched them sheepishly get to their feet, dust off their clothes and continue their patrol. Satisfied, she began slogging through the paddy toward the dike.

"Here, let me help you," Pete said as he hurriedly tried to catch up to Tess and help her negotiate the steep dike.

Tess turned and halted. She watched the pilot flail around in the muddy paddy, in danger of losing his precarious balance at any moment. "Captain, take your time. That mud will suck the boots off your feet if you try to go too fast."

"But you should have help climbing that dike."

Tess's smile broadened. The pilot continued laboring in the sucking mud for a moment—then promptly lost his balance, falling back into the water. She tried to stop from laughing, but couldn't help herself. His handsome features had gone thundercloud black with disgust and fury as he dragged himself upright again. Tess held out her hand to him.

"Come on, Captain, grip my hand. I'll help *you* out of this paddy before you drown yourself." His attitude might be surly, but there was nothing not to like about the way he looked, Tess thought. He was more than six feet tall, with a lean, tigerlike body. Tess had to stop and laugh at herself. Some men had interested her, but most of them, upon realizing her independent nature, quickly fled. Still, she told herself as she stood waiting for him, it didn't hurt to appreciate someone of this pilot's bearing.

Spitting and coughing, Pete dodged Tess's long, slender hand. Less than two feet separated them now and he glared at her. Laughter made her eyes sparkle like emeralds struck by sunlight, her red lashes making long curved frames around them. There was such a freshness and sense of joy around her that Pete momentarily forgot some of his own awkwardness at the embarrassing situation.

"Naw, you go on up first," Pete muttered. Wrinkling his nose at the smell emanating from his wet clothes, he followed her up to the top of the dike.

Tess turned and waited for the lumbering pilot as he slipped and slid his way up the dike wall. She smiled benignly at him and extended her hand. "Put a chopper pilot on the ground and he's like a big, fat goose that's too heavy to fly. I'm Tess Ramsey. Hell of a way to meet, isn't it? Who are you?"

Taken aback by her aura of confidence and her easygoing manner toward him, Pete stared at her proffered hand for a moment. It was reddened and chapped, the nails cut short. Her slender fingers were covered with many small, white scars. Hesitantly, he gripped her hand.

"I'm Captain Pete Mallory. Your brother, Major Ramsey, sent me down here to get you." He was shocked again by the strength of her returning grip as they shook hands. Tess Ramsey was tall and raw-boned, just like her older brother, but it took nothing away from her obvious femininity despite her bedraggled, foul-smelling clothes and her slender, almost boyish figure.

Releasing his hand, Tess nodded. "Rats. That's right, there's a small party at Marble Mountain tonight, isn't there? I'd forgotten all about it." She saw conflicting emotions in Pete's penetrating blue eyes, and she suddenly had the feeling that he was assessing her as a tiger would its next quarry. More than used to appraisal by the military advisors with whom she worked, Tess didn't take his perusal as an insult. She merely ignored it.

Pete stared at Tess. "You forgot?" Normally, Pete didn't care for women with freckles. And Tess had her share: large copper sprinklings across her high cheekbones and well-defined nose. But on her, they looked like delicious raindrops, merely serving to emphasize her gorgeous eyes and patrician nose. Because she was a redhead, her skin was a pale ivory, and Pete wondered how on earth she managed not to be sunburned by Vietnam's blisteringly hot sun. Maybe that was why she wore that ugly bamboo hat.

With a shrug, Tess turned. "Yes. Tell Gib I can't make it, that I'm sorry. I've got a sick child I'm taking care of right now."

Flabbergasted, Pete quickly caught up with her. "You can't make it? After all I just went through to get here to pick you up, you can't make it?"

Tess slanted him a glance, more than a little aware of his height compared with her own. Despite his current bedraggled appearance, Pete Mallory *was* a heart stopper. Perhaps it was those cobalt eyes that sparkled with devilry, or the shape of his mouth. With a shrug, Tess tried to shake off the effect the pilot had on her. "That's right. I can't make it, Captain. Gib will understand. He always does."

Gripping her arm and bringing her to a halt, Pete muttered, "Hey, look, lady, *I* don't understand. I mean, it's not exactly a lot of fun bumping over a ten-mile dirt road to reach this miserable place and then get covered with water buffalo dung to find you. I think you damn well ought to show up after all I've been through."

A flicker of anger went through Tess. She pulled her arm from his grip. "Captain, I'm staying. Is that clear enough for you?" She turned and continued off the dike onto a well-beaten path that led back to Le My, less than a quarter of a mile away.

Angrily, Pete caught up with her. It was on the tip of his tongue to tell her how bullheaded she was. He'd never met a woman like her before—so damned independent and confident! Her red hair was plastered against her neck and shoulders, and she stank no less than he, yet she carried herself proudly, as if it didn't matter. "You're something else," he groused. "No girl in her right mind would miss a party." He gestured to her clothes, which looked like castoffs from the Salvation Army. "And how can you feel good about yourself as a woman running around in these things? I thought US AID advisors had a one-piece khaki uniform they were supposed to wear."

Tess glanced at him and continued toward the village. "First of all, I don't like being referred to as a girl, Captain. I'm a full-grown woman. Secondly, clothes do *not* make a person what they are." She grinned slightly, her lips curving into a teasing angle. "Look at you."

"What do you mean, look at me? What's wrong with the way I'm dressed?" he snapped irritably.

"It's obvious you don't respect the Vietnamese people or me, Captain. Yet, you're dressed impeccably well under the circumstances."

Stung, Pete glared at her. Damn, but she had a long stride. She didn't even walk like a woman should! He didn't like her candor or the way she saw him, either.

Scrambling to save what little was left of the deteriorating situation, Pete tried another angle. "My friends call me Pete."

"I'm not your friend, Captain."

"You can be, if you want. I'd like that."

"Oh, please! I know your type. You'd be better off chasing some poor Vietnamese bar girl who needs your money to put food in her family's mouths. You forget: I've been over here for fifteen months. I'm on my second tour. There's nothing you marines can put over on me that hasn't been tried by the male military advisors I worked with long before you chopper jockeys landed. So, let's put the games away. I don't play them. Life's too short, too important, to play games."

"Anyone ever tell you you're outspoken?" Pete demanded hotly.

"Plenty of times."

"And that doesn't bother you?" he asked, incredulous.

Tess shook her head. "Captain, I'm twenty-six years old and I've kicked around the Far East the last four of those years. There's not much I haven't seen, done or been part of. I'm not your typical American girl out of college, okay? The sooner that fact lodges in that brain of yours, the better we'll get along."

Pete said nothing more as they walked back to the village. Well, he'd wanted a challenge, and Tess Ramsey was certainly all of that—and more. He thought of giving up. Obviously she could see straight through his usual routine. Then he shook his head. Any woman he'd ever wanted, he'd gotten—it was that simple. He could pursue a girl better than any of his buddies. His reputation was on the line, anyway, because he'd made several bets at the O club last night that he'd bed down Tess Ramsey. Of course, her brother didn't know it. That wouldn't bode well for Pete's career as a helicopter pilot. Besides, Gib Ramsey was a prude in Pete's opinion—a man who didn't chase the bar girls at the O club as most of the pilots did.

Tess led Pete to the back of a large thatched hut—literally, a wooden frame roofed with a blend of dried grass and woven palm leaves. Behind it ran a small stream about four feet deep and six feet wide. She gestured to the water.

"This is where you can clean up. I suggest you strip out of that flight suit, wash it out and put it back on."

"Hey, wait! Where are you going?"

"To my hut to get cleaned up," Tess said wryly. There was something vulnerable about Pete Mallory in that moment. It struck Tess acutely, and she mentally assimilated the discovery. For all his macho bravado, suddenly he looked helpless. "When you get washed off, come to my hut. I've got a comb you can use, and some soap, plus a small bowl."

He grinned suddenly. "Sounds good."

"That's an invitation to clean up, Captain, not chase me. Okay?"

"Anything the lady wants," he returned, flipping a smart salute in her direction.

Tess shook her head and turned away.

Things weren't looking too bad despite the embarrassing situation, Pete decided as he stripped out of his smelly flight suit and threw it into the stream. Luckily, he wore a regulation olive green cotton T-shirt and boxer shorts under the suit, but those were going to have to come off, too. The stream was surrounded by tall elephant grass, a profusion of shrubbery and a few rubber trees, so he was relatively hidden from any curious eyes as he stripped naked and stood in the lukewarm water of the clear stream.

Humming to himself and plotting his next strategy, Pete knelt down and began sluicing the clean, clear water over himself. It was hell without a washcloth—more than ever he missed the amenities that Americans back in the States took for granted. Finally cleaned up, he struggled back into his wet clothes and zipped up his flight suit. Running his fingers through his dripping wet hair and pushing it off his brow, Pete turned and walked back into the village.

Damn! He came to a halt, realizing that Tess hadn't told him which hut she was in. He grimaced, taking in the number of thatched dwellings. Just then, a young boy, thin as a proverbial rail, approached him curiously.

"Missy Tess said you come," the boy said in pidgin English. He gripped Pete's hand and tugged on it.

Extricating his hand from the boy's small, thin one, Pete followed him, whistling cheerfully. Maybe the day wasn't lost after all. Maybe, if he was diligent enough, persuasive enough, he'd talk bullheaded Tess Ramsey into coming to that party tonight—as his date.

Chapter Two

Tess's hut looked like all the rest: woven rice grass hung around the outside of a wooden frame. Carefully woven palm spikes had been thatched to make a thick, impermeable roof to keep the rain at bay during the monsoon season, which would begin shortly. The boy pointed to an opening covered with a faded orange cotton cloth.

"Tess?" Pete called hesitantly at the door.

"Come in."

He pushed the cloth aside. The three small windows were open to allow air and light into the hut, but he had to stand still for a moment to let his eyes adjust. Tess sat cross-legged on a rice mat with a child in her arms. She had cleaned up and changed out of her black pajama outfit into a pale pink cotton blouse and khaki pants that looked threadbare. Her hair had been washed and brushed, and it lay in damp strands down her back. Long hair meant sweet exploration, Pete thought as he imagined his fingers combing through that rich red, gold and copper carpet. The image sent a sharp shaft of longing through him.

The child in her arms was a little girl, no more than four years old. Frowning, Pete stepped closer.

"What's wrong with her?"

Tess glanced up at him. In the shadowy light, Pete's face showed the first genuine concern she'd seen in him for someone other than himself.

"She stepped on a rusty nail the other day." Tess ran her hand worriedly down the child's spindly leg to where a dirty bandage covered her small foot. Feeling the child's damp brow, she murmured, "She's running a fever."

"Has she had a tetanus shot?"

Tess held his troubled stare. Maybe he wasn't as shallow as she'd first thought. Maybe there was a shred of depth and concern for others in his life. Maybe. "What tetanus shot? Captain, out here we don't have such things." She gently unbandaged the girl's foot. The flesh was red and swollen around the puncture wound.

Pete came forward and crouched next to Tess and the girl, frowning. "Damn, but that looks ugly."

"It is," Tess said softly as she gently stroked the girl's sweaty cheek and head. "I washed it out the best I could this morning. The supply truck comes by tomorrow. I could send her on it to the hospital at Da Nang."

"Did you use soap and water?"

"Yes."

"That's all you have?"

"We didn't get soap until about six months ago, Captain, so I'm not complaining. It's a step forward."

Pete's heart went out to the little girl, who sleepily rubbed her eyes, then nuzzled deeply into Tess's arms, her face pressed against Tess's breast, as if she were her mother. "Where are her parents?"

"The mother's dead. She stepped on a mine meant for an ARVN soldier in one of our rice paddies earlier this month."

"Oh."

"This is the frustrating part of being over here. I know about tetanus shots, antibiotics and everything else available in the real world. But they don't exist here." Tess's voice lowered with pain and weariness. "In fifteen months I've seen so many needless deaths just for lack of simple things like vaccines and antibiotics."

Bitter memories surfaced in Pete, and he struggled to keep them at bay. He watched almost with jealousy as the little girl in Tess's arms gradually fell asleep, warm, obviously loved and protected.

Looking at Tess in the dim light, her damp red hair curling softly as it dried, Pete felt his heart respond powerfully to the expression on her face. In the shadows her features glowed with such care and concern for the child in her arms. Each stroke of her long, work-worn fingers across the child's injured extremity tore at his closely guarded heart. It was the look of love on Tess's face that suddenly gripped him, held him as nothing ever had in his entire life. There was such compassion in her large green eyes fraught with anguish. The richness of her mouth, her lips parted as if in a silent cry for the helpless child, startled him.

Shaken deeply, Pete suddenly got to his feet and backed away. He scowled, feeling a mixture of pain, hope, anger and need. It was a stupid array of feelings to have churning within him, but he wanted to be in Tess's arms, being stroked by her caring hand, seeing that look in her eyes for him. Muttering a curse under his breath, Pete walked to the door of the hut, unable to sort through what was going on within him. Why should this particular scene, a not-unfamiliar one, get to him? Why now? Was it Tess? Him?

"I hate Vietnam," he ground out in frustration. "Everywhere I look, there's nothing but stinking poverty and suffering." He gripped the orange curtain with his fist and pulled it aside to stare blindly out the opening.

Tess looked up. "Captain, some things, with time, you'll get used to." She glanced lovingly down at the child in her arms. "Others, you never will."

"How could you have signed over for a second tour?" Pete demanded in a strangled voice.

Leaning down, Tess pressed a small kiss on the sleeping child's brow. Looking up to meet his tortured gaze, she whispered, "How could I not?"

Pete froze at her softly spoken words. He saw the hope of the world in her eyes, and realized that she was one of those people who had a heart larger than her body, larger than her brain, and that it was going to get her into trouble someday. She gave more than she ever got. He tore his gaze from her lustrous eyes. Pete took more than he gave, and he knew it. But then, everything had been taken away from him since birth—he wasn't about to give any precious piece of himself back to anyone or anything that might run away with it, hurting him all over again.

"You know what a scrounger is?" he said abruptly.
"No."

He jabbed his thumb into his chest. "I'm one. Every squadron has a guy who's good at getting things, scrounging up whatever is needed from God knows where."

A slight smile hovered around Tess's mouth. "Is that more or less like a wheeler-dealer? A used-car salesman?"

A thaw went through Pete as her smile gently touched his walled heart. How could her one, sad smile, get to him so easily? Completely off balance in Tess's quiet, serene presence, he nodded. "Yeah, I'm the guy who can double- and triple-talk anyone out of anything. Look, why don't you come back to Marble Mountain with me? While you're there, I'll scrounge up some tetanus vaccine and antibiotics for this kid."

Tess gasped. "You could do that?" Even her brother, Gib, who wasn't immune to the recent suffering of the Vietnamese people, hadn't been able to requisition any medical supplies for her villages—as much as he'd wanted to.

Grinning cockily, some of his old spirit returning, Pete nodded. "Honey, I'm the best scrounger in the world. What you need, I can get." Without reason, he wanted her to come back with him. A hunger ate at him to know Tess better—much better. Normally, he didn't care what was in a woman's head, it was always her body that got his undivided attention. But curiosity about Tess transcended his normal needs regarding women, and Pete was at a loss to explain why.

"Well—"

"Come on. You can't do this girl much good here. If you come with me, I'll make sure you get your medical supplies. Now, how can you pass up a deal like that?" he cajoled.

Smiling with relief, Tess nodded. "You're right: I can't. Not for her or the people of the three villages I work with. Okay, I'll go with you."

"According to Gib, you're supposed to come back to Da Nang every night, anyway."

Tess gently placed the girl on a sleeping mat and rummaged through a large rice-mat chest. She felt more than saw Pete draw near to look over her shoulder at what she was doing. "Gib would like me to go to Da Nang every night, but I don't," Tess said. Her precious supply of bandages—thin cotton strips that she'd torn from her old shirts, washed and then boiled thoroughly—were almost gone. With care, she took a vial of iodine from the chest.

Pete snorted as she laid out her meager medical items. "God, is that all you have to work with?" He looked at the strips of cotton in lieu of true bandages or dressings, a lousy one-ounce bottle of iodine, a pair of scissors and a set of tweezers.

"That's been it ever since I arrived here." Tess set to work scrubbing out the girl's infected foot with cool, soapy water. Afterward, she placed more iodine into the puncture wound, bandaged it, then covered the girl with a thin excuse for a blanket and allowed her to go to sleep.

Tess got to her feet. "She'll sleep for a while. Let me go next door and ask the woman to check in on her while I'm gone."

"Where's the rest of this kid's family?"

"Her father is a sergeant in the South Vietnamese Army, her two older brothers have been kidnapped by

VC, and you know what happened to her mother. She has no one. I'll be right back."

Pete stood in the hut, alone with the sleeping child. As much as he wanted to bar the raw, rising emotions from his heart, he couldn't. Looking down at the girl, her small hands gently curled in sleep—some of the pain she was suffering eliminated through Tess's care and love—he felt tears flood into his eyes.

"What the hell?" he rasped, and took a step back toward the door. Blinking furiously, Pete retreated, unable to deal with the quandary of feelings that Tess had unknowingly evoked within him. What was the matter with him? Why should he feel anything for this little rug rat?

Tess met him outside. The late afternoon sun shot through the lush vegetation that surrounded the busy village. The fragrant scent of cooking pots filled with rice and vegetables, the wood smoke and the singsong voices of the people impinged upon Pete's heightened awareness. Although Tess wore baggy clothes, in his opinion barely suitable for a beggar, nothing could hide her obvious femininity.

Perhaps it was her shoulder-length red hair—now caught up in a haphazard ponytail with tendrils touching her high cheekbones—that made her so beautiful. Pete blinked, and stared at her as she approached. Back Stateside, a buxom chick in a mini-skirt *always* got his attention. Now this woman, who wore Third World garments and no makeup, somehow looked more beautiful than any of those women he'd ever chased and caught.

"I'll get my knapsack and be with you in just a second," Tess promised. She saw a confused and penetrating look in Pete's eyes as she walked past him.

There was something going on between them, and Tess wasn't sure what it was. As she went into her hut and picked up the olive green knapsack that had literally been around the world with her, she wondered what it was about this cocky, narrow-minded pilot that touched her heart. One moment he was such a hard case, yet the next he seemed an angel of mercy.

As Tess walked with Pete back to where the jeep was parked, she asked suspiciously, "So what's in this for you if you get me the medical supplies I need?"

Pete grinned. "You."

She shot him a withering glance. "I'm off-limits."

"Not to me, you're not."

With disgust, Tess muttered, "You can't *demand* a person do or be something you want, Captain."

Pete laughed and opened his hands in a peaceful gesture. "But look at me: here I am, twenty-eight years old, a bachelor, handsome as hell and unattached. What more could you want, Tess?"

Inwardly, Tess offered grudging agreement. He was terribly handsome, and when his mouth lifted into his boyish grin, his dimples and smile lines deepened, giving his face a wonderful character. "I would think an intelligent man would want a woman to come to him of her own volition, not because she was blackmailed."

"Some women just don't know what they're missing until they get it."

Tess halted next to the jeep and tossed her knapsack in the back. She climbed in. "'It' being a roll in the hay?"

With a shrug, Pete climbed in and started up the jeep. The vehicle coughed, sputtered, then roared to life. "I can't think of anything better than sharing my bed with a woman. Can you?"

Tess gazed at him in utter shock. The jeep jerked twice, then they were off down the rutted dirt road, heading toward Marble Mountain, only a few miles south of Da Nang.

"Are you for real? I mean, are you serious about this trade-off—medical supplies for me?"

Pete backed off at the angry fire in her verdant eyes. He was an artist of sorts when it came to manipulating a woman into his arms. Too much pushing and Tess would tell him to take a walk. "Well," he hedged, "let's just say I'd hope you'd entertain the thought of letting me into your life a little."

"Going to bed with someone isn't a 'little' thing, Captain."

"Couldn't you call me Pete?"

Tess crossed her arms. "I guess...if you want." She scowled at him. "Where I come from, women save themselves for marriage, and engagements are in order."

Chuckling, Pete said, "Hey! Now, I'm not getting *that* serious, honey."

"I didn't think so."

For some reason, Pete winced inwardly at her bitter tone. For some reason, he wanted Tess's respect, not the disgust written so eloquently on her lovely features. "Look, don't take this so seriously. Just let me get to know you a little better."

"What does 'better' mean?"

"A date at the officers club? Maybe we could do some dancing? It's not much of an O club yet, just a couple of tents, but we've got a plywood dance floor and a mean jukebox. We could have a couple of drinks."

"I don't drink. And I haven't danced in years. I'd probably step all over your feet and break one of your toes. At the very least, I'd break your healthy ego." Tess looked at the surrounding vegetation, in every shade of green ranging from yellows to nearly black. "And as for partying, I'm a stick-in-the-mud. Back at Texas A & M, I was one of those girls who stayed in the dorm and studied. I wasn't out every night with the frat boys."

"Well, let's just start with a talk over some ice water at tonight's party. Fair enough?" Pete gave her his best little-boy look, guaranteed to get him an affirmative response. This time, however, he felt a bit guilty, because he knew Tess was leveling with him, and he wasn't with her.

"Tonight?"

"Why not? You'll be at the party at our squadron. I'll requisition a jeep and drive you back over to Da Nang. You can return to the village tomorrow morning."

"I was hoping you'd get me the medical supplies and I'd hop a ride back to Le My with a convoy going this direction tonight. Or maybe Gib could authorize me a helicopter ride back to the village. That little girl needs the tetanus shot and antibiotics as soon as possible. My conscience would eat me up alive if I stayed overnight, knowing she could die without the medicine."

She was right. Pete realized Tess was extraordinarily sensitive to those around her, not necessarily to herself. "Man, we're complete opposites," he muttered as the jeep bounced along the road. "Every time

I get off a chopper flight, I hit the bar and have a good time. There's no guarantee I'm coming back from any one of those flights, and I'm not putting my life on hold because of it.''

"What I do is relatively safe," Tess said. "So that kind of good time isn't high on my list of important activities."

"Like hell your job's safe. It isn't. The VC are getting aggressive, and Intelligence says they're gonna start getting real nasty real soon. You're a white American woman, and you're gonna be in their sites." Pete glanced over at her profile, wildly aware of the innate gentleness of her mouth and the softness in her eyes. "Don't ever think you won't be a target, Tess."

With a shrug, she said, "Listen, everyone knows me—friend and foe alike. They know my work. I've helped the Vietnamese increase rice yields, gotten them more food and improved their existence. I'm here as an AID advisor in an agricultural capacity. No, Pete, I'm safe. They won't hurt me."

"Brother, are you an ostrich with your head in the sand." Shaking his own head, he looked both ways, then turned onto the asphalt of Highway 1. Gunning the jeep on the smooth road, he relaxed slightly, knowing there was less chance of VC attack on the highway, too.

Tess smiled absently and leaned back against the less-than-comfortable jeep seat. "So, will you get me the supplies as soon as we get to Marble Mountain?"

"Yeah, I suppose."

"I'll go over and see Gib about a chopper flight back while you do that."

"No, don't. I'll fly you back."

Tess stared over at Pete in surprise. His mouth flat, the corners pulled in. "Thanks," she said, meaning it.

"Yeah, don't mention it."

"Maybe you're not such a bad guy after all." Tess grinned. When Pete glanced over at her, he didn't look very happy. "And don't worry, as soon as I can, I'll have that glass of ice water with you at the O club."

Heartened, Pete suddenly couldn't remember when he'd wanted anything quite so badly. He wanted to know a hell of a lot more about what made Tess Ramsey tick. She was a lone American woman in a Third World country, surrounded by escalating danger and hardened military men. But none of these things seemed to register with Tess. With a sigh, he realized that Tess wouldn't be in his arms tonight. He'd be spending time with her, albeit with him in the cockpit and her in the rear with the door gunner. Still, the hope in her eyes, the awe that he could finagle medical supplies for her, had won him some of her respect and approval, and Pete knew it.

It was early evening when they arrived back at the Marine Air Group at Marble Mountain. To Tess's disappointment, Gib was out on a helicopter flight, so she wouldn't be able to see him. Pete insisted that Tess walk with him over to the group of olive green tents, wood-backed and set on platforms to keep them above the sandy ground, that housed thousands of boxes of supplies for the base. She stood to one side as Pete corraled a marine gunny sergeant, a position she knew to be very powerful in the military system.

"Look, Gunny," Pete cajoled, "I need a box of vaccines—all kinds—and a box of antibiotics for this pretty young lady here. She works with the villagers. What have you got for her?''

The gunny, a grizzled, lean man with sharp gray eyes, sized up Pete and then Tess. "What have you got for me, Captain?''

Grinning affably, Pete looked around the dark, silent reaches of the tent. "What do you need, Gunny? Name it, and it's yours.''

The gunny snorted. "How about a case of Johnnie Walker Red?''

"Done." Pete thrust out his hand.

The gunny shook it, then gave him a wary look. "When am I gettin' it?''

"I gotta make a milk run down to Saigon next week. I'll pick it up and deliver it to you on my return. How's that sound?''

"Good," the gunny growled. .

Pete smiled triumphantly over at Tess as the marine sergeant disappeared between the aisles. "Well? What do you think?''

Tess shook her head, awed. "I think you're an angel in disguise.''

"Me? An angel?'' Pete laughed deeply. "I've been accused by my ladies of being many things—a bastard, a devil, a swindler, a liar—but *never* an angel.''

Tess tilted her head and studied him in the tent's shadowy gloom. There was such a wall around Pete that she could almost feel it. Why? It was as if he wanted her to think the worst of him. What about the good he also carried within him? "That's quite a list of adjectives.''

"Yeah, well, the ladies were right. I'm not the nicest guy in the world." Pete shook his finger in her direction. "And stop looking at me with those beautiful green eyes with the hope of the world in them. I'm a bastard. I make no bones about it. Life's short and I intend to play hard and work a little. I'm not an angel, Tess Ramsey, and don't you ever forget that.''

Sitting on the nylon seat in the rear of the Sikorsky helicopter on the way back to Le My, Tess held both precious cardboard boxes of medical supplies on her lap. Darkness had fallen, and all she could see in the reddish light from the cockpit display up front was the bare outline of Pete's helmeted head. He sat in the pilot's seat, his gloved hands busy with the controls, keeping the aircraft stable as they sped toward their destination. Night flights weren't a helicopter's strong point, Tess knew, although they often did fly in the murky darkness.

Pete had assured her that he could make this short hop blindfolded. Well, that was close to the truth. Tess's awe of him had risen a notch by the very fact he was willing to fly her back to the village. Knowing full well he could have refused, she rummaged around in her heart, trying to understand what made him run the way he did. He was an enigma. Verbally, he was telling her he was a bastard to every woman he'd met. Yet, he was flying a mission of mercy for her and the little girl. Of course she hadn't forgotten that Pete was probably counting on the chance to seduce her at a later date.

As the helicopter landed outside Le My, many of the children came running out to see it. Pete gave orders to his copilot, Lieutenant Joe Keegan, and his door gunner, Lance Corporal Jerry Random, to keep their eyes peeled for trouble in the form of roving VC while he escorted Tess into the village. Tess climbed out of the aircraft, her precious cargo cradled in her arms as the powerful blades whipped up dust and debris all around her. Pete unhooked his communications jack and, leaving his helmet on, climbed out of the front seat. Leaping down, he gripped Tess's arm and hurried her away from the buffeting wind.

The children ran alongside them, their voices high with excitement. Tess was wildly aware that Pete hadn't released her elbow as he shepherded her along the dirt path into the village. The air seemed charged with energy as he grinned down at her.

"See, I told you we'd get you here with no problem."

"You've got eyes like a cat," Tess agreed breathlessly.

"Here, let me help you." Pete took one of the supply boxes and tucked it under his left arm. He looked around, feeling edgy. This flight wasn't authorized by anyone. He doubted Gib would have okayed it. Night flights were strictly planned, and little jaunts like this one were forbidden. Pete didn't trust the VC buildup he knew was taking place, either. If he got the helicopter shot up or one of his crew wounded, all hell would break loose and his career would go down the tubes.

In the village, some of the adults came out to see who had arrived. Tess halted at her hut and quickly moved the curtain aside. An old kerosene lamp sputtered in one corner, shedding meager light. On the grass mat the little girl still slept. Going over to her, Tess touched the child's brow.

"How is she?" Pete asked, kneeling next to Tess and opening the box of antibiotics.

"Terribly hot. Her temperature must be 102 or 103."

Taking off his helmet, Pete set it aside. "Here, let me help." He saw the worry in Tess's shadowed eyes, and the way her mouth was pursed to hold back her real reaction to the girl's deteriorating condition. Ripping off the top of the cardboard box, Pete located the antibiotics. "Start her with 500 milligrams of penicillin."

"That's a heavy dose," Tess protested.

"Yeah, but honey, you ain't got no choice." He motioned to the little girl's foot. "Look at the red lines moving up her leg. The kid's got blood poisoning."

"Oh, God..." Tess looked more closely. Her hands shook as she took the syringe and needle from Pete.

"Hey, relax. She's gonna make it. Just give her this shot, keep her cooled down with water, and by morning she'll be a lot better."

Tess gave him an odd look. "Are you a doctor?"

Shyly, Pete shrugged. "Nah, I'm just the kind of bastard that knows a little about a lot of things. Go on, give her the penicillin." Gently he turned the girl onto her side so that Tess could give the shot.

Relief cascaded through Tess afterward. Pete had also wrangled an entire box of syringes and needles, so she wouldn't have to keep boiling and using the old ones over again as she had in the past. "Thanks," she murmured, her voice wobbly with feeling. "You really are a knight in shining armor to us."

Pete snorted and slowly rose. "Don't go putting me on any pedestals, honey, I'll sure as hell fall off faster and quicker than you could ever believe. Listen, I gotta hoof it out of here. I don't like leaving my helo crew sitting ducks on the ground."

Immediately, Tess stood. "I—thanks, Pete. Thanks so much...."

Gone was the brusque, hard-talking woman of this afternoon. In her place, Pete was privileged to see the real Tess. And sweet God, did he like what he saw. With a shrug he placed his hand on her shoulder. "It's nothing."

"I don't call helping a little girl 'nothing.'" There was such vulnerability in his eyes now. Tess felt her breath become suspended and her heart start to beat fast at the discovery. Pete's hand felt good, steadying her spinning emotions.

"Then," Pete whispered, devilry dancing in his eyes, "I intend to collect for my good deed sooner or later." The urge to lean forward those few inches and kiss the hell out of her parted, soft lips was almost Pete's undoing. But something cautioned him not to do it—at least, not yet. Patting her shoulder, he said, "I'll see you around, honey."

He was gone. Tess stood in the center of the hut, the syringe still in her hand. Whatever powerful magic was at work made her feel dizzy and not of this world. Trying to shake off Pete's overwhelming presence, she turned and knelt down by the little girl. Tess's night would be spent bathing the child to keep her temperature down until the antibiotic took hold—if only it would. Some of Tess's hope diminished as she heard the helicopter take off, the heavy whap, whap of blades cutting through the humid air that always hung over Vietnam.

She began to gently bathe the girl, and her hope continued to erode as the last sounds of the helicopter bearing Pete Mallory back to Marble Mountain faded into nothing. It had been a crazy day in so many ways. Pete had crashed into her life, quite literally. Tess couldn't understand how his hard line toward women in general went with such a compassionate streak toward children. It didn't make sense. *He* didn't make sense.

Still, as she remained awake through the early morning hours, bathing the delirious child, Tess couldn't forget Pete. There had been moments when his eyes had revealed another side to him—and it was that side she wanted to know. Tess sighed. She'd already lost her innocence about life and men. Three years ago, she'd been engaged to Eric Hampton, a Peace Corps volunteer. So caught up with being in love, Tess had given herself—body, heart and soul—to him.

Tess struggled to shake off much-needed sleep to stay up with the girl. By 3:00 a.m., the child's temperature was beginning to drop. Relief shattered through Tess as she lay down and drew the girl into her arms. She closed her eyes, but sleep refused to come. Pete's unexpected entrance into her life had stirred up a lot of unsolved feelings toward Eric.

Eric had been the exact opposite of Pete: quiet, sincere and hard-working. Somehow, the engagement had fallen apart. What had gone wrong? Had it been her? Was she incapable of being loved? Or of knowing what love really was? Now Pete was saying he was a bastard, making no bones about it, and yet there was such a discrepancy between his words and his actions. Unable to figure it all out, Tess sighed again and gave the little girl a gentle squeeze, just to let her know she was loved and cared for.

Pete Mallory was a hunter with few morals or values when it came to women. The pain in Tess's heart widened as she broached the twilight zone between sleep and wakefulness. So how could she be drawn to him? How? Resolution wove with sleep as she surrendered to the security of the darkness. Under no circumstance would she allow herself to be manipulated. No way.

Chapter Three

"Man, things are getting bad out in the bush," Pete's copilot, Joe Keegan, confided. The Sikorsky helicopter's blades were turning slowly, the engine already shut down. Pete finished flipping off the rest of the switches on his side of the cockpit and sat back in the uncomfortable seat, perspiration running down the sides of his face beneath his helmet. Sweat poured off him from the humidity that hung like a heavy, wet blanket around them twenty-four hours a day.

"Yeah," Pete croaked, loosening the helmet strap. "Things are getting worse." With a groan, he took the heavy helmet off, fresh air cooling him momentarily. Running his fingers through the wet hair plastered against his skull, he glanced back at the glum marine second lieutenant—a green twenty-three-year-old kid. This was the officer's first month in Nam and into what was known as the "bush," a place where lives could be and were lost—especially to VC land mines and snipers. The war—and it was a dirty war, in Pete's opinion—was heating up daily.

Keegan glumly lifted his hand in farewell and exited out the right side of the Sikorsky, heading toward the flight shack to file their flight report.

Pete's gunner, Random, a red-haired marine lance corporal with dancing gray eyes, glanced over at him. "Want me to check for holes in the fuselage, Mr. Mallory? I know we took hits."

"Go ahead. Just don't tell me how many you find." Pete sat there, letting the shakiness pass before he attempted to move. His knees felt like jelly.

"You don't want to know?"

Pete shook his head. "No way." He didn't want to know how close one of those bullets had come. The VC knew the man sitting in the right seat of a helicopter was the pilot, and they aimed for him first. He tipped his head back, closed his eyes and took in a ragged but deep breath, trying to still his pounding heart.

"It wasn't very groovy out there today," Random added, just as shaken as Pete from the ground fire. "Hot LZ's are the armpits of the universe."

"No argument from me, and groovy isn't a word I'd use for a wartime situation," Pete whispered. His mind, his heart, circled back to Tess. Damned if she hadn't haunted his dreams for the past five days. And not an hour went by that her image didn't gently intrude upon his world of harsh reality, of life and death, giving him a moment's serene peace. How was the four-year-old girl? he wondered. Had she survived with the help of the tetanus vaccine and antibiotics? How was Tess?

With a sigh, Pete opened his eyes, stuffed his helmet into the green canvas bag that he stowed behind his seat during flights, and slowly moved out of the cramped, confining cockpit. All around him on the tarmac was the busy-bee activity of ground crews servicing the birds and tanker trucks, refueling them for the next flight. Weary flight crews were dragging their butts back to the flight line shack to file their reports and discrepancy logs.

At the flight shack, Pete joined his copilot. "What're your plans?" Keegan asked as he handed him the report to check and then officially sign off. "Beers at the O club?"

Normally, that's exactly what Pete would do. Only an ice-cold beer took the edge off his thirstiness and dulled the adrenaline from a rough flight. He quickly read Keegan's report, noticed how wobbly the printing was on it, and signed it off with his own trembling signature. Pete handed the report across the desk to the flight chief. "No," he said. "I gotta check out some things. Maybe later."

Gib Ramsey was at his desk in the hard-back tent that served as headquarters for the Marine Air Group helicopter squadron. The air in the tent was squalid, and hung like a damp sheet within the gloomy interior. Gib looked up as Pete sauntered in.

"How was it out there today? I heard you took ground fire."

Pete shrugged. "Yeah, my crew chief counted fifteen rounds that stitched up my bird. No casualties, though."

"Good," Gib said, putting the pen and paper aside. "We aren't always going to be so lucky."

"No..."

"Hey, I want permission to buzz on over to Le My for a couple of hours."

"Oh?" Gib cocked his head, his eyes curious.

With a burgeoning grin, Pete added, "I scrounged up some more supplies for your sister."

"I thought so."

His mouth stretching into a full smile, Pete said, "This *is* business."

"Oh?" Then Gib shrugged. "She knows your type anyway, Mallory, so I'm not worried. Tess has been able to take care of herself in situations far worse than you horning in on her life."

Pete laughed good-naturedly. The major knew he was the best scrounger at Marble Mountain and relied on him heavily to get badly needed items for the squadron. Every once in a while, Pete took advantage of this relationship, but his CO usually allowed it to happen by way of thanks for his heroic efforts in the area of procurement.

"So, you got some stuff to go to Le My?" Gib teased.

"Strictly business." Giving Gib an innocent look, Pete opened his hands. "Hey, Tess called me an angel of mercy a week ago."

Rolling his eyes, Gib muttered, "You? With *your* reputation?"

"Believe it, Major. Well? Can I have about three hours? We're not due for another mission until tomorrow morning. I'm all caught up on paperwork."

Gib nodded, then scowled. "Yeah, go ahead. I'm up to my armpits in local politics with that rubber plantation estate owned by Dany Villard."

Joy coursed through Pete. He hadn't realized how much he truly wanted to see Tess again until he heard permission granted. "Out of sight. See you later, Major."

"Pete?"

He turned on his heel. "Yes, sir?"

"When you 'accidentally' run into Tess, will you tell her to get her rear back to Da Nang at night? Things are heating up out there." The scowl on his broad brow deepened. "She's supposed to stay at Da Nang every night, not out at those villages."

"I'll tell her that." Pete recalled vividly her earlier refusal to stay at Da Nang. "But I don't know if it will do much good."

"Do me a favor? Use your considerable charm, sweet talk and any other kind of leverage you can think of to get my baby sis to see the light of day? Tell her there're VC massing west of Le My."

Pete shared Gib's belief that Tess should stay at a safe haven each night. "I'll do what I can."

"If you succeed, I'll owe you, Mallory."

Grinning, Pete nodded. "Maybe a weekend's worth of leave in Saigon?"

With a groan, Gib shook his head. "Get out of here, Captain Mallory."

Chuckling, Pete sauntered out of the tent and into the humid noontime heat. He threw his utility cap on his head, the broad brim shading his eyes from the always brilliant, burning rays of the sun. Whistling softly, his spirits lifting so high he felt as if he was walking on air, Pete requisitioned a jeep from motor pool, then went about collecting all the little things he'd scrounged all week—just for Tess. When she saw these gifts he'd managed to wrangle, he thought with a deepening grin, she wouldn't be able to say no to anything he asked.

* * *

Pete found Tess at one end of the village of Le My, sitting on a rubber-tree stump and holding what looked like some sort of impromptu medical clinic. Spread out on a cardboard box next to her were syringes, bottles of vaccine and the cotton strips she used for bandaging. In front of her, standing patiently in line, were about thirty women with children hanging onto their clothes or tucked away in their arms.

"Hey!" Pete called as he approached, "you playing nurse now?"

Tess's head snapped up. Her eyes widened. She'd just finished inoculating a five-year-old boy, and she used a piece of cotton dipped in alcohol to clean away the spot of blood on his arm.

"Pete!"

He grinned broadly and set a large box down beside her. "You're a sight for sore eyes, honey. How are you? And how's that little girl with the bad foot?" It took everything Pete had to stop himself from reaching out to touch Tess's cheek—which was smudged with a bit of red dust. Her hair was caught up in a haphazard ponytail, and today she was wearing her "official" AID uniform, a one-piece khaki outfit replete with badges on each shoulder that proclaimed her as a civilian, not a military advisor.

"I'm fine. Oh, and the little girl, Lee, is much better—thanks to you." How stalwart Pete looked in his dark green flight suit, his hands settled confidently on his hips and that rakish smile on his face. The look in his dark blue eyes made Tess feel overwhelmingly special for a moment—but then she reminded herself that Pete had the ability to make each woman feel special, desirable and one-of-a-kind just so he could get her into his bed.

"Looks like today is shot day. Lucky people," Pete teased. "Glad it's not me."

Tess glanced at the long line in front of her. "Well, if I had some help, the vaccinations could go faster."

"Is that a hint for me to roll up my sleeves and get to work?"

She smiled up at him as his shadow fell across her. "You seemed to know a great deal about medicine last week. Sure, pitch in. If you can fill the syringes, hand them to me, this will go twice as fast."

"If I do, will you take an hour out of your schedule and visit with me?"

Tess shook her head and managed a sour laugh. "Do you always have to bargain with a woman, trade something for her attention?"

Pete moseyed on over to her "table" and methodically began to do as Tess asked. "Well, now remember, most ladies just fall into my arms without a fight. I only make trade-offs with tough lady customers who have to be convinced of my being a good thing in their lives."

"Oh, boy," Tess said, rolling her eyes and laughing as the next person in line, a mother with three small children, stepped up to her.

Occasionally, Pete looked up from his duties. Tess knew Vietnamese fluently, and her voice was soft and rhythmic as she spoke to each woman and child. She had such gentleness. Pete wished mightily that Tess would touch *him* like that. It was obvious to him that the Vietnamese worshipped Tess. But he knew they could never really appreciate her fully—the way he could.

"So, Lee is getting better, huh?" he asked, handing her another syringe filled with vaccine.

"Yes, much better. Thanks to you."

"You promised to have a glass of mineral water at the O club with me on that one."

Tess gave him a wary look. "I haven't forgotten."

"More importantly, have you been looking forward to it?"

With a delicate shrug, Tess said, "Would a monkey look forward to being trapped and eaten by a tiger?"

"You've been in Nam too long. You're already beginning to sound like a Zen Buddhist—answering a question with a question."

She grinned and swabbed down the next boy's arm. "Just answer my question, Mallory. Why should I allow myself to be trapped by you?"

Pete had the good grace to blush, something he'd not done in a long, long time. Placing two more filled syringes next to her, he muttered, "Since when is kissing or making love a trap?"

Tess hooted, and several of the villagers smiled even though they didn't understand enough English to know what had been said. "Real love is never a trap. Is that how you see love?"

Uncomfortable, Pete shrugged. Only five more people stood in line and then they'd have time to themselves, time for him to woo Tess with his array of scrounged gifts. "I'm not sure what love is."

Giving him a curious look, Tess said, "What an odd thing to say." What had happened to Pete to make him that doubtful of one of the most beautiful feelings in the world? "There are so many kinds of love," Tess began softly. Smiling up at her next patients, she said, "The love of a mother for her child. The love of a brother for a sister. The love of a husband for his wife.''

Scowling heavily, Pete fixed the last syringe and handed it to Tess. ''Yeah, well, I'm not too well acquainted with any of the above. Maybe that's why I don't put much stock in this thing called love that everyone thinks is so great.''

The vibrating anger beneath his words made Tess turn and study him for a moment. She returned to the last few vaccinations. ''Tell me about your mother. What kind of woman is she?''

Pete snorted violently and shoved his hands into the pockets of his flight suit. ''A bitch.''

Tess froze momentarily beneath his grated words, then finished the injections. She slowly turned around to face Pete. His eyes refused to meet hers, but the anger banked in them was very real. And so was the thundercloud-dark expression on his hardened features. Instinctively, Tess knew she was treading on some very painful ground.

''Tell me about her,'' she coaxed gently as she gathered up the used syringes and empty vaccine bottles.

He shrugged and his mouth quirked. ''What's there to tell? I was the unwanted brat. The minute after I was born, my mother gave me up. She abandoned me, according to her older sister, because she was only sixteen years old at the time. I was a mistake that happened, and believe me, her whole family thought so, too. No one in the family would take me for various and sundry reasons, so I ended up in a string of foster homes until I was twelve. By that time, I was past the cute and cuddly stage, so no one wanted me. I spent time in a Chicago orphanage until I was eighteen. When I got out, I headed to college to make something of myself. I never wanted to look back. I never wanted to hear from any of my so-called 'real' family again. They didn't want me, so I don't give a damn about them.''

Pete nailed Tess with a lethal look. ''Don't talk to me about love. I don't know what the hell it is. I never did. Now, rejection—I can tell you a whole lot about that. And quitting—that, too. I come from a family of gutless wonders who would rather let a little kid go than try to keep him.'' Darkly, he looked down at his dusty flight boots. Why the hell was he telling Tess about himself? It was the cardinal rule in his book of life never to divulge anything of himself to anyone— especially a woman. She could do too much damage with that kind of information.

Tess packed the medical supplies into the small cardboard box, at a loss for words for several moments. She felt Pete's pain as if it were her own. Glancing around the village, where so many children played happily, she looked up at him, her face filled with compassion. His mouth was a tight line holding back a deluge of suppressed feelings. Somehow, somewhere in her heart, Tess knew she could unlock that buried grief and pain for Pete. But at what price to herself? He didn't acknowledge love, and with good reason. He could take, but he wasn't going to give to her or anyone.

''I'm sorry if I touched a raw nerve.''

''Hell, that nerve's been dead a long time,'' he said explosively. Exasperated, he added, ''Look, I didn't mean to talk about myself. Let's forget it.'' He moved like a tightly coiled spring to where he'd set the box, and brought it back to the makeshift table. In an effort to shake off all mention of his dark and unhappy past, Pete struggled to put on a smile and tuck away all his emotions. "I've been gathering things all week for you. Go on, take a look."

Hesitantly, Tess stood up and moved over beside Pete. As he folded open the flaps of the cardboard box, she gasped. There was an incredible array of medical supplies—adhesive tape, several thermometers, huge rolls of gauze, brand-new scissors, Mercurochrome and at least fifty bottles of penicillin. With a gasp, she reached out, barely touching the items.

"Pete..." she breathed disbelievingly. "How—"

"Now, honey, don't go asking a scrounger how he got what he got for you. Those are trade secrets." He forced a smile he still didn't feel, although Tess's glowing features assuaged some of the pain that lingered in his chest. Still in shock that he'd admitted his anger toward his mother to Tess, he felt awkward.

"This is wonderful! Oh, look! Typhoid, diphtheria and whooping cough vaccine! The babies won't die from any of those, now." She held up a huge amber bottle. "And malaria tablets!"

A hot, powerful feeling moved through Pete as Tess made a big deal over the supplies. Something good and clean flowed through him, erasing much of the ugliness that roiled within him. Her joy was genuine, the look in her lovely green eyes telling him everything. It struck Pete that Tess simply didn't play the games other women played back in the States. There was a straightforward simpleness about her, that soft Texas drawl of hers touching him like a heated fever, changing him in ways he'd never be able to logically categorize. But his body was responding of its own accord, and the ache building in him was more than just physical. He ached to capture and tame that smiling mouth of hers, to absorb the beauty and happiness he saw in her eyes. In that moment, Pete felt like a man bound for hell getting his first and only look at what heaven might have been like.

"This is incredible, Pete. Wonderful!" Tess turned and threw her arms impulsively around his broad, powerful shoulders and gave him a hug. "Thank you," she whispered, her voice off-key. "Thank you for your gifts."

The shocking touch of her body against his own made him dizzy. Automatically, Pete reached out to place his arms around Tess, but she was gone as quickly as she had embraced him. Her cheeks were flushed, the freckles across her cheeks darker, making her look even more desirable, if that were possible. Her red hair, straight by nature, was slightly curled and damp against her temples. Pete longed to touch her hair, just a strand of it, to see what it felt like. Would it be strong yet soft, like Tess?

His mouth went dry, and his heart picked up in beat as he met, held and drowned in her gaze, now awash with tears. Tears?

"Now," he muttered gruffly, "don't cry! I can't stand it when a woman cries. It bothers the hell out of me."

Tess blinked them away and managed a sliver of a laugh. "They're tears of happiness, Pete. Don't tell me you don't know what that feeling is, either."

Bashfully, he shrugged and turned away. If he kept staring down into Tess's upturned face, he'd do something they'd both be sorry for later. The blinding urge to kiss her, to take her bodily and bury himself in her loving depths, nearly unstrung all his carefully made plans to woo Tess into his bed. Fighting to get a hold on his unraveling feelings, he felt Tess's hand grip his arm.

"Pete?"

"I'm okay."

She smiled up at him. "And you keep saying you're such a bastard." A flood of incredible light and heat swept through Tess. "You foster such a bad-boy image, yet you turn around and do this. Pete, something's not making sense here."

"It's just a way of getting your attention, is all," he muttered defensively, aware of her firm grip on his arm. Her touch was galvanizing, hot coals against his flesh. "Don't read anything more into it than that."

"When a man courts a woman, he usually brings chocolates and flowers," Tess teased and glanced at the box, "not medical supplies." If she didn't let go, Tess knew she'd want to keep touching him—to raise a hand to his implacable features, smoothing and softening them once again by taking away the tension that hung around his mouth and eyes. How easily touched he was. That was a happy discovery. He wasn't half as bad as he tried to make people think. Releasing his arm, Tess whispered, "Well, whatever your intentions, you'll be saving lives with these medical items whether you know it or not."

"And for that, you'll have dinner with me tonight at the O club?" he pressed, taking advantage of her lowered guard. Never had he wanted anything more.

With a laugh, Tess shook her head. "I can't go tonight. One of the women is in labor, and I promised her I'd stay with her. It's her first baby, and I want to be here for moral support as well as for medical purposes." Tess touched the box. "Now, with the Mercurochrome, I can disinfect the baby's navel. Do you know how many infants get infection right after they're born because of lack of iodine?''

Pete shook his head. But he saw the seriousness in Tess's vulnerable eyes. "There's more," he said abruptly, hurt that she wouldn't go with him to the O club.

"More? Of what?"

"Supplies. Come on, they're in the jeep. They're too bulky to carry all at once." He turned on his heel, trying to salvage his hurt pride. A part of him understood Tess's reason for staying at Le My. There was a mother having a baby—and he was sure the baby was wanted and wouldn't be given away to some stranger as he'd been. He saw something commendable in Tess's decision to stay, but the selfish part of him wanted her regardless of the situation, and that was the part he wrestled with as he walked back to the jeep.

Tess quickly caught up with Pete. "I can't believe this! What other things did you bring?"

"Oh, just odds and ends I found."

At the jeep, Tess halted, her mouth dropping open. There were ten half sheets of plywood in the back of the vehicle. In another cardboard box were six colorful comforters, in quiltlike patterns. The third box contained six marine-issue green Snoopy blankets, in camouflage jungle green-and-brown, a blend of nylon quilted with an inner layer of polyester down. Tess was speechless.

Pete felt an incredible tidal wave of pleasure sweep through him as he saw the effects his gifts had on Tess. She was like a child at Christmas. He patted the plywood.

"After looking at your hut, which is more like a sieve than a house, I figured plywood walls would be best." He pointed to the box of comforters. "And all you had to lie on are those lousy grass mats. You're sleeping on a dirt floor, for all intents and purposes. At least now you'll be able to have some padding under you and a blanket to throw on top of you when it gets chilly in the early morning hours."

Pete's thoughtfulness overwhelmed Tess, and she fought back tears of gratitude. Some of the harshness had left his features, and she saw a little boy standing in front of her, wanting so badly to please his mother, wanting so badly to be held and loved for what he'd gotten her. All of these realizations cascaded through Tess: how much Pete needed to be held and loved, to be told *he* was worthwhile and needed. The only way he knew to get approval was to buy someone with gifts.

Sadness moved through Tess as she gently touched the comforters and then the blankets. "You are," she whispered unsteadily, on the verge of tears, "an angel of mercy, Pete Mallory." And without thinking, she put her arms around his neck, drew him close and simply held him. She buried her head next to his jaw. "Thank you," she whispered.

A shattering sensation broke around Pete's heart as Tess went slowly into his arms. This time she didn't move away. This time, her loving body filled with a strength he craved, she remained within his tightening embrace. Closing his eyes, Pete savored her length against him, as if she were a prayer that had finally been answered. A ragged sigh tore from him and his nostrils flared to take in her very feminine scent. It was a perfume far more dizzying and beautiful than the orchids that clung to the trees in the jungles.

Just her simple act, an act of innocence, made him savor Tess as he had no other woman. Pete felt the rapid beat of her heart against his chest wall, the firmness of her small breasts. He was wildly aware of the shallow rise and fall of her breathing, and even more aware of how Tess fit beautifully—perfectly— against his tall frame.

Tess slowly extricated herself from Pete's tight embrace. Shocked by her own impulsive gesture, she touched her flaming cheek as she looked shyly up into his hooded eyes, smoldering with raw need of her. "I—I'm sorry... I don't know what happened...."

"I'm not sorry at all," Pete rasped, his voice roughened with desire. Tess looked incredibly vulnerable right now, wide open for any attack he might make on her. But something stopped him from taking advantage of her—for now. She was shaken. So was he.

The moment was broken when the shortwave radio in the jeep began to squawk. Cursing the bad timing, Pete picked it up and called in.

Tess stepped away and crossed her arms, as if to hold herself together after the unexpected embrace. Disappointment washed through her: Pete was needed immediately back at base to fly an urgent mission.

Apologetically, Pete put the radio on the seat of the jeep. He began to transfer the goods from the vehicle and Tess pitched in to help him. "Sorry I can't stay, Tess."

"I am, too," she admitted. They placed the sheets of plywood against the trunk of a rubber tree. In moments, the jeep was unloaded. Tess wiped her dusty hands against the thighs of her uniform. "Will it be dangerous, this mission?"

Pete shrugged, not wanting to leave. The need to capture Tess's provocative mouth was real, overriding. "I don't know."

"Well," she cast about, "Gib said you guys fly one mission a day. This would be your second one."

Forcing himself to climb into the jeep, Pete started up the cantankerous vehicle. "Don't worry about me, honey. I'm too damn mean to die. Didn't you know? Only the good die young. I'm going to be around until I'm a dirty old man of ninety."

She laughed and stepped away from the jeep. "You're such a hard case, Mallory. When will I see you again?"

Pete grinned belatedly. "When do you want to see me?"

"As soon as possible. I could use another set of strong, capable hands to turn that plywood into a small room we could use as a school."

With a groan, Pete complained, "So you only want me for my body."

It was her turn to smile. "Isn't that what you only want from me? What an interesting turn of the tables...."

In that instant, Pete liked Tess more than ever. She had spunk and wit, not to mention an unquenchable spirit. He laughed. "All's fair in love and war, and honey, we're in a war. I'll drop by and loan you myself as soon as possible. Okay?"

Sobering, Tess said, "Be careful, Pete."

"I always am."

"No, I mean, be really careful."

"For you, I will be, honey. See you later."

Tess watched the jeep disappear, leaving a cloud of reddish dust in its wake. So much was happening to her when it came to Pete. He was incredibly complex—one moment the jokester; the next, hauntingly human and emotionally fragile. Turning around, Tess looked at all the equipment he'd brought. A number of children had come up to eagerly sift through the contents and finger the soft, clean material. Their faces were filled with awe over the array of rainbow colors. With a shake of her head, Tess moved toward the expectant and excited children.

"You're something else, mister. Something else," she muttered, hoping against hope that she would see Pete much sooner rather than later.

Chapter Four

"**Y**ou're turning into a bear," Gib Ramsey noted of Pete as they slowly walked off the tarmac toward the line shack to finish off their flight reports. The afternoon sun beat down thickly upon them. Pete's flight suit clung damply to his body.

"Yeah, well, this damn Tinkertoy war is getting to me," he griped. "Since I last saw your sister two weeks ago, we've been flying three to four missions a day. I haven't had *any* time off to go visit her." Pete ignored the constant movement of trucks and men, and jets taking off in the distance. Fatigue lapped at him, but despite it, his thought and, incredibly, his heart, centered on Tess. "And she never stays at Da Nang at night. What's with her, anyway?" If Tess would come back to the base at night, Pete would have ample opportunity to see her, to chase her. It would be easy to take a jeep from Marble Mountain and drive over to the main marine facility a few miles away.

With a laugh, Gib slowed his walk as they approached the line shack. "Now you know how I feel. I wish she'd stay here at night, too—for different reasons." Gib gave Pete a significant look laced with amusement. "But Tess is committed to her villages and the people in them."

"She's a one-woman show out in the bush," Pete muttered, opening the creaking screen door to the stuffy line shack. A number of other pilots were already at the counter filling out discrepancy logs for the crew chiefs. Pete and Gib went to the small refrigerator and pulled out two bottles of soda pop.

"I get concerned about her," Gib admitted.

"She could walk on a damned land mine out in a rice paddy at any time," Pete said. "Or get shot at by these VC snipers that are cropping up more and more every day."

"Or get kidnapped by the VC."

Scratching his damp hair, Pete pursed his lips. "She's trying to do too much. Last time I was there, she was playing doctor. Isn't being an agricultural advisor enough?"

Gib shook his head. "No argument from me, but Tess has a great love of these people. I worry about her. This place has really drained her emotionally. I wish she hadn't signed up for a second tour. She needs a rest...."

Sourly, Pete looked around. "Well, if you ask me, these gooks aren't worth that kind of attention. They live in the Stone Age, they're backward.... They don't even have plumbing in their homes, or a commode!"

Frowning, Gib said, "Look, Pete, I know you don't like the Vietnamese but don't call them gooks. At least, not in front of me."

Warned, Pete sank into silence. He reminded himself that Ramsey was exactly like his sister: a sucker for the underdogs of the world. After they'd finished debriefing and were walking back to the headquarters tent, Pete decided to test Gib.

"Hey, let me have permission to drive over to Le My. I want to see if Tess has got those pieces of plywood up."

Ramsey shrugged. "Go ahead. Ask Tess if she'll consider coming in tonight. Tell her I'd like to see her and catch up on what she's been doing out there."

The gloom that had surrounded Pete immediately dissolved. With a grin, he said, "Yes, sir, Major." Rubbing his hands together, Pete could hardly wait to see how his gifts had made Tess's life easier. How would she respond to him? Would she be glad to see him?

On the way over in the jeep, Pete frowned at himself. Since when had he ever felt *this* good about seeing a woman? His heart felt expanded, and happiness kept throbbing through him, catching him off guard. Trying to tell himself it was the "chase" that had him so pumped up, Pete ignored the other possibilities. All he wanted—no, needed—was to see Tess again. What a lucky bastard he was.

Pete went straight to Tess's hut at the far end of the village. The children, half-naked, skinny, their eyes dancing with joy, ran all around him. Ordinarily, Pete hated the kids following him, but something was changing inside him, and he permitted them to hang around him.

"You're a bunch of little ragamuffins," he told them.

They looked up at him with wide smiles on their faces.

"Poor rug-rats," he added.

More smiles.

With a grimace, Pete dug into the pocket of his flight suit and threw out five packs of gum and some chocolate bars. As the gifts hit the red dirt, the children scampered after the treasure.

By the time he got to Tess's hut, Pete was alone. Behind him, he heard the screeches, laughter and shouts of the children vying for the cherished gum and candy. He tried to ignore the good feeling his lousy little present to the kids had created.

"Tess? It's Pete...." He pulled the orange curtain aside. A frown gathered. She wasn't home, but then neither were any of the gifts he'd given her. The same old worn rice mats were on the floor, and the sides of the hut were just as breezy as before. What had she done with the supplies?

Turning, Pete spotted Tess coming into the village, her black cotton pants rolled above her knees, her legs and bare feet glistening with water. She'd just come out of a rice paddy, no doubt. Even in that god-awful bamboo hat she insisted on wearing and her baggy Vietnamese clothes, she looked lovely in his eyes. Her red hair was caught up in a ponytail. He watched with studied intensity to see what kind of expression she'd have on her face when she realized he'd come to see her.

"Pete!" Tess's heart leaped wildly, and she automatically raised her hand. He stood uncertainly by the opening of her hut, a frown on his handsome features. With a laugh, she moved into a loping trot, covering the distance more quickly. As she drew near, Tess took off the bamboo hat and ruefully touched her hair, sure to need a brushing.

"Hi, there!" she greeted warmly, coming up to where he stood. Under one arm he had a package. "This is a wonderful surprise. When did you get here?"

Hungrily, Pete drank in Tess's open, glowing features. Momentarily, he lost his voice. How could she possibly have grown more lovely in these two long, miserable weeks? She had. All the sourness he felt washed away beneath her welcoming smile. He wanted nothing more in life than to taste those deliciously curved lips.

"Hi...just a few minutes ago." He jabbed a thumb toward her hut. "Hey, where's all that plywood and stuff I brought to you? You were supposed to take them for yourself."

With a laugh, Tess ducked into her hut. "I did. Come on in for a moment."

Grudgingly, Pete followed her. Tess set her hat down on a rice mat and then knelt before a large, rusty tin bowl. She poured water in it from a chipped ceramic pitcher and sluiced the liquid over her face, neck and arms. She used the towel—if the cotton rag could be called that—to pat her skin dry.

"Actually," Tess said, glancing up at him as she dried her cheek with the towel, "all of it has been used."

"Not here," he protested.

"Others needed it a lot worse than I did, Pete."

Unhappily, he sat down cross-legged on one of the rice mats where he could watch her. Each of her movements was economical; there was no wasted motion about Tess. "What about you?"

"I get along fine with what I have here. Don't look so unhappy, Pete. The comforters were distributed to six mothers with babies. The Snoopy blankets went to several families who had nothing."

"And the plywood?"

"Remember? I told you we'd use them to start building a school?"

Glumly, Pete nodded. He handed her the sack. "Here, this is for *you*, not these damned people."

She quickly dried her hands and hung the towel up on a nail driven into one of the main beams of the hut. The paper sack was badly wrinkled and she smiled.

"What have you scrounged up now?" Tess came and sat down next to him, the sack resting on her crossed legs.

"Some little things," Pete hedged, trying to pretend not to be too interested in her excitement.

"Jams! Jellies! And look at this: all kinds of makeup!" Tess looked over at him, once again struck by the expression on his features. She placed the six jars of preserves to one side. "These I can definitely use."

"*You* use them. Don't you dare give them away."

She grinned. "Now, Pete, if you give a gift to me, it's mine, right?"

"Yeah."

"And I have the right to use it any way I see fit. Right?"

He didn't like the merriment in her dancing green eyes. "You're leading up to something."

With a chuckle, Tess nodded. "I'll keep one jar, but I'll share the rest with the people."

With a sigh, Pete shook his head. "What about the cosmetics? I even managed to get some Chanel perfume for you. And there's lipstick in there, not to mention makeup."

Wryly, Tess held his gaze. "First of all, the water buffalo go crazy if I 'smell' like an American. When I first came over here, I used to wear lipstick and a little dab of perfume. The first water buffalo I encountered tossed his horned head, snorted and charged me. Later, after I climbed down out of the nearest tree, the village chieftain told me they hated the odor. I also found out that the mosquitoes and other insects *loved* my perfume, and I ended up with more bites per square inch on my body than you could believe." She smiled softly and touched the makeup. "To tell you the truth, Pete, I've never been one for much makeup. Remember? I was that string bean of a Texas girl who hid away in her dorm studying and making good grades instead of partying like the prettier, more popular girls?"

Disgruntled, Pete stared down at his clasped hands. Any of the Viet women at the O club would have been thrilled with these presents. "I thought all women used makeup."

"Some do, Pete. I just never did." Tess pointed to her copper freckles. "I kinda like the natural look." She laughed gently. "Look at me! I don't think very many American women would approve of what I do or how I look. I can't say I blame them, but I'm happy."

She was. Pete drowned in her rich verdant eyes, hotly aware of her ability to share her incredible warmth with him. The ache in his body heightened to a painful degree. How many times in the last two weeks had he dreamed of bedding down with Tess, taking her? Too many.

"Well," he groused, rallying as he took the paper bag back into his hand, "I know some bar girls who will kill for this stuff."

"Oh," Tess hooted, getting to her feet, "and I imagine you'll extract a price from them for it, too."

He grinned. "Everything in life has a price tag on it. Can I help it if I'm great at exchanging goods?" He stood. "Your brother would like you to come back with me. He needs to see you."

Tess nodded and released her red hair, brushing it quickly. "I do owe Gib a visit. Time goes by so fast out here, Pete. There's so much to do."

Pete reveled in the sight of Tess brushing her rich, red hair. Even in the half light of the thatched hut, he could see highlights in the strands. The ache to tunnel his fingers through that thick, shoulder-length mass seized him.

"Like what?" His voice had thickened.

Tess quickly rewrapped her hair with a rubber band, the ponytail back in place. She leaned down and filled her ever-present green knapsack with a few articles. "Well, I'm trying to get the local Vietnamese government to approve my application for a pump. The people in Le My have a lousy water source that carries raw sewage in it, and I've gotten them to dig a well. We hit water today, and now, if I could get my hands on some pipe and a pump, they'd use it." She frowned and turned back toward him, the knapsack slung across her shoulder. "Of course, that means a generator to generate electricity, otherwise the pump wouldn't work. Sometimes it all seems so impossible. I don't want them drinking that filthy water. I can't get them to understand that it's causing disease among them."

"What if you did have a generator and a pump?" Pete asked, walking at her side as they left her hut. The hot midafternoon sun poured through the village, with no trees to give shade.

"As soon as the novelty wore off, the villagers would use the generator."

"Positive?"

Tess gave him a shrug. "Pretty much so. Why?"

"Because I happen to know where I can get my hands on a pump. Now, a generator's another thing. Those babies are at a premium here in Nam because of the U.S. buildup."

Gripping his arm, Tess whispered, "You can get these things for us?"

"Sure."

Releasing him, Tess gave him a guarded look. "How much will it cost?"

"A date in Saigon with me, honey. Now, is that too much to ask?"

With a laugh, Tess climbed into the jeep. "I'll have to think about this, Captain Mallory. I already owe you some time at the officers club. Let's just see how that goes first, shall we?"

Triumphantly, Pete smiled. The jeep roared to life and he quickly backed out of the area and headed down Highway 14 toward Highway 1. The vehicle bounced along the rutted road, a cloud of dust rising in its wake. "It will be a date you'll never forget," he promised her wolfishly.

With a roll of her eyes, Tess tipped her head back and laughed fully. Still, another part of her, the part curious about lifting that wall around Pete, was intrigued and she wanted to know more.

At the row of tents reserved for civilian personnel at Da Nang, Tess had one all to herself. Outside the nondescript olive green tents was a line of showers made out of wooden walls with shower heads attached. It wasn't pretty, but it was functional. Tess stood under the tepid water and scrubbed herself clean with a bar of French milled soap. Drying off, she took the set of civilian clothes she'd hung over the plywood partition and dressed. Pete had promised to pick her up at 1700, to take her to dinner at the O club, replete with that promised glass of ice water. Glancing at her watch, she saw it was already 1700!

"Darn..." Tess hurried back to her tent, rummaged around and located her toiletry items. She brushed her still-damp hair, grabbed her clean knapsack and hurriedly left her tent. The area was deserted, although Tess knew a number of American technical advisors, all men, also lived in this section of the barracks. They were still at work. The rows of tents behind her housed the officers that comprised headquarters staff for the marine effort at Da Nang.

Pete Mallory was sitting in the jeep when she exited the tent row.

"Don't say it," Tess said, walking over to the vehicle. "I know I'm late."

He smiled, observing the dramatic change in Tess. She wore a short-sleeved pink cotton blouse, white cotton slacks and sandals. Her hair was thick and full, and framed her face to make her glorious green eyes just that much more beautiful. And to his surprise and pleasure, Tess even wore some pink lipstick and a set of dainty white earrings! When she came to sit in the jeep, he inhaled a spicy scent of her perfume.

"I expect a woman to be late," Pete teased with a smile. "Anyone ever tell you that you're a knockout, Tess Ramsey?"

Heat flowed up her neck and into her cheeks as she avoided Pete's hooded stare, desire written in his eyes. She placed the knapsack on the floorboards between her feet.

"Thank you, Captain. You don't look so bad yourself." And he didn't. He was wearing a bright Hawaiian-print shirt with red, blue and yellow tropical flowers, a set of loose khaki slacks and dark brown loafers—a far cry from his uniform. His smile was very confident. Very male.

"Yeah, I clean up pretty good when I want to." He reached over and barely grazed her flaming cheek. "But, honey, so do you. Man, you are a knockout. Those boys over at the O club are gonna drool all over themselves when they see you come in on *my* arm."

"So what do you see in living in Third World countries?" Pete wanted to know over dessert much later at the O club. He'd paid the Vietnamese waitress to put them in a corner where conversation and privacy were possible. Everywhere else in the dining room of the club—a large tent with a plywood floor—groups of various men, mostly marine officers, filled the tables. Pete was the only one with a woman—and an American, at that.

Tess sipped the hot coffee, holding the gold-rimmed china cup in her slender fingers. "As John Kennedy said before he was assassinated, we can all make a difference, remember? I liked his concept of the Peace Corps, and his commitment to the world at large. What about you? What made you join the Marine Corps?"

Pete always got edgy when the conversation went back to him. "You know—the image."

"Come on," Tess said, hooting, "give me the truth, Pete. You're evading me—again."

"Well...maybe. I received a degree in aerodynamic engineering, and I wanted to fly. After officer's candidate school, I went to Pensacola, Florida, to try and win my wings, and I did. Helicopters fascinate me."

"Why?"

"You can do so much more with them than you can a fixed-wing aircraft." He used his hands to show her. "You can get that bird to stand on its nose if necessary, to squeeze into some tight places. I like the versatility of the chopper."

"And the marines? Why them? You could have joined the army."

"The doggy army?" He groaned. "No way, honey."

"I know Gib joined the corps because our dad was a marine. It was a family tradition." She skipped lightly over the family matter, never forgetting Pete's explosive and negative response about his mother. "What made you choose the marines?"

He eyed her. "You don't give up, do you? When you want something, you just keep chipping away until you get it."

It was her turn to grin. "I'm like a bulldog, Pete."

"No argument from me. The reason I liked the marines was their pride and esprit de corps. It was like a tight-knit family, I guess." He frowned and moved the fork absently around on the white linen tablecloth in front of him. "To tell you the truth, I grew up having no pride in anything. All my friends had families...parents...a mother and father who were proud they were in college, or at the naval flight facility in Pensacola getting their wings...crap like that. I had no one who cared about what I was or wasn't doing, so I wanted to join something that had an inbred pride. Just being a marine was a big deal. It made people stop and look at me with respect. They knew I was someone special because I'd made it through boot camp and all." He snorted and glanced up at Tess. "Sounds corny now that I've said it."

"No," Tess offered gently, "it sounds fine. With your background, you could've turned out a lot different. Maybe a lot worse, you know."

He gave her a curious look. "Why is it when I get around you, I become a bleeding-heart liberal baring my dark, hopeless soul?"

"Gib always said I was a good shoulder to cry on. Maybe that's why. And you're far from hopeless."

He ignored her comment. "What about you, Tess?" He waved the fork in her direction, frustration evident in his voice. "You've got looks, you've got brains and yet you're here—in Nam. Why? Why not be back in the States, married with a brood of kids like other American women?"

"I come from a large Texas ranch family, Pete. I'm the youngest of the brood of four, and the only girl. After Dad died unexpectedly, I watched my mama work, slave over a hot stove, and raise us." She sighed and smiled slightly. "Maybe I wanted more, I don't know. I didn't want to be tied down like she'd been. I loved adventure and challenge, so I went out and got it after graduating with honors from Texas A & M. My first assignment as a government AID official was in the Philippines. I helped those people improve their farming methods and saw the contribution increase their food yield and better their way of living. It made me feel awfully good about myself."

"So there's more to life than baking bread, having a husband and kids?"

"Some day, I intend to have that, too," Tess said, meeting his sour smile.

"Do you know how different you are?"

"Yes."

"Does it bother you?"

With a laugh, she asked, "Why should it? I'm happy with what I'm doing. I'm proud of what I've been able to accomplish. I feel needed. I belong."

Pete sat there mulling over Tess's fervency, and her very clear-cut values. There was a confidence shining in her eyes, and well-earned pride in her work. He understood all too well about those needs being fulfilled.

"You got a boyfriend?"

Tess laughed. "Nothing like being blunt, is there?"

"Well?"

"No. Not presently."

"You ever been engaged?"

Tess laughed lightly, as if it were no big deal. "Once," she admitted. "When I was over in the Philippines, I met Eric Hampton. He was a Peace Corps volunteer. A really nice guy. We fell in love. It was that simple." And that complicated, Tess wanted to add, still hurting and confused as to why Eric had drifted away from her.

Pete mulled over her story. The lights above shone on her loose, beautiful red hair. The need to touch her hair with his hand shook him. There was such gentleness in Tess. She was a strong woman, there was no doubt, but it was a woman's kind of strength.

"I can't believe any man in his right mind would have let you go," Pete hedged, watching her facial features closely. Although she'd tried to pretend that her past love affair meant nothing to her, Pete saw differently. He saw a shadow in her eyes, pain.

"Well . . ."

"What did he do? Set you up to get you into his bed by dangling the right carrot in front of you? An engagement ring?"

Anger tinged her voice. "Eric didn't become engaged to me just to get me into bed. I was in love with him—or so I believed."

He nodded thoughtfully, interested in Tess's reaction. "I don't want to burst your bubble, honey, but most men will do anything to get the woman they want into their bed. Look at me—I'm the same way."

Tess stared at him, outraged that Pete would even suggest such a thing of Eric. "Not every man lies, Pete. Eric didn't. He was honest and so was I. It just didn't work out, that's all."

Picking up her work-roughened hand, Pete held her wavering gaze, filled with hurt. Gently, he squeezed her fingers. "Honey, there's one good thing about me: I'll never lie to you. I'm up-front all the time. I had so many lies told to me growing up that I promised myself when I was old enough to escape the orphanage I'd never lie to myself or anyone else." Leaning down, he pressed a kiss to the back of her hand. Her flesh was warm and fragrant. "I want you, Tess Ramsey, in my arms, in my bed and with me as much as I can possibly wrangle under the circumstances." Pete sat back, surprised by the emotion behind his line. And that was all it was—a line. Or was it? Where the hell had all these unexpected feelings come from?

Tess colored and withdrew her hand from his. His light, provocative kiss made her skin tingle wildly. His statement was just a line, Tess thought sadly. She wanted to believe Pete, and the powerful feelings his words aroused, but she didn't dare. "Actions always speak louder than words," she challenged.

Her response hurt him. She was wary of him, justifiably so. Still, Pete had wanted Tess to believe him. "How about the rest of what I want from you?"

She took a sip of her coffee. "I don't trade myself for anything, Pete."

"But I can get you a generator."

"No."

"And a pump."

"No."

He sighed. "You drive a hard bargain, lady."

"You can't buy love or affection."

Pete slanted her a wry look. "There's no such thing as love. An hour in bed together and we can share a lot. How about it?"

With a shake of her head, Tess laughed. "You're incorrigible, Pete Mallory."

"But you like me anyway? Just a little bit?"

Tess studied his shadowed face, very much aware of his vulnerability. "If you'd shed that wall you're wearing around you like a good friend, there's an awfully nice guy under there with a big heart. *That's* the guy I'd like to get to know."

"Then there's hope!" he crowed triumphantly.

"Only if you shed that image," Tess warned, still chuckling.

Pete touched his shirtfront where his heart rested. "I don't know if I can ... or if I want to."

"Why? Because you're afraid of getting hurt?"

He nodded. "That's right."

She became serious and set the coffee cup aside. "Why all this tough-guy come-on, Pete? What made you throw up this kind of image to women? The guy hiding under there's pretty nice, in my opinion."

He tapped the fork on the linen. "When I was a kid, every foster home was like a new possibility that a family would adopt me ... want me...." He avoided the word *love*. By that time, he'd had no idea what the feeling was supposed to be all about. The tapping grew quicker on the table. "At every house, I found out I was wanted to a certain extent, but usually I was an errand boy doing this, that and the other thing. I felt like a damned servant more than a part of the family." He lifted his chin and stopped tapping the fork. "So, I got tough. I quit trying to reach out to be something for them."

Tess's heart ached for Pete. Reaching over, she took the fork out of his hand and put it aside. "I like the man inside the wall he hides behind." She placed her hand over his and held his dark gaze. "In some cases, you're all talk, and I know that, Pete. Your actions have spoken for you sometimes, and I like what I see."

He gripped her hand, her voice ladened with emotion. "Yeah?" he croaked. Something about Tess made him want to come out from behind that wall.

"Yeah." She leaned over and pressed a chaste kiss to his recently shaven cheek. "Come on, I've got to get back to the tent. I have to get out to the village early tomorrow morning. We're starting to lay bamboo pipe from the well."

Just the soft brush of her lips against his flesh sent a bolt of heat and longing through Pete. He sat there for a moment, stunned by her ability to fearlessly show herself and her feelings. The fact that she'd kissed him made him feel great. As he released her hand—reluctantly—and stood up to slide her chair back for her, he gazed down at her.

"No sack time for that pump, huh?"

She stood and smiled. "No."

"I had to try."

"I know."

"Damn, woman. Come on, I'll drive you back to the barracks."

Tess left the O club with Pete, his hand resting lightly on her elbow. A feeling of danger moved through her. She was on highly unstable emotional ground with Pete. He'd finally leveled with her, finally trusted her with a small bit of himself. The discovery made her giddy and cautious. There was a fine human being under that rough Marine Corps pilot facade, and she wanted to know him. But at what cost to herself? And to her heart?

Chapter Five

A week later, Pete found Tess standing near a dike, up to her knees in a rice paddy. He had counted the days, hours and minutes until he could see her again. As he sauntered out onto the dike, dressed in his flight suit, he smiled when Tess looked up and spotted him.

"Hi, Pete," she greeted, straightening.

The late-morning sun slanted and Pete was glad he had his dark aviator glasses and utility cap drawn low to shade him from the blinding glare. He grinned and came to a halt, his hands resting arrogantly on his hips.

"Now, what kind of people get turned on by rice?" he wanted to know.

Standing in the murky, muddy water, Tess said archly, "Brides, ministers and agricultural experts."

He thrilled to her welcoming smile and the warmth in her eyes that he knew was for him alone. These once-a-week visits were for the birds. Pete wanted to see Tess a hell of a lot more often. "You really find this exciting?" he asked with a flourish of his hand to the surrounding squares of water holding the thin blades of rice.

"Rice has a certain charm," Tess said, wading closer to the edge of the paddy.

"Compared to what?"

Grinning, Tess leaned over and stroked one of the long slender blades. "Compared to jocks like you."

Pete shrugged, thinking how lovely Tess looked despite her damned Vietnamese dress. "You know, if you eat rice, it'll slant your eyes."

Tess laughed and stared up at him. Pete looked so proud and confident standing there. A smile lurked at the corners of her mouth. "Are my eyes slanted?"

"No. Do you eat rice?"

"Every day. Shoots down your prejudicial theory, doesn't it, Mallory?"

"How do I know you haven't had cosmetic surgery to correct the condition?"

"You're impossible." Tess laughed as she placed her foot on the dry soil of the dike to climb out.

Pete extended his hand and grabbed hers. With a haphazard grin, he flung back, "So are you."

Once up on the dike, Tess unrolled the damp, dark blue baggy slacks until the material brushed her bare feet. She looked over at Pete and felt heat cascade through her under his predatory gaze. The sensation was exciting and unnerving. She pushed the damp red tangle of her hair away from her cheek.

"You have a gloating look on your face," Tess decided.

"Now, is that any way to greet the man of your dreams after not seeing him for a week?"

"Oh, brother."

"Tess..." Pete reached out as she started to walk past him. He gently snagged her arm and brought her around until she was standing inches away from him. He gazed down into her lustrous green eyes. "Not even a little hello kiss?"

Her eyes glimmered. "You're such a rascal," she said, and turned away. "Come on, let's get down off this dike."

He followed and caught up with her. "You sound worried. Has there been sniper fire?"

Tess nodded. "Yes, but please don't tell Gib, or he'll come out here and get into a rip-roaring argument about me staying at the village at night instead of my tent in Da Nang. We've had enough fights about it in the past month."

Once they were down off the dike and standing in the greenery that skirted the area, Pete gripped her arm worriedly and slowed her to a stop. "Hey, what's happened?"

With a grimace, Tess muttered, "Two days ago the VC stole the chief's youngest son, Do Hung. We don't know where they've taken him. The chief thinks it's their way of punishing the village because more and more marines are walking across his farmlands in order to hunt VC."

"Did you report this to the base?" Pete demanded, genuinely worried more for Tess than for the son.

"Yes, but the marines will never find Hung." Frowning, Tess whispered, "I'm afraid they'll kill him as an example to the chief and other villagers to stop fraternizing with the Americans."

The terrible realization that Tess could be kidnapped or killed drenched Pete. His hand tightened on her arm. "Then you have to start coming in at night, Tess. Now, don't give me that look, dammit. You know I'm right. If the VC captured Hung, what makes you think you won't be next? Or what about that sniper you just mentioned? You could be killed. Be reasonable for once, will you?"

Tess wavered. "Part of me knows you're right, Pete." She gave a small shrug, enjoying the firmness of his hand on her arm. "But if I change my routine, that's a signal to the VC that their strong-arm tactics are working, and they're liable to kidnap more young boys from the villages or continue their sniper activity." She tried to give him a smile that would ease the care burning in his dark blue eyes. "This is just one isolated incident. I'll be fine."

"But Tess—"

"Why did you come? Did you find my well pump?" she asked quickly, wanting to head off any possible argument with Pete. It was the last thing she wanted to do. The terrible shock of losing Hung, and realizing the boy of fifteen was probably already murdered, hung heavily over her.

Pursing his lips, Pete led Tess toward his jeep in the distance. "Changing subjects isn't going to do it, Tess," he growled, his hand still on her arm. "The marines are devising a new program, a village pacification, where about twenty marines will come and live in a village and protect it. Not only that, but there will be a navy corpsman with the unit, and the village will get needed medical supplies and attention. It's a good program, one that I think respects the Vietnamese way of life and still gives them protection from these damned VC."

"That's a better idea than the other one I've heard, where they're taking whole hamlets and villages and moving them to another so-called 'safer' area."

"Marines are always on top of things," he teased. "That's an army concept you're talking about, and one that I don't agree with. Resettlement isn't the answer. Education, food, medicine and protection where these people live is the answer."

Tess feigned shock. "My heart be still. Pete Mallory isn't as prejudiced as I first thought. Will miracles never cease?"

"What a smart, lovely mouth you have, Miss Ramsey. You'd better be good or I'll do something I've been wanting to do ever since I met you."

Slowing as they approached the jeep, Tess grinned. "Oh, more threats, Mallory. What are you going to do?"

He turned her around, his hands resting lightly on her shoulders. Gently, he cupped them and drew her forward. "Kiss you," he rasped. And before she could protest, he brought her fully against him and claimed her parted lips.

The instant Pete's mouth sought and found hers, Tess knew it was impossible to resist. Heat exploded between them as his lips slid across hers, testing, tasting and exploring. A swift intake of breath lodged in her throat and for an instant, Tess froze. But then, the cajoling insistence of his assault on her ripened senses won out. As his hands moved slowly, reverently, down her spine to her waist, she felt the wild thud of his heart against her breasts. His ragged breath flowed across her cheek and neck as Tess responded instinctively to his invitation to taste and explore him.

Moments spun into a texture of combined heat and light. Her entire body vibrated with need, with a fierce awakening memory of what it was like to be loved after so many years of denial. That thought caused Tess to break the fiery, searching kiss with Pete. He held her, not allowing her to escape, and she was violently aware of his need of her as he opened his stormy blue eyes and stared down at her.

"I—this is wrong, Pete," Tess whispered breathlessly.

"No," he said thickly, "everything's right about it. We're right for each other, Tess." Never had he wanted a woman more than Tess. Part of it was the challenge, Pete acknowledged, but dammit, his heart was hammering away, strident in its need of her, too. No woman had ever captured his heart, his feelings—until now.

Her body—her emotions, desert dry—agreed with his growled words, but her head and her moral values told her differently. "Please . . . let me go."

"You sure?" Pete enjoyed her weight against him, enjoyed where their bodies merged into oneness at their hips. The urge to grip her by her nicely shaped hips and hold her tightly against him was nearly overwhelming.

"Very sure." Tess struggled a bit, frightened of the feelings Pete's kiss had awakened in her.

Releasing her, Pete studied her in that awkward moment afterward. Tess had enjoyed the kiss just as much as he had. That discovery alone was worth the risk of kissing her in the first place. The look in her dazed green eyes confirmed so much, as did her glistening, well-kissed lips.

Touching her hair nervously, Tess whispered, "You shouldn't have done it."

"Sure I should have. I can tell you enjoyed it."

"Stop gloating," Tess muttered, giving him a defiant glare, anger in her voice. Shaken to the core, she added in a trembling voice, "You planned this."

"Sort of. I've been wanting to kiss you from the day I met you."

Tess took several steps away from him. Grasping wildly at any topic except the present one, she pointed to the large cardboard box in the rear of the jeep. "What's that?"

Pete ambled over, pleased with himself, and with her hot, vivid response to his overture. "The pump I promised for your well."

Gasping, Tess whirled toward him. "Really? It's a pump?"

He grinned cockily. "Of course it is. Remember? I told you I was the best scrounger in Nam. You're not a flowers-and-candy kind of girl. I gotta scrounge up a pump to get your attention." A pure feeling flowed through him when he saw the anger over his kiss turn to tears of gratitude in Tess's eyes. How easily touched she was. How hungrily he absorbed each of her moods and expressions of emotions. Pete felt like a thief stealing precious moments from her.

Shocked, Tess touched the thick cardboard box. "If we have a pump, we need a generator to generate electricity so it can be used."

"That's next," he promised, walking over to her side. "But there're some strings attached to that baby."

"I'll bet there are," she growled, giving him a glare.

"Hey," Pete protested, holding up both his hands, "I didn't plan this. If you want a top-of-the-line generator, you have to fly down with me on a C-130 flight to Saigon. I found out from my buddy on the black market that there's a shipment of generators belonging to a consortium of American construction companies scheduled to arrive in a week. He promised me if I got in early enough, I could probably find one sitting all by itself. What do you say?"

A turbulence of emotions, some of longing, some of distrust, warred within Tess as she studied his happy features. When Pete smiled, it was as if sunlight were cascading through her in warm, wonderful waves. The man could make a stone statue come to life with that smile of his, Tess thought grimly, and she certainly wasn't immune to his powerful, persuasive charms.

"Okay, but I'm not going with you to hop in the sack. I want to make that perfectly clear, Pete."

"I read you loud and clear." He grinned wickedly. "But I've already got us a room over at the Caravelle Hotel, the best American-run hotel in Saigon."

"Two rooms, Pete."

"Oh, Tess."

"Two or I don't go, Pete."

"Damn, you're a tough horse trader."

"You haven't seen anything yet," Tess warned him grimly, watching the hope die in his eyes. "This isn't a vacation, Pete. We're going down to Saigon to pick up a generator—*nothing more.*"

"Hey, anything the lady says." He patted the jeep. "Hop in. This ought to make your chief a little happier when he realizes what I brought to him."

As Tess climbed into the vehicle, her heart bled for the chief. What Pete didn't realize was that the whole village was in mourning over the loss of Hung. No gift, no matter what its importance, ever transcended the Vietnamese people's closeness with their family and relatives. Still, as she glanced over at Pete's profile and saw the smile pulling at the corners of his mouth, Tess couldn't begrudge his feeling good about his gift. Once again, the man behind the walls had proved he had a heart of gold.

Tess mulled over the idea of flying to Saigón with Pete. The unexpected kiss they'd shared moments ago lingered hotly in her memory and her body still vibrated with need. Touching her tingling lower lip, Tess closed her eyes as the jeep bounced along the dirt road toward the village. How could one kiss from a man who was intent on stealing anything he could from her, shake her so? What kind of crazy magic was going on here? Tess had no answer. Her heart pounded not only in anticipation of going to Saigon with Pete, but also with fear. Fear of her own vital reactions to him, as a man who excited her as no other ever had.

That evening, Tess caught a ride with a small marine convoy heading back to Marble Mountain. She had the lieutenant drop her off at the marine helicopter squadron tent area to see her brother, Gib. Thanking the officer, Tess hopped out. She was dressed in her khaki jumpsuit with the patches that identified her as a US AID official.

Just as Tess stepped onto the dirt path that led to the hut where her brother worked, a loud, irritating bell started clanging through the hot, humid evening air.

Turning, Tess saw Gib running out of the tent, his face grim. He spotted her, hesitated and then halted.

"Tess."

"Hi...what's going on?"

He settled the utility cap on his head. "Trouble. One of my choppers has been hit by VC ground fire. It's got engine trouble." Gib pointed toward the west, a frown on his long face. "We don't know if it will make it back or not. There's wounded on board."

Tess walked swiftly at Gib's side, his stride longer because of his height. "Well...who is it? Someone I know?" Tess knew a good number of the pilots and crews of Gib's squadron.

"It's Pete Mallory and his crew."

Terror rooted Tess momentarily to the spot. "Pete?" she gasped.

Gib gripped her arm. "Yeah. Come on. You can stay at the line shack. I'll be coordinating the fire rescue team. He ought to be flying in here in about ten minutes if that chopper of his hangs together that long."

Her head spun with questions and a terrible, sinking fear. "Who's hurt?"

"I don't know. One, two, maybe all three of them. My radio man reported hearing them take heavy fire at the landing zone where they were delivering supplies to a dug-in marine company. Radio comms with them is sporadic." Gib gripped her by the arm and forced her stop at the line shack. "No matter what happens, you stay here."

Trembling inwardly, Tess nodded. Her brother, always calm and cool in emergency situations, brushed by her and started issuing a series of orders to the men standing tensely at the line shack counter. Immediately, men sprinted to waiting fire trucks, donning bulky asbestos suits that would protect them from a possible aircraft fire if the helicopter crashed.

The line shack was all but deserted in a matter of moments. Gib had ridden out in one fire truck to coordinate the possible crash sequence. Placing her hands on the wooden counter, Tess watched out the window. She couldn't see Pete's aircraft yet. The young black man who'd remained behind the desk, a marine lance corporal, turned to her.

"He'll be coming in shortly, Miss Ramsey."

Tess nodded tensely. She tucked her lower lip between her teeth. Was Pete wounded? Dying? Closing her eyes, she leaned her full weight against the counter, her knees suddenly shaky.

"I hate this," Tess whispered. "I hate war."

The lance corporal glanced up from his radio duties, his eyes sad. "It doesn't make anyone's day, if you ask me."

Tess saw the ambulance scream by, its siren wailing as it headed toward the landing apron area.

"Mr. Mallory's a fine pilot," the lance corporal went on. "He's got wings instead of arms. If anyone can bring in a crippled helo, it's him. He's got what it takes."

Some of the marine's confidence soothed part of Tess's fear. "But what if he's wounded...dying...?"

"You gotta take this one step at a time, Miss Ramsey. Let's get Mr. Mallory and his crew here on the ground in one piece, first."

Words were so damned useless. Tess stood, her joints frozen, her muscles going tight with fear. Oh, why had she been so breezy and teasing with Pete? Underneath, she knew he was a good man, a man lost in a jungle of emotions and feelings like so many other men, that was all. That kiss. That one heated kiss slammed back to Tess, and she shut her eyes tightly, remembering the feeling of it ... of Pete.

The kiss wasn't like the ones Eric had given her, soft and chaste. Pete's one kiss had been searching, and dominating. There had been taking *and* giving as they'd stood in each other's arms. Opening her eyes, Tess realized that even though Pete wanted her to believe he was a selfish son of a bitch like most other men, he really wasn't.

Her hands tightening into fists on the counter, Tess jumped when the lance corporal leaped to his feet.

"There!" the marine told her, pointing to the west. "There he is!"

Her eyes riveted on the pale golden sky, where the clouds hung along the jungle horizon like cotton balls, Tess saw the limping helicopter slowly closing the distance toward the base. Huge roiling clouds of black smoke poured from the engine located in the nose. Tess's pulse skyrocketed, and sweat bathed her, mingling with her fear.

"Oh, man, that dude's in big trouble," the lance corporal whispered, coming around the counter to stand next to her. "Those Sikorsky helos are tough birds, but I'm afraid Mr. Mallory took a bad hit."

Tess moved blindly toward the door and jerked it open. She ran far enough away from the building so that she could have a full, unobstructed view. She heard the Sikorsky's sputtering engine and saw the helicopter dancing jaggedly up and down in the sky, about a thousand feet in the air. As it drew closer, Tess could see that the side of the fuselage had huge holes torn through the skin. The cockpit windows had been shattered.

"Oh, my God," she whispered. Around her the sirens stopped wailing and the men stood tensely by hoses near their trucks as the helicopter limped toward the chosen spot, attempting to land less than a quarter mile from the line shack.

Just as the helicopter began to descend to the white-painted landing circle on the tarmac, the engine sputtered and died. The bird flailed, the nose suddenly dropping downward. The deadly silence was filtered by the whooshing of the blades. Tess gave a cry, her hands pressed hard against her lips. At the last possible moment, the nose was yanked upward, the helicopter's dying blades found an invisible cushion of air as they sluggishly flailed around and around. Instead of crashing, the helicopter steadied, caught the last bit of available air in the autorotation mode and sank with a loud clanking sound onto the apron.

Tess stood shakily watching as men ran forward with hoses, spreading foam retardant across the nose of the aircraft to put out the smoke and flames in the engine compartment. Her gaze was riveted to the cockpit where she saw only one man moving. The other man was slumped in his seat, held by an array of harnesses, his helmeted head against his chest. Who was it? Pete? His copilot, Joe Keegan? She didn't know.

For the next five minutes, Tess lived in a hellish limbo. Once the smoke and flames were extinguished, an ambulance hurriedly backed up to the fuselage door. Only one of the three men was moving around in the helicopter. She saw navy corpsmen scrambling from the truck to the helicopter to get to the wounded men. Was Pete one of them?

The wait was excruciating. After the ambulance careened away, siren screaming as it headed for the nearest MASH unit tent complex, Tess saw Gib get out of a jeep in front of the line shack. His face was gray, his eyes dark.

"Pete?" Tess asked as he drew up to her.

"They're all wounded," he muttered as he gripped her arm. "They're going over to the MASH unit, Tess. I'm going over now to see how they are."

"How bad is Pete?"

"He was the least injured, I think. I don't know how bad or good, Tess. There was blood everywhere inside that bird...on the crew.... I just don't know."

"I'm going over there. I've got to see Pete."

"No."

"Let me go, Gib."

He gave her a doleful look. "That's no place for you, Tess."

"It's no place for anyone!" Tess cried, pulling her arm out of his grasp. "I like Pete. I care for him. I want to know how he is!"

Stunned, Gib stared at her. He started to protest, then shrugged. His face mirrored his own exhaustion. "Okay, you can come with me. But just wait outside until they get them stabilized. Lieutenant Commander Leslie Simmons is the head of OR over there. I'll try and find her. She'll answer any questions we have."

Tess could see the surprise and question in Gib's eyes at her concern for Pete. She'd told no one of the feelings boiling up inside her. How could she have? This crisis had only just revealed the real truth to herself. She smiled weakly and leaned over, giving Gib a hug. "Let's go."

Pete was sitting on a gurney in the emergency section of OR when he saw Tess walking hurriedly toward the huge tent. Lieutenant Carolyn Purser, who had dressed the wound to his arm, stood next to him. She gave him a penicillin shot to combat any infection.

"That arm will be sore for the next couple of days, Captain. Do you want a sling for it?" she asked.

"God, no," Pete said. He slid off the gurney, pulled his blood-soaked flight suit back on and awkwardly zipped it with his left hand. He was trembling badly. He wanted to hold Tess and escape the unraveling horror twisting in his gut and chest. "Just help my buddies," he pleaded to the young navy nurse.

"They're getting the very best attention, Captain, believe me." She hurriedly walked away through the swinging doors to the triage area that held the worst of the injured crew.

Pete stood there, torn between staying near his friends in the unit, who were being worked on by a separate group of doctors and nurses, and going to Tess. Gib had come in to visit him earlier and make sure he was all right. Pete had assured him he was fine. It was a lie, but he wasn't about to cry in front of his commanding officer. His mouth dry, the metallic taste of blood in it, Pete hung his head and tried to get a grip on the terrible avalanche of fear now thrumming through him. He felt himself wavering.

The doors to the left swung open and then quietly whooshed closed. "Pete?"

Tess stood there uncertainly. Her voice was low and urgent. The trembling sound of it impinged upon his spinning, shocked senses. He opened his eyes and slowly turned his head. She stood three feet away from him, her hand extended to him, her face pale and her eyes huge with fear.

"Don't come any closer," he joked weakly, gesturing toward his flight suit. "I'm covered with ketchup. Somebody in the bird spilled ketchup all over the place...."

Wincing inwardly, Tess realized Pete was trying to cover up the horror he'd just experienced by joking about it. She gave him a wobbly smile and tried to play along. "I can see that." The front of his flight suit was soaked with blood. Tess knew Pete was in shock.

"It's Joe's, my copilot. We...uh...we were delivering C-rats to the guys at an LZ when the VC started shooting. Joe and my gunner, Jerry Random, bought it." Pete looked down at his drenched flight suit, the flies buzzing around him, the smell cloying and making him nauseous.

Girding herself, Tess saw Pete's face go waxen, all color draining from it. She stepped forward, gripped him by his good arm and guided him over to a chair next to an empty desk. It was probably the receiving nurse's desk, but Tess knew she'd understand. She helped Pete sit down.

"You're going to faint," she whispered.

"No, I'm not."

"Don't argue with me, Pete. Where the hell's some water?" She looked around.

"Dunno."

Anxiously, she saw his eyes go dull. "Put your head between your legs."

"...What?"

He was in shock and going deeper by the moment. Angry that there was no one to care for him, Tess pushed his head down between his legs. "Stay there. The blood will come back to your head," she muttered. Where her hand rested, blood was splattered up across his neck and matted in his hair. Swallowing hard, Tess placed tight control on her own emotional reactions. Pete needed her help, not her weakness, right now. "Just stay that way until your head starts to clear," she croaked. "I'll be here. I won't leave you."

Chapter Six

Pete shut his eyes tightly. When Tess returned with a paper cup containing water, he was sitting on the chair, elbows dug deeply into his thighs, head hanging down between his legs.

Kneeling beside him, her hand on his slumped shoulder, Tess whispered, "Here, Pete, drink this."

Her shattering words, "I won't leave you," spun in his aching head as he lifted his gaze. She was a woman, someone fully capable of abandoning him, just as his mother had. Barely twisting his head to the right where she knelt next to him, he studied her drawn features.

"You came back," he rasped, his voice barely above a whisper.

"Of course I did. Here, drink this, Pete. You're in shock."

With a trembling, bloodied hand, he reached for the water. The paper cup slipped through his fingers. Pete watched the contents splash across the plywood floor.

Grimly, Tess stood up. She gripped his shoulder. "It's all right. Let me go get another for you." She would have to walk to the next tent and get it.

Shutting his eyes, Pete waited until Tess was gone. A terrible coldness was spreading through him, a door flung open from the past beneath the shock of the mission, flowing into the present. He had to get away. Staggering to his feet, Pete stumbled back on the heel of his black flight boot, then moved drunkenly toward the swinging doors of the MASH unit.

The world tilted crazily around him as he moved in a daze away from the tent. He had to get clean. The smell of the blood was making him gag, and more than once on his way to his tent, he stopped, vomited and moved on.

As he staggered into his tent, empty since Joe Keegan, his roommate, was still in surgery, Pete jerked at the zipper of his flight suit. He had to get the suit off! He had to get away from the smell of blood. At the shower stalls at the end of the row of tents, he leaned against the wall and fumbled with the laces on his flight boots. His right arm had taken a piece of shrapnel, and his fingers weren't obeying him as well as they should. Making a frustrated sound, Pete tore wildly at the black laces.

Finally, the boots came off, and then so did the flight suit. Both ended up in a gory pile on the sand outside the entrance to the shower, and Pete staggered into the stall. He turned on the shower, feeling the tepid water. It didn't matter what temperature the shower was. He stood, shaking, as the streams of water washed across his head, face and shoulders, rinsing the foul-smelling blood from his hair and skin. Goose pimples rose on his flesh as he hunched over, hands pressed against his face. As badly as the emotions wanted to tear loose from him, nothing would come out. His mouth, dripping with water, stretched into a twisted shape, a fist of rising emotion lodged in his chest. The sound refused to escape his throat and be born into a primal scream of rage, grief and frustration.

How long Pete stood there, his feet spread apart on the glistening plywood floor to steady his shaking body, he didn't know. Just the sound of all that cleansing water gradually cleared his mind. Like a robot, he sought and found a bar of Ivory soap. Looking at the clean white object, Pete remembered the commercials on television about how the bar of soap would float. His fingers curved around it.

First, his hair. It hurt like hell to raise his right arm, and the dressing was now soaked with water, but he did it anyway. The smell of the soap filled the air around him as he scrubbed. He vaguely remembered shrapnel exploding into the cockpit, pieces of it flying around like scattershot. His helmet had taken a direct hit, nearly jerked off his head but for the strap beneath his chin.

Almost an hour later, Pete emerged from the shower and, naked and dazed, walked back to his tent. He left the bloody flight suit and boots exactly where he'd dropped them, not even looking back. Two single cots and metal lockers furnished his small rectangular tent. Pete sat down heavily on his cot before his knees gave out. Shivering, he reached over and found an olive green towel at the foot of the bed. He began to dry himself with shaky, convulsive movements. Somehow, he had to get himself together. Part of his functioning mind knew that his copilot and gunner were in surgery. He didn't know anything more about their condition and probably wouldn't for some time. He'd have to wait.

When he'd dried off, Pete went to his locker, found a clean flight suit and put it on. He had to get rid of the blips of the explosion, of the screams in the cockpit. Locating his second pair of flight boots, Pete grabbed a pair of socks and struggled several minutes before he was able to put them on. He left his boot laces untied. The officers club was where he wanted to go. There, he could drown out the horrible pictures flashing in his head. He could drink enough alcohol to anesthetize himself.

Gib looked up from his desk in squadron headquarters. After he'd spent two hours tensely waiting at the MASH unit, the head nurse had gently suggested that he go back to work. Surgery on the crewmen was going to take a long time. Gib reluctantly left, his heart and mind still back at the MASH unit with his men. His sister, Tess, came in, looking worried.

"I thought you were with Pete," Gib said as he laid his pen aside on a stack of papers that desperately needed his attention.

Tess shook her head. All around Gib, the heart of the helicopter squadron continued to throb—men at various desks doing the necessary paper-chase jobs to keep it functioning. It was two hours after Pete's near crash, and everything appeared to be back to normal. But Tess could tell by the looks on the faces of Gib's men that it wasn't really so. Everyone was affected by the crash. As she halted at Gib's desk, she lowered her voice.

"I'm trying to find Pete. When I went to get him a cup of water, he disappeared on me."

Grimly, Gib nodded and gently pushed back his squeaky wooden chair. "I'm not surprised."

"Why? I was there for him, Gib. I was someone who cared, who would listen if he wanted to talk. Why did he take off?"

Gib's mouth stretched into a sad smile. "Baby sis, this is the side of my business I hoped you'd never get tangled up in."

"It's a little late for that. You're in it."

Gib hesitated, then nodded. "Being part of the service means taking the good with the bad, the peacetime with the wartime, Tess."

"Being squadron commander means twice as much responsibility, too," Tess griped, her emotions frayed.

"Every flight is potentially dangerous, Tess." Gib kept his voice low so only his sister could hear him. "Look, things are heating up out in the bush. I've been trying to tell you that for the last month, but you wouldn't believe me." He gave her a pleading look. "Please come in every night from the villages. Pete was out on a milk run, a flight that was supposed to be routine and boring as hell. According to the company commander, just as his helo was lifting off, the VC opened up with a rocket attack, Tess. A rocket went off right in front of him. It shredded the aircraft like a sieve." Gib grimaced, his voice dropping even lower. "The copilot, Joe Keegan, just died in surgery."

"Oh, no!"

"And from what Lieutenant Commander Simmons, the head of OR just told me, it doesn't look good for Random, the gunner, either. He's critical and unstable.''

"Then," she whispered, "Pete was lucky."

"Yeah, according to Lieutenant Purser, he has a couple of scratches. She dug shrapnel out of his right arm and his neck at the base of his skull, plus some Plexiglas splinters from his left leg. He's the one who will remember this.''

Anguish soared through Tess. "I've got to find him, Gib. He needs someone.''

"Don't we all," Gib said softly. "Pete might be over at the O club, Tess. That's where we go after a bad mission—to drown the pain in alcohol. And don't go giving me that look. I do it, too.''

"I hate this damned war, Gib! We're pawns of two governments who both think they know what's best for Vietnam. Why don't they ask the people?"

"Take it easy, baby sis," Gib soothed, getting up. He came around the desk and placed his arm around her, then led her toward the door. "Look, this has been a shock to you, too. Why don't you go back to Da Nang? Take a nice, long shower and try to forget what happened here. You're looking pretty frayed.''

Tess leaned wearily against her older brother. Gib had always been the strong one for the entire Ramsey clan. She allowed him to lead her out of the tent and into the darkness. He closed the door behind them, and they were alone. When he offered her the solace of his embrace, she stepped into the circle of his arms.

"I'm so scared, Gib," she moaned, burying her face in the folds of his damp flight suit. "I'm scared for all of us . . . but especially for Pete."

He squeezed her gently. "Does this guy mean something special to you?''

Tess nodded. "You know how long he's been chasing me and how long I've been telling him no. He just won't take no for an answer, Gib. I—I guess this crash showed me my real feelings."

Gib pressed a kiss to her hair. "Be careful, baby sis. Mallory's got some serious problems." He gazed down at her shadowed face and huge, pain-filled eyes. "I've seen him break too many women's hearts already. I don't want that to happen to you."

Sniffing, Tess forced back her tears for Pete. "You're right. But it isn't like he hasn't warned me, Gib."

With a sigh, Gib released her and gave her a worried look. "Every time a woman gets serious about him, he abandons her."

Tess stood there, her brother's strength a bulwark for her. "Just like his mother abandoned him."

"What?"

"...Nothing. Just something Pete told me. It might be a key to why he is that way, that's all."

"You're looking tired, Tess. It's been one hell of a day on everyone."

Tess nodded. She reached up and placed a kiss on Gib's scratchy cheek. "How are you and Dany Villard coming along?"

It was his turn to shrug. "I don't know. I know where I want it to go, but she's frightened, and she's got other issues staring her in the face." He smiled tiredly. "Nobody said loving someone was easy, did they?"

Tess knew all too well what Gib meant. What she felt for Pete deep within her heart was much more than friendship. But was it love? Did she dare call it that? Or was it the war overdramatizing her and everyone else's fragmented emotions, extruding them to some invisible breaking point where the only option was to reach out to another human being for support and stability? To reach out for sanity's sake? "No," Tess finally said, "love is never easy."

Gib snorted softly and placed his hands on his narrow hips as he studied the star-studded sky above them. "I remember Pete telling me one time that falling in love was like a shadow on the sky."

"What an odd thing to say," Tess murmured. "What did he mean by that, Gib?"

"I dunno. He muttered something about love being like a shadow in his life, blotting out the sun. I guess he sees love like a bad stain." He smiled slightly. "Pete's a man who lives, eats and breathes flying, Tess. So he sees everything in terms of the sky, I guess. It's where he feels safest, feels strong." With a shake of his head, Gib put his hand on the doorknob. "I've heard of love being a lot of things, but never a shadow on the sky."

Once again Tess felt anguish. "I understand what he meant," she said, her voice roughened with unshed tears. "And it makes sense."

Gib gave her a pat on the shoulder. "Glad it does to you, because frankly, love to me is the sunshine, not the shadow. Get some sleep, Tess. I'll see you tomorrow night?"

"Yes . . . I'll come in tomorrow night," she promised, and melted into the darkness. Pete's analogy of love spun in Tess's mind. Right now, she knew he needed someone to talk to, to share the horror of what had happened today. Grimly she headed toward the officers club in the distance. Maybe she'd find Pete there, and they could talk. Maybe.

* * *

With a groan, Pete opened his eyes. It was morning, and the sunlight was pouring through his tent flaps. His head felt like it was about to split open, and he was sweating freely in the humidity. He turned over and discovered he was still in his flight suit and boots. Rubbing his face, he slowly made it to a sitting position, squinting in the bright light. Over the next half hour, bits and pieces came floating back to his groggy senses. A couple of his buddies had helped carry him back to the tent long after he'd drowned himself in Johnnie Walker Red. He'd blacked out on the cot, and that was the last thing he remembered.

Yesterday his stomach had been clenched like a painful fist, but Pete felt nothing there now. There was a sense of safety in feeling nothing at all, and he closed his eyes, a sigh escaping from his lips. What day was it? He looked at the Playboy calendar taped to his locker. Well, they sure as hell wouldn't schedule him to fly a day after the crash. Good, he wouldn't fly today. And then the scenes of the rocket attack slowly encroached upon his spongy mind.

Joe...how was Joe, his copilot? The kid was just out of marine OCS and navy flight school, and he loved to fly as much as Pete did. Had he made it through surgery?

And Jerry? What about his gunner? God, Random had been assigned to him a year before he'd shipped over with the squadron to Marble Mountain. The lance corporal was a good marine who was gung ho and fiercely loyal. Before he'd shipped to Nam, Jerry had become engaged to be married to Maria back in New York. How many times had Random showed him a picture of that good-looking Italian chick he was going to tie the knot with?

"Damn it," Pete rasped, rubbing his face. He had to get over to the MASH unit and find out how his crew was doing after surgery. Guilt shredded through him as he slowly got to his feet. He should have checked on them last night. The pain in his head increased tenfold. No matter how rotten he felt, he had to make it over to the MASH unit. His crew needed to know he cared. Men stuck together in times of crisis. They didn't abandon one another.

Fumbling for and finding his utility cap, Pete settled it on his aching head. Putting on his aviator glasses to protect his sensitive eyes from the brutal sunlight, he staggered out the tent door. His crew needed to know he was there for them. Men stuck together.

"I'm sorry," the nurse at the entrance desk said, "neither of your crew made it out of surgery, Captain Mallory."

Pete stood thunderstruck. He stared at her, open-mouthed. "But—"

"They're dead," she said as gently as possible. "The body bags are already over at—"

"No!" The cry lurched from his constricted throat. Dazed, Pete turned and ran out of the tent. Back out in the sunlight, he stumbled to a halt. His chest hurt, his eyes burned and he felt a scream clawing up through him, one that demanded to be released. He wavered, both hands pressed against his chest as he tried to absorb the nurse's words, absorb the reality of war. Joe and Jerry were dead. And he was still alive to remember what had happened, how they'd lost their young lives.

Whirling around, Pete moved drunkenly down the flight line toward the nearby beaches. They would be devoid of people, and he needed to be alone. This time he couldn't escape the pain. This time he couldn't go far enough, fast enough, to escape the terrible anguish exploding deep inside him.

Tess's image hovered before his eyes. Tess, who was strong and vulnerable at the same time. As he ran, the humid wind tearing at him, Pete knew he had to see her soon. Somehow, only Tess could protect him against these terrible, overwhelming feelings.

Tess thanked the jeep driver who had given her a lift to her tent from the convoy staging area. The evening was beautiful as she stood outside the tents, looking up at the sky. Lavender and gold stained the horizon, although the serene beauty was ruined by jets taking off and the whap, whap, whap of helicopter blades cutting into the dusk around her. As she trudged into her tent, she worried how Pete was getting along.

Last night she'd gone to the officers club only to discover that he wasn't there. Some of Pete's buddies told her they'd carried him back to his quarters after he'd drank himself into a stupor. As much as she'd wanted to see him, Tess knew it was stupid to try under the circumstances. Early this morning, she'd hitched a ride back out to Le My, and had worked steadily through the day. But not an hour went by that she didn't think of Pete—of the pain he carried over the death of his friends. Tess had gone back to the MASH unit last night, only to find that neither Joe nor Jerry had made it. The discovery had strengthened her realization about how tenuous a hold a person had on life. By the grace of God, Pete had escaped most of the injury. But it could just as easily have been him, Tess acknowledged.

In her tent, she changed into a light cotton wrap and went to take a shower. She had promised to meet Gib for dinner at the officers club at 1800. Yesterday's crash had made her realize that even her brother, whom she loved with a fierceness that defied description, was vulnerable to being shot down.

Tess changed into a light blue cotton skirt that nearly brushed her ankles, a pair of sandals and a simple white cotton blouse with short puffed sleeves. Her mind, and if she admitted it to herself, her heart, were really centered on Pete. Perhaps after dinner she could hunt him down and talk with him—see how he was handling the deaths of his friends and coping with the crash.

Pete Mallory was sitting at the officers club bar when he saw Tess step through the door of the large tent facility. The shot of Johnnie Walker Red hesitated midway to his lips. His heart thudded powerfully in his chest as she stood there uncertainly, as if looking for someone. Him? He tipped his head back, gulped down the whiskey, and placed the shot glass on the varnished plywood surface. Tossing piasters to the Vietnamese bartender, he slid off the stool. The bar was always filled with off-duty marine officers, plenty of Vietnamese bar girls in skimpy miniskirts, loud music and thick clouds of cigarette smoke. The overall odor was a mixture of alcohol and cigarettes, something Pete could tolerate over the memory of other smells that haunted him.

He went to intercept Tess, who stood uncertainly, holding a small leather purse. A huge part of him reached out toward her. His gaze stripped her, and he felt like a starving, predatory wolf devouring her simple beauty with his eyes. What he really wanted—needed—was to bury himself in her warm, loving arms.

"Well, if it isn't my favorite lady," he teased.

Tess whirled to her right at the sound of his voice. "Pete!" She quickly looked him over, her heart beginning to hammer. He was in his wrinkled green flight suit and black boots, the garrison cap tucked beneath one shoulder epaulet. It was his face, the terror lurking in the depths of his blue eyes, that shattered her heart. His skin was pale and beaded with sweat, his mouth drawn into a smile that didn't reach those tortured eyes.

"The one and only. Lady," he whispered as he gripped her by the shoulders, "you look good enough to eat. Come here, give your favorite pilot a kiss."

The odor of whiskey assailed Tess as Pete pulled her toward him. "Pete...no!" She placed both her hands against his chest to stop him. "You're drunk!"

Pete's grin grew. "Me? Drunk? No, honey, not drunk, just forgetting a few things. Come on, how about that kiss? The last one wasn't so bad, was it?"

Heat flew to Tess's face and she struggled out of his grip. "Pete, get ahold of yourself, will you?"

Confused, Pete cocked his head in her direction. "I thought you wanted me."

Tess looked around, afraid someone would overhear their conversation. "Pete, straighten up! You're drunker than a skunk, and I've got no intention of kissing you in this condition!"

Hurt, he muttered, "Well, I just thought you'd be glad to see me. I'm glad to see you."

Tess couldn't stand the hurt-puppy-dog look he gave her. He certainly knew how to manipulate her emotionally. Gripping his arm, Tess turned toward the dining room. She was a bit early for dinner with Gib, so she hauled Pete along with her.

"Come on, mister. There are only two things you're getting from me: hot black coffee and some food in that gut of yours. And don't you dare fight me on this, Pete! Don't you dare!"

He gave her a loose grin and shrugged. "Far be it from me to say no to a lady."

The hostess gave Tess a table in a corner away from most of the other patrons. Tess ordered coffee and hamburgers for both of them, then, after the waitress left, she turned grimly to Pete, who sat at her elbow, the same silly smile on his features.

"You're drunk."

"Naw, I'm not drunk, honey."

"Have you been drinking since yesterday night?"

With a shrug, Pete muttered, "No. I got up this morning and...well, I started drinking late this afternoon." He looked blearily at the watch on his right wrist. "About an hour ago, honey, so don't look so upset. I drink every night. Everyone does."

Her heart wrung with compassion for Pete, but Tess was angry with him, too. "You've been through a lot the last couple of days," she said softly. And then the anger leaked through. "Drinking is just another form of escape, Pete." And there was no doubt he was trying to hide.

Pete held the beaded, cool glass of water between his trembling fingers. Maybe they wouldn't shake as much if he held onto something, he thought. "In this business, it's a healthy thing to do," he said stubbornly.

Tess lowered her voice, tense. "Do you know about Joe and Jerry?"

He winced and refused to meet her eyes. "Yeah..."

Tears flooded into Tess's eyes and she forced them back. "They were your friends, Pete. I'm so sorry you lost them. You've got to be feeling horrible about it."

"Honey, in this business, you don't make friends. It don't pay," Pete muttered darkly. "It's just like women: you love 'em and leave 'em. You don't get tangled up with them personally or they'll end up hurting the hell out of you." He glanced over at her. "War's the same way. You don't get close to anyone, Tess. You don't dare, or it'll rip you apart."

Staring over at the suffering so visible on his features, Tess realized how hopelessly crazy she was to think anything lasting could ever happen between them. "People who care are a shadow to you, aren't they?" she whispered bitterly.

He smiled. "Shadow? Sure, honey, anyone who wants a piece of me is a shadow on my life. Shadows are like blights, you know?"

Tess felt utterly hurt and helpless. No one needed to be held more than Pete did right now, yet he was pushing her away. Staring at him, she tried to determine how to help him. She took his cool, sweaty hand between her own.

"Pete, you're worth more than that, and so am I."

He blinked. "What are you talking about?"

"You and I," Tess whispered, "are worth more than this crazy idea you have in your head. I'm not a shadow on your life! And you certainly aren't on mine, either. Feelings, Pete, are good. Even ones that hurt us aren't necessarily bad." Her fingers tightened on his. "Have you been able to cry for the loss of your crew yet? Have you let yourself?"

With a curse, he jerked his hand away. Glaring at her, he rasped, "You don't know the first thing about feelings!" Pushing to his feet, Pete nearly overturned the table. *Run!* The word pounded through his head. *Run!* Blindly, he staggered around the table and headed toward the door. He heard Tess call him once. Her voice, the awful tone of pain laced with care, washed through him. He had to escape. Blindly, Pete ran through the foyer of the officers club and threw open the door.

Chapter Seven

Pete stood uncertainly by the jeep, staring angrily at the village of Le My. It had been three weeks since he'd last seen Tess, after the crash and loss of his crew. He'd left her at the O club and hadn't looked back—until now. Rubbing his cheek, feeling the bristle of beard beneath his palm, he sighed and stared down at the red dirt beneath his booted feet. What the hell was he doing here? Why didn't the image of Tess's vulnerable features ever leave him—even during his worst nightmares?

A huge part of him wanted to let the past remain buried, as he always had before, but something invisible was pulling him to confront Tess. The village children began to gather around him, giving him curious looks. Occasionally one of the smaller tykes smiled.

Pete watched them slowly surround him and the jeep. These were the children Tess loved so deeply, little ragamuffins caught in the middle of an escalating war. He'd already heard of several children being instructed to carry hand grenades from the VC to some unsuspecting marine who was part of a pacification team in a village or hamlet. Pete shook his head. He never wanted that to happen to him with one of these innocent children. The thought of having to kill a child in order to save himself from being blown up was just too overwhelming to contemplate. War was a filthy thing, he decided.

"You little rug-rats," he muttered, and dug deep into one of the pockets of his flight suit. "Here." Producing six packs of gum, he tossed them among the awaiting children and watched them scream and yell with glee as they fought to get his gifts. As he walked toward the center of the village, Pete felt disgust and anger. It wasn't fair. The kids were caught in the middle. But at least they had one champion: Tess. As he walked, his heavy heart began to feel lighter. Pete couldn't explain why the awful feelings that had hung around him like a dark cloud were suddenly beginning to dissolve. What kind of hold did Tess have over him?

Finally, a small girl dressed in a cast-off cotton dress led him by the hand to where Tess was working. Pete paused at the door of the hut. The curtain had been pushed aside, and Pete peered into the gloomy depths. Tess was on her hands and knees bending over a small boy. He was sick, there was no doubt. Pete stood awkwardly for several moments before he spoke. Just seeing Tess made his heart swell with such a fierce tide of emotion and longing that a lump formed in his throat, blocking his words.

Tess was wearing her Vietnamese clothes once again—loose black pants and a dark blue top. Her hair was haphazardly pinned into a chignon at the nape of her slender neck, and tendrils stuck damply to her temples and cheeks as she worked over the boy, dipping a cloth into a small tin bowl, then wringing it out and bathing the child with it.

Pete's gaze moved to the boy, who couldn't be more than two years old. His left arm was in a dirty bandage, and he was delirious, his extremities moving and jerking of their own accord. Only Tess's soothing voice and the touch of her hand seemed to quiet him. On the other side of the child knelt the mother, who looked to be barely out of her teens. Pete wondered if the child was a by-product of some GI, since he looked almost white and his facial features didn't appear Vietnamese.

"Looks like I came at a bad time," Pete said from the doorway.

Tess gasped. She straightened and gazed toward the door. "Pete!"

He nodded but had no smile for her. Still, the look in her widening green eyes melted his hardened resolve not to let her affect him. Ducking through the entrance, he came and crouched close to where she knelt.

"What's going on with this kid?" he demanded.

Tess felt an incredible warmth suffuse her. "The baby was bitten by one of the village dogs a week ago. The mother didn't tell me about it, because kids get bitten all the time." Sadly, Tess touched the baby's hot, feverish brow and thin strands of black hair. "The dog has rabies."

"Damn." Pete saw the terrible anguish in Tess's eyes as she returned to bathing the child. "How about rabies vaccine?"

"Sure. I'll just run down to the doctor's office and get this poor child that series of shots."

Pete heard the sarcastic edge to Tess's throaty voice. Studying her closer, Pete saw she looked drawn and exhausted. "What can I do to help?"

Tess's hands shook, and she tried to hide her reaction. It had been three long weeks without any contact with Pete. Her emotions were frayed from staying up with the baby last night. "Help or run?" she snapped.

Stung, Pete glared at her. "Look, this rug-rat needs help. I'm offering to do what I can."

Slowly she turned her head. She met and held his angry gaze. "I didn't think you'd want to get involved in anything that might leave you open to hurt."

Grimly, Pete looked into her defiant green eyes, shadowed with fatigue. In that moment, he realized just how much Tess needed to be held. She had to be strong for everyone. Right now, the distraught Vietnamese mother was looking at her as if Tess could cure her child of rabies. Pete knew she couldn't. Putting away his hurt at her accusing words, he muttered, "Did you contact Gib for help?"

"Yes," Tess said wearily, "but he couldn't budge any medical help loose. Now he's down in Saigon with Dany Villard on business."

"What do you need?"

Tess shrugged. "I think it's too late for this little one. Even if we could get him the series of shots, I don't think he'll survive." Pushing a strand of red hair out of her eyes, Tess went on in a dull voice, "What could help in the long run is rabies vaccine for the dogs in the villages I work with. Then we wouldn't have rabies victims."

"Who is the little rug-rat?"

Tess looked down at the baby while the mother took over bathing her child with the washcloth. "His father's an American advisor. Lee, the mother, danced at one of the clubs in Saigon to make enough money to survive."

"She did more than dance."

"She's doing what's necessary to survive," Tess said tightly. "And the American GIs aren't helping the situation. They use these poor women, then throw them away. When Lee got pregnant, the club owner fired her."

"Who's been taking care of her since then?"

"Me. Lee's family is either dead, kidnapped or in the South Vietnamese Army. She and a lot of other young women are falling through the cracks of the system as their families are broken up." Tess smiled softly over at the mother, who looked terribly worried. "I helped Lee deliver her son."

Pete saw the danger in Tess's relationship to the baby. Why didn't she pull away from emotional things like this? Why did she insist upon getting involved when the kid could die, leaving Tess wide open for heartache and grief? Scratching his head, Pete said, "Look, if a helo flies in wounded refugees, they accept them at the MASH units on base. How about if I bring a chopper in here so you can transport the kid and his mother to the base? That way, he's assured of quick medical help."

"Oh, would you, Pete? Could you?"

He shrugged at the sudden hope in her voice and shining green eyes. "I'll do what I can."

"Could you get in trouble for this?"

He grinned sourly. "Hell, I'll just rig an emergency call. Nobody will know the difference back at Marble Mountain."

"But . . . if you get caught . . ."

"I won't. Don't worry about it."

"When can you come?"

"Tomorrow morning."

Tess studied the baby, her brow wrinkled. "It might be too late, Pete."

He straightened to his full height. "It's the best I can do. In the meantime, I'll go back to base and see if I can round up some rabies vaccine for the mutts around your villages."

Tensely, Tess got to her feet, telling the mother she'd be right back. Moving over to Pete, she followed him out of the hut.

"Thank you," she whispered. She reached out to touch his arm, then drew back, remembering he'd been wounded in that arm. Wondering why he'd suddenly stepped back into her life, Tess asked in a low voice, "How are you, Pete?"

He glanced at his healing arm. "Mean as ever. Come on, you can walk me back to the jeep." He looked up at the sky. "You coming into Da Nang tonight?"

Tess hesitated for a long moment, her heart at war with her head. Finally, she fell into step with him. "No, and don't tell Gib when he gets back from Saigon, either."

Pete met and held her gaze, confused by her sudden coolness toward him. "I won't tell him, but you ought to come back with me."

"I want to stay with Lee and her baby. She needs the support."

With a shrug, Pete muttered, "You're just as bullheaded as ever, aren't you?"

Tess glared at him. "Seems to run in our family." Then she gave in to her aching heart, the part of her that was lonely without Pete. "How are you?"

"You already asked me that."

"You never answered."

"I said I'm fine. Mean as ever."

"That's a cover, Pete," she said angrily. Tess halted at the jeep and held his blue gaze, still seeing the remnants of the crash in his eyes. "I want the truth."

He threw his hands on his hips, a scowl on his tense face. "My arm's healed, and I'm back to flying two or three missions daily. I've got a new crew, and I'm trying to train them so they don't get blown away. It's a pain in the ass because I'm afraid of losing them."

Tess tried to fight the need to walk into his arms. Just to be held by Pete would help. "So far, so good. Go on."

He gave her an uneasy look. "What do you mean, go on? That's everything." Dammit, he didn't want to fence with Tess. He wanted to kiss that lush, sinner mouth of hers.

"You haven't said anything about you."

Pete's mouth quirked. "Why do I feel like I'm in a dentist's chair and you're pulling my teeth one by one without novocaine?"

Hurt and angry, Tess touched her damp brow. "Because I care about you, and you know it!"

"Honey, we're on dangerous ground again," he growled. "Quicksand for me. Remember?"

"Life is quicksand," Tess parried hotly. "Ever since the crash, I've been worried for you, Pete."

"Don't waste your worry on me, Tess. I'm not worth it." He gestured toward the village. "Worry for that kid. He needs your care."

"You're such a bastard at times, but you don't fool me with your cheap talk and blustering." Tess poked him in the chest. "Remember? I'm the one who can see through that wall you try to scare everyone off with. Now, level with me," she ordered. "Has the crash left you with nightmares?"

He pushed dirt around with the toe of his flight boot. "Yeah...sometimes."

"Just sometimes?" Her voice went off-key in disbelief.

"Okay...I get them almost every damned night!" he snarled. "Are you satisfied?"

Tess leaned against the jeep, trying to control her anger and frustration. "What else?"

"There is no 'what else,' dammit!"

"Why do you get so upset at giving little bits of information about yourself, Pete? Don't you know it's normal in a relationship to share private things with the other person?"

Pete glanced over at Tess's tense, shadowed features as the sun set behind the rounded, green-velvet hills. "I get upset over anyone knowing how I really feel, okay?"

"And what do you think I'm going to do now that I know about your nightmares? Go tell Gib? Blurt it all over base to embarrass you?"

"You could," Pete muttered, crossing his arms over his chest and leaning against the jeep near her.

Tess whispered tautly, "Not every woman is to be mistrusted! Don't judge me by what your mother did to you." Her voice became strangled with emotions that begged to be released. "I like the guy underneath that tough facade. Can't you begin to look at me? Tess Ramsey? I'm sorry your mother abandoned you, Pete, but not every woman after her is planning on doing the same thing."

He eyed her warily. "You have a damned irritating way of getting under my skin. I'm sorry I told you about my mother."

"I'm not. If anyone has skirted our on-again, off-again relationship, it's been you, Pete, not me."

Cold anger stirred in him. Grumpily, he stared down at the ground, refusing to meet her gaze. "Dammit, Tess, you want a lot."

"No, I want what any normal person does in a relationship: intimacy, honesty and sharing."

He snapped a glance over at her. "Can't have you any other way, huh?"

"No." She held his frustrated gaze. "Pete, I'm serious about you! I want to know about you, the person, not the Marine Corps pilot, okay? I don't consider this a game, and I hope you don't, either."

"Life's a game, honey."

"Some things in it aren't," Tess blazed. "Look, if all you want is a toss in the hay with me, Pete, then you'd better quit coming to visit. But if you want something more, to share something worthwhile between us, then let's continue seeing one another when our schedules permit."

Pete cursed softly. "Tess, I can't live with you, and I can't live without you!"

"Then something needs to change between us, Pete," she rattled.

"It's scary, Tess."

"What is?"

"You and me."

"Don't you think I'm scared, too?" Tess demanded. Had she said too much? Shocked by her vulnerable emotions, Tess stepped away from Pete.

He held her gaze and realized there were tears in her eyes. He winced. Stunned by Tess's outburst, he stood tensely for a long moment. "I don't like making a woman cry. I can't stand tears."

"Because you don't want to feel, that's why," Tess shot back hotly, wiping the tears away and forcing the rest back. "I want to share something with you, Pete. I loved Eric, and I thought he loved me." Wearily, Tess raised her hand in a signal of surrender. "And then, one day, he broke off our engagement. I never could pull the reason out of him." She closed her eyes, all her raw feelings tearing loose. "Maybe it's me. Maybe I'm not lovable. I don't know. I've spent so many sleepless nights wondering why. What did I do wrong? Is there a flaw in me?" Tess forced herself to look into Pete's shadowed blue eyes. "I have a lot of doubts about myself."

Pete wrestled with very real anger toward Eric. He saw the pain in Tess's eyes, and heard a reflection of it in her voice. Clearing his throat, he whispered, "You've got a lot to offer a man, Tess. You're bright even if you are bullheaded. You're easy on the eyes, and you have a nice way about you."

"Thank you—I think." She rubbed her brow and shrugged. Pete had already hurt her, and he could hurt her more. But Tess didn't know what else to do with all these powerful feelings lunging through her.

Stunned by her honesty and trust in him, Pete shrugged. "Hell, I'm not perfect, either, Tess."

"No kidding."

He managed a sour, tenuous smile. "I had that coming, didn't I?" Silence settled around them. Finally, the words were forced out of Pete. "Look, it's going to be hard to learn to trust a woman—you."

"I know that."

He saw how much he'd already hurt her, and it dug at his conscience. Of all people, she deserved happiness. "I don't have a choice, though," he admitted hollowly. "I like you...."

A part of Tess leaped for joy, but she knew Pete was able to wound her even more if she capitulated to her crazy, nonsensical need of him. "It's a step in the right direction." Tess turned and rested her hand on his arm. "Pete, let's learn to be friends first. No demands, no expectations of each other. Don't see me as some girl to be chased down and bedded. I'll try not to let my own doubts about myself interfere. Fair enough?"

"I guess...."

"Listen to me. In this world everyone is hurt by someone or something, Pete. What's important, I've discovered, is going on despite the scars we get by living life. We can't let a wound stay open and fester, because in the end it'll stop us from living life to the fullest. Eric nearly killed me in one sense, just as your mother nearly did you." Her grip on his arm became firm. "Aren't we worth more than that? Why let shadows from the past block the sunlight of what we can possibly be to each other? The only way we're going to find out is to trust each other—fully."

Her hand on his arm sent a heated wave of longing through him. Pete stood, mesmerized by her upturned face bathed in the pale pink of the sunset. There was such hope in her eyes. He ached to lean those scant inches closer and kiss her, to feel her heat and giving once again. Restraining himself, he looked up at the cloudless sky. "No promises, Tess."

"I didn't ask for any."

"I'll try," Pete finally whispered, meeting her lovely emerald eyes. "That's all I can do, and I don't know if it's enough."

Tess reached up on tiptoe and pressed a chaste kiss to his cheek, rough with five o'clock shadow. "It's enough for now," she whispered unsteadily. "More than enough."

Just the brush of her lips against his flesh broke his control. Pete blindly reached out and grabbed Tess. The driving need to kiss her, to feel her soft, womanly heart, shattered through the barrier of his fear.

Tess gasped, felt Pete's hands settle on her shoulders and pull her hard against him. His mouth smothered hers in hungry urgency, taking her softness, giving back his heat, his starving desire for her. With a moan, Tess surrendered and sagged against his tall, tense frame. His mouth moved like fire across her lips, his tongue quickly finding entrance. The world exploded before Tess, and her moan was lost in his growl of triumph.

"God, woman," Pete breathed as he drew away, "you're enough to try a saint, do you know that?"

Tess felt herself go weak beneath his stormy blue gaze. Her lips throbbed with the power of his male kiss. Dizzied and shaken, she took a step away from him because she wanted to kiss him again. And if she did, all would be lost. Tess stared up at him, words jammed beneath the volcanic urgency building within her. "There won't be any lines between us anymore," she warned breathlessly.

"That's going to cramp my style," Pete rasped. He saw the luster in Tess's eyes, and God help him, he wanted her more than ever. The kiss hadn't solved a thing. Instead, it had stirred his hungry longing to even more urgent life.

"Then," Tess whispered unsteadily as she raised her hand in farewell, "you'll just have to be plain old Pete Mallory—the man I like."

With a shake of his head, he reluctantly slid into the jeep. "Music to my ears."

"It better be to your heart, Mallory."

With a laugh of relief, he started up the jeep. Tess had kissed him just as eagerly as he had her. "Hey, are you sure you don't want to come into Da Nang for the night?"

Tess hesitated. "No, but thanks anyway. See you tomorrow morning?"

"Roger that, lovely lady."

Tess headed back toward the village, her heart singing. She'd risked everything with Pete, and miraculously he hadn't thrown it back in her face. Hope raced through her.

Some of her euphoria dissolved as she neared Lee's hut. The baby's deteriorating condition quickly snuffed out her sunny emotions. Tess wondered bleakly as she entered the hut if her world would ever stop being this roller coaster of highs and lows. As she knelt next to the baby and smiled over at Lee, Tess prayed for the morning to come quickly. The waxen pallor of the boy was frightening; she knew his small life hung in the balance.

Pete gave his crew orders that if any shooting or rocket attacks began as they sat on the ground near Le My, to take off without him. They could pick him up later when it was safe. As he unplugged the phone jack to his helmet and slid out the rear door of the Sikorsky, he thought he'd be damned if he'd place another crew in jeopardy.

Pete jogged through the village. The smiling Vietnamese children welcomed him as he headed to Lee's hut. It shouldn't take long, he thought, a little perplexed that Tess hadn't been waiting with the mother and son. She knew how dangerous it was bringing a chopper into a village area. The VC were really turning up the heat, getting more aggressive by the week.

"Tess?" Pete shouted as he neared the hut. A huge crowd of people surrounded the opened door. Confused, he threaded through the Vietnamese, calling again for Tess.

At the door, he halted, his eyes adjusting to the dim light within the thatched hut. Lee, the mother, was wailing and holding her son in a blanket to her breast. Next to him, her eyes red-rimmed, was Tess. Pete opened his mouth to speak, then realized with a sinking sensation that the boy had died.

Damn. He hesitated. His instincts told him to avoid the situation. To stay meant to feel. He clenched his teeth, torn. Emotions were dangerous, pulling him apart in ways he never seemed able to recover fully from. But one look at Tess's vulnerable face, the raw emotions written there, and Pete knew he couldn't leave her—no matter how much it hurt him. Grimly, he turned on his heel and ran back to where the helicopter sat, its blades still kicking up huge clouds of dust. Pete stopped beside the new crew chief and motioned him to hand over the spare communications cable. Pete plugged the jack into his helmet connection and ordered the copilot to dust off and leave him behind. The younger man, a twenty-two-year-old with blond hair and hazel eyes, gave Pete a thumbs-up. It would be his first flight without the pilot on board. Pete knew he was breaking a lot of rules by staying behind, but he couldn't turn his back on the look on Tess's face.

As he hunched and quickly moved away from the whirling blades, Pete thrust his hand up in the air, moving it in a circular motion to tell the copilot to lift off. His thoughts and his heart centered on Tess. Why was he doing this? He didn't have to stay behind. He could have avoided an emotional confrontation. But he hadn't. With a grimace, Pete pulled the tight-fitting helmet off his head as he watched the dark green Sikorsky whump skyward.

As the helicopter banked and headed back to Marble Mountain, Pete breathed easier. At least his crew was safely away. Turning, he hurried back through the village. Tess needed someone, a shoulder to cry on, and he could provide it. God knew, he wasn't an expert on this. As a matter of fact, Pete ruminated as he drew near the hut and the wailing cries, this was the first time he'd run *toward* something painful instead of away from it. Hope flared in his heart as he carefully wove through the tightly packed villagers, their shrieks and cries rending the air.

Maybe Tess's courage was rubbing off on him; Pete didn't know. Right now, something was pushing him to stay. Some indefinable emotion, as deep as it was startling, was forcing him to hold ground—something he'd never thought he'd do with any woman.

His heart picking up in beat, he made his way to the entrance of the hut. Tess was still in a kneeling position, her face stark and pale, her eyes like wounded holes, mirroring her grief over the baby's death. She was comforting the mother. Pete knew what Tess needed: to cry. And then he laughed at himself—he, who never cried, knowing what was best for her. Moving inside the hut, his hands stretched toward her, Pete ignored his old instincts, still hammering at him to run away. For the first time in his life, he allowed his carefully protected heart to come out from behind that wall he'd built around it since childhood. He reached out to help someone else who was hurting just as much as, perhaps more, than he.

Chapter Eight

Tess cried brokenly with Lee as the mother rocked and held her baby to her breast. It was only when Tess felt Pete's hands settle gently on her shoulders that she looked up. His mouth was grim, his eyes shadowed with pain, her pain.

"Come on," he ordered thickly, lifting her to her feet, "let's get out of here for a while. You've done all you can."

Tess stumbled forward, then sank against Pete. She caught herself, and through a veil of tears, followed him out of the hut and beyond the gathered, grieving villagers. His arm was around her waist, propelling her forward, and she blindly followed, too lost in her own anguish to care where Pete was taking her.

Tess found herself back in her hut, the orange curtain thrown aside to allow bright morning sunlight to stream across the mats on the floor. Pete sat her down and moved behind her, his arms encircling her. His caring broke through the last remnants of grief she had been trying to hold back. Leaning against his body for support, Tess raised her hands, covered her face and began to cry in earnest.

Pete tried to remain immune to Tess's sobs as he slowly rocked her back and forth in his arms, but he couldn't. Anger mixed with his own discomfort, because tears had always disturbed him badly. He tried to figure out why as he rocked Tess and murmured words of solace he knew couldn't possibly assuage her grief. In those minutes of holding her and feeling her tremble, Pete's initial discomfort dissolved.

There was something good and warm about being able to share Tess's pain and comfort her. Eventually, as her tears lessened, Pete turned her around in his arms so that, like a small child, she huddled against him, her face buried against his shoulder, her hands pressed to the wall of his chest. An incredible flood of new, awakening feelings flowed through Pete as he held her, stroking her tangled hair. Pete knew Tess had been up all night with the baby; her loyalty would drive her to do that.

"Such care," he whispered gruffly, his hand resting on her hair. He pressed a kiss to the top of her head. "Tess, you're bleeding yourself dry for these people. You can't keep doing this to yourself, honey. You've got to save something of yourself for you...."

Pete closed his eyes as he felt a tremor pass through her. He held her a little tighter. That was the real problem with her, he realized: Tess had been in the country too long. He knew enough American advisors who were on their second or even third tours in Nam, and it was a damning situation. After a while

they no longer felt comfortable back in America—
some unknown force drove them to come back to
Vietnam. They felt better here. They no longer fit into
the fabric of American society. Gently, he stroked
Tess's shoulder and back with long, smooth motions.
Vietnam was taking every ounce of emotion from
Tess, and she was close to running dry.

He sat on the floor of the hut with her for half an
hour with the sunlight spilling like gold into the darkness, chasing it away—and Pete discovered something else. Tess was *his* sunlight chasing away the
shadows. Savoring the closeness, the intimacy of
holding her in the aftermath of her grief made him feel
humble and good about himself in a way he'd never
before experienced.

"I—I'm all right," Tess whispered brokenly as she
finally eased away from Pete. Touching her bedraggled hair with her trembling fingers, she wiped the last
of the tears off her face.

Looking around, Pete found a brush and comb on
top of a small wooden chest. "Yeah, I know you are,"
he said wryly. "Come here. Turn around and just sit
here for a minute."

Tess allowed him to maneuver her around between
his thighs so that her back was to him. "What are you
doing?"

"Cleaning you up. You look like hell, Tess." He
gently eased the bobby pins out of the messy bun of
red hair. The strands, curled slightly by the constant
humidity, tumbled into his awaiting hands. There was
something incredibly beautiful about the moment, and
Pete absorbed it like a starving man. "I haven't
brushed a woman's hair before, but yours needs it. Sit
still. I hope I don't hurt you more than help you," he

joked weakly as he began to run the brush through the disheveled copper strands.

Sniffing, Tess relaxed as Pete gently brushed her hair. "I am a mess," she admitted, her voice strained.

"In more ways than one." Pete grimaced. "Honey, you need to get away from here for a while."

With a shrug, Tess closed her eyes. "I don't want to be anywhere else." Each hesitant stroke of the brush through her hair seemed to take away a little layer of pain. Pete's hands were healing, whether he realized it or not.

"Yeah, I know advisors who have been over here two or three times who say the same thing. It's an obsession, Tess. It grabs you by the throat and it doesn't let go."

She looked out the door of her hut and heard the cries of grief echoing through the village. "These people are worth caring about, Pete. Forget about the damned government and politics."

"I understand," he soothed. The luxury of skimming his hands across her tamed, shining hair was sensual and exciting. The gleaming strands curled across her slumped shoulders. "There," he said with smug satisfaction, "now you're looking better."

Tess turned around and took the brush from his hands. "Thank you. It's the first time a man has brushed my hair for me."

He grinned shyly. "For me, too. It was different . . . good."

She placed the tortoiseshell brush on the chest. "This is what I was talking about before: intimacy, Pete. The small things, meaningful things shared between a man and woman."

Leaning over, he stroked her waxen cheek with his finger. "I like sharing with you."

"The good and the bad?"

"Yeah. All of it."

Tess gave him a wary look. "It can get rough between two people, Pete. That's when you dig in for the duration and you don't quit."

His smile deepened as he held her reddened eyes. "Honey, I just did two things I've never done with a woman before, and it felt kinda nice. In the past, every time a woman would start to cry, I'd leave in a hurry. And I never held anyone who was in trouble before, either."

"I'm just glad you were here, Pete. It was nice to be held. Usually, I'm the one doing the holding and soothing." Turning around on the rice mat, Tess brought over a small bowl of clean water and retrieved her washcloth from the chest. Her face felt hot and gritty with dust. She hadn't bathed last night as she usually did.

In the quiet of the hut, Pete watched Tess bathe her face, arms and hands. Her graceful gestures sent a building ache through him. In his mind, he pictured her in a hotel room with him, taking a shower together after making wild, heated love. Just the way the sunlight caressed her hair and brought out the living fire of it suggested she was a passionate woman. But Pete knew his thoughts and feelings weren't appropriate for the moment, and he forced himself to address the reality.

"I'm sorry the baby died before I could get here, Tess," he told her in a low voice.

"You tried, that's what counts," she whispered softly as she folded the washcloth and set the bowl aside.

"The kid was too far gone."

"I—I know. I just didn't want to accept it. I thought maybe I'd start to get used to it somehow." Tess pressed her hand against her heart. "But each death gets harder to take."

Pete reached over and captured her hand. "Listen to me, Tess, you need a break from this place. How long has it been since you've had any R and R?"

"I went Stateside between my two tours." And then she shrugged. "Well...actually, I went home to our Texas ranch, went out of my mind with worry about my villages and flew back to Saigon a week later."

"Foolish woman," he taunted gently and lifted her hand to press a kiss to it. "You need time off. Even a thick-headed guy like me can see that. I've got that line I told you about on a portable electric generator in Saigon. How about taking a trip down there with me on a C-130, and we'll see what can be done? I've got to go down for the squadron, anyway. We're not getting certain spare parts for our choppers, and Gib wants me to requisition them right out of the warehouse. They store parts there, then send them to the units through a paper jungle. When the parts finally do make their way north to us, half of them have disappeared. It's tough to keep the birds flying without them."

Tess rallied beneath his cajoling and care. This was the real Pete Mallory, the man who felt deeply, and was able to share his heart with her. For once, Tess had to admit to herself that she *was* exhausted. She couldn't continue. She needed a reprieve from her highly emotional world. She nodded. "Okay, I'll go. Maybe you're right—I need a break."

Rolling his eyes, Pete said dramatically, "Look out, Saigon. Here we come!"

"When's the plane leave?"

"Eighteen hundred from Marble Mountain." Pete didn't want to let go of her hand because intuitively he felt she needed the human contact right now. There wasn't anything sexual about it, but it made him feel warm inside just to hold her hand. Maybe Tess was right, and there *was* more than sex in the world.

"That's so soon," Tess protested.

"Yeah, but we might be able to get that generator you need," he baited. Her features were distraught and pale. "If you want a well for these people, we've got to move fast, Tess. Generators don't grow on trees."

"Okay..."

"Don't worry, I've made all the plans. We've got a reservation at the Caravelle. All I need is you, honey."

Tess was too mired in her grief to rally much beneath Pete's sunlit smile and good-natured teasing. She didn't even question whether the reservation was for two rooms or one. She'd find out soon enough.

"This is pure, unadulterated luxury," Tess said with awe as she stepped into her hotel room at the Caravelle. Next door was Pete's room—connected by an interior door, he'd already informed her, a gleam in his eye.

They'd flown for several hours and landed at Tan Son Nhut air base just in time for a late dinner. Pete had the porter put her suitcase down and paid him in piasters. "Yeah, it's not a bad joint," he said, after the porter had left. He motioned to the large double bed covered with a gold silk spread. "Most important piece of furniture in the place."

Pete's teasing had lifted so much of her darkness. Tess gave him a sideways glance. "You never give up, do you?"

"With someone as pretty and nice as you?" Pete whispered conspiratorially, placing a small kiss on her cheek. "No way." He saw her eyes widen beautifully at the stolen kiss.

"Pete!"

"Tess!" He laughed. "Get a hot shower, honey, change and meet me in the lobby in an hour. I plan to wine and dine you proper."

After Pete had sauntered confidently through the door that led to his room, Tess shook her head. Everything was dreamlike, from the carpeted floors to the glass-enclosed shower to the fragrant lilac-scented French milled soap. She was so used to taking a quick bath in the stream that ran behind the village and using a scratchy cotton cloth for a washcloth. Here, the hot water alone was a sensual luxury. Wrapped in a soft, thick towel after her shower, she padded out to her small suitcase. Inside was her only decent dress: a sleeveless white cotton concoction with an empire waist. She put it on and stared at herself in the floor-length mirror.

With her recently washed hair up in a French twist, a few tendrils softly touching her flushed cheeks, she didn't even recognize herself. The woman staring back from the mirror was another Tess, she thought with a wry smile. Placing small white-and-gold clip earrings on her earlobes and sliding her nylon-clad feet into a pair of white sandals, she was ready to meet Pete. Miraculously, she was looking forward to this night with him, her heart silencing her head, which warned that he was still on the make trying to woo her into bed.

Pete's eyes widened in appreciation when Tess stepped out of the elevator. She looked demure, slightly flushed and shy as she walked over to him.

"Honey, you're knockout material. I hope you know that." He grinned.

"I'm uncomfortable enough, Pete. Don't rub it in." She looked down at herself. "Look at me—in nylons of all things! Nobody wears nylons here, it's too hot and humid."

"This place is air-conditioned, so it's a moot point." He gazed appreciatively down at her long, slender legs. "What a set you've got," he said, and whistled softly.

"You're not exactly bad-looking, either," Tess teased, a fierce sense of longing catching her off guard. Just the way Pete's mouth moved, the hunter-like look in his intense blue eyes, stole the breath from her. He was so very male in the navy sport coat, white silk shirt and paisley tie with ivory chino slacks.

"Thank you." He cupped her elbow. "Come on, I've got the best seat in the house reserved for us. We're going to do some heavy celebrating tonight."

The coffee after dinner warmed Tess. As the waiter cleared away the dessert dishes, leaving a pristine white linen tablecloth between them, she smiled at Pete. "This has been wonderful. You were right. This is exactly what I needed."

Pleasantly full, Pete leaned forward and captured her work-worn fingers. "What I needed was a good dose of you to cure me of my Vietnam blues."

His hand was strong without hurting her fingers. In the candlelight, Pete's handsome features took on a craggy, shadowed appearance. Tess wondered if he still saw her as a shadow on his life.

"Tell me about tomorrow morning. Where are we going to get this generator?"

"I'd rather talk about tonight."

"I wouldn't."

He grinned. "I had to try."

"No, you didn't."

Squeezing Tess's hand, Pete released it and sat back. "We're going down into a district where they stash items for resale."

"Black market?"

"Yeah." He scowled. "I'd rather you stay here at the hotel, get your beauty sleep and let me go. It gets kinda dangerous down there at certain times... Vietnamese gangs and all that."

"Won't you need someone who speaks Vietnamese?"

With a grin, Pete said, "Honey, these guys get along just fine with pidgin English, lots of hand gestures and real greenbacks instead of piasters. They know how to count in every language, believe me."

Tess could believe it. Vietnam, for good or bad, ran on greed, corruption and a very active black market.

"What about the rabies vaccine?"

"I got a supply sergeant at another depot that has what we need. The vaccine will be easy to get. After that, I've got to drive over to a third district and make sure our helicopter supply parts get loaded on that C-130 we're taking back tomorrow evening. I'll be gone most of the day. Why don't you rest, maybe do a little shopping, and I'll meet you for lunch?"

The idea was tempting. Tess discovered how tired she was beginning to feel, from accumulated stress, lack of sleep for weeks on end and the trauma of the war. "Okay. I'm falling asleep, Pete. All of a sudden, I feel like somebody poleaxed me."

Pete stood up, swallowing his disappointment. Tess looked luscious in her dress, and he hadn't been able to help but entertain thoughts of making slow, beautiful love to her. But he could see the darkness in her eyes, and the exhaustion in her face. "Come on," he urged. "I'll walk you back to your room."

"Thanks," Tess said wearily. "I'm sorry to be a wet blanket, but I'm ready to sleep."

"Combat stress," Pete assured her as they walked out of the restaurant. And before she could protest over his choice of words, he added, "What you do *is* combat oriented, Tess, so don't argue with me. A VC sniper is just as capable of blowing you away as one of the marines. You're an American, even if you keep forgetting it."

"Well, all arguments aside," Tess told him in the elevator, "that generator is going to make a world of difference at Le My. I can hardly wait to see it working."

Sometime after midnight, Tess awoke screaming. The nightmare that suffocated her had to do with a young boy and water buffalo stepping on a mine in one of the flooded rice paddies. As Tess sat up in bed, trembling, her hands pressed against her face, she could see it all over again. The shorty cotton pajamas she wore were damp with perspiration. Oh, why wouldn't these nightmares leave her alone? Sobs tore from her.

Rubbing his eyes sleepily, Pete opened the inner door to Tess's room and staggered toward her. She was sitting up in bed crying. He'd heard her scream, a haunting cry that had shaken him out of his light, restless sleep. Clad only in a pair of drawstring pajama bottoms, he moved to her side.

"Hey, honey, what's wrong?" he asked, sitting down and gathering Tess into his arms.

As Tess felt Pete's arms go around her, pressing her against the hard warmth of his body, she wept even harder. His voice was husky as he held and rocked her.

"It's gonna be okay, Tess," he crooned, feeling each convulsion shake her. Dammit, the stress of yesterday, of the baby dying, was still haunting Tess. Lights from the street entered the half-drawn silk drapes, sending a cascade of gauzy iridescence into the room. Maybe because he was reeling from months of tiredness due to combat—or emotional fatigue he hated to own up to—Pete coaxed Tess to lie down on the bed next to him. She came trustingly, without a fight.

"Let's just lie here," he soothed, his hand moving in slow circles across her shoulders and back. It seemed the most normal thing in the world to have Tess in his arms. This was where she belonged, Pete realized humbly. For the first time in his life, he discovered the pleasure of being there for someone other than himself. Reaching out, giving, wasn't bad at all, he discovered as he pressed a kiss to her fragrant hair.

Tess felt the dam of terror and grief gradually dissolve beneath Pete's voice, caressing hands and lingering kisses. As Tess gradually came out of her weeping, she became hotly aware of his hard length against her own. She was lying on her back, with his arm beneath her neck, cradling her head against him.

His other hand moved tenderly, stroking her arm, torso and hip in an effort to assuage her pain. But his trembling hand was eliciting other responses, and Tess moaned. It was a sound born of desperation coupled with desire, and unconsciously she tilted her chin upward to receive one of his kisses on her lips instead of her hair, temple or cheek.

Pete's response felt completely natural as Tess eased away just enough to give him access to her mouth. For an instant out of time, he froze. When she opened her tear-bathed lashes, Pete lost the last of his reason and control. Just having Tess tucked against him, her long legs, hips and breasts pressed against him, was eating him alive. Their eyes met. He saw the shadows in hers, but he also sensed her need to bury herself in the present, in something good and clean instead of hurtful and filled with pain.

''Come here,'' he ordered thickly, and he bent his head. Never had he wanted a woman more in his life. Tess whispered his name, and it sent a tremor racing through him, snapping the last of his disintegrating control. She wanted him. Sweeping her into his arms, holding her tightly against him, Pete claimed her lips with a heat and force that surprised even him. He wanted to drown in Tess's goodness, her warm body, pulsing and alive. All the good things about life were in her, and God help him, he needed her.

His mouth moved strongly against her lips, stealing her breath, infusing her with his heat, his urgency. As his tongue stroked her lower lip, as he bit it gently then soothed the flesh once more, Tess surrendered to the explosive storm bursting through her. Eagerly, she returned his searching kiss, meeting, matching and drowning in his response. His breathing was ragged and moist against her and she felt his hand dig into her shoulder, gripping her, his other hand pinning her hip hard against him. A moan, a little cry, became trapped in her throat as he broke the wild, feverish kiss and trailed a series of wet, moist patterns down the length of her neck with his tongue.

Thrashing her head from side to side, Tess became mindless beneath his onslaught. As he slid his hand beneath her thin cotton top, a lush heat blossomed between her thighs, and her breath jammed. The material was pushed aside, exposing her, and Tess felt no shame beneath his burning, intense gaze.

"You're so beautiful," he rasped, as he stroked the curve of her small breast with his hand. The nipple was puckered, begging to be tamed, and he lowered his head, his lips capturing it.

A ragged cry tore from Tess, and she tensed against Pete, her fingers opening and closing against his taut shoulders now damp with perspiration. He suckled her, drawing upon the nipple, teething it gently and sending electrifying sensations throughout her. The fire burning between her thighs seemed a liquid thing as he tasted and teased her. Each lazy stroke of his hand along her bare skin incited her demand of him. Her legs moving restlessly, Tess sobbed for breath, begging him silently to continue his lush exploration.

Pete moved his hand across the soft carpet of hair at the apex of her thighs. She was hot, trembling and just as famished as he was. All of these things instructed him to slow down, to take his time and love Tess the right way. But just her womanly form against him shattered his control. Caught up in the scent, sound and texture of her, he eased her taut thighs apart.

A bolt of heat swept through Tess as his fingers glided into her. Never had Tess felt like this, so hungry, so wildly in need. She heard Pete groan as he began to explore her depths, and she arched shamelessly against him, wanting him, wanting more of the rapture he was wreaking in her.

"Easy, easy, my beautiful woman," he whispered. Humbled by her wild abandon, Pete took off her cotton briefs. The pearl quality of her belly, the slenderness of her hips and long, curved thighs made him shaky with need. He removed his drawstring pajamas and they fell in a heap beside the bed on the floor. As he covered her, his knee coaxing her thighs apart, he saw the pleading urgency in Tess's large eyes. Before this, he'd always taken what a woman offered and run, but that was the last thing he wanted to do with Tess. No, he thought, as he settled his hand beneath her hips and moved forward, he wanted to share himself, not just take from her.

The instant his flesh met her heat and moistness, Pete groaned, his lips pulling back from his clenched teeth. Perspiration stood out on his taut face as he slid into her. Her cry wasn't of pain, but of utter pleasure. Pete couldn't stop his thrust forward, her hips meeting, melding and drawing him deeply into her confines. There was such hunger between them, a starvation so long unfulfilled, that he lost all thought of entering her slowly. Placing his full weight down upon her, he captured her, taking her, falling into a frantic, savage rhythm.

He tasted the saltiness of her perspiration, the living sweetness of her mouth as he captured it beneath his own. Their ragged breathing increased, moist flames against each other's faces. His fingers tangled in the thick, red strands of her hair as he held her captive and thrust again and again into her, taking and giving as she matched his starving immediacy.

Tess's world narrowed to breathing and the trembling power of Pete's body against her own. Their needs combined in an inferno raging out of control. She capitulated to her own animal instincts as a woman, and to him as a strong, potent male. All she was aware of was them, coupled, straining and reaching for the dizzying heights of pleasure together. The building storm broke within her, and she arched, tense in his arms. He held her tightly, giving her all the beauty and pleasure she'd ever experienced. Wave after wave tremored through her, and she surrendered to it and to him.

Moments later, Tess felt Pete tense against her. His growl was low, like an animal, and she met each of his strokes with equal fervor. Night and day melded together as they fell into each other's arms, damp and spent in the aftermath. Tess closed her eyes, loving Pete's weight against her, a sense of security blanketing her. Savoring each second, she absorbed the feel of Pete's fingers as they gently tried to untangle wet strands against her temple.

Easing to one side, Pete gazed down on Tess's flushed features. As she opened her eyes, he saw the sparkle and luster in them, and he felt humbled as never before. He knew he'd given Tess enjoyment, and it made him feel damn good. For once, he'd shared the act of love, not run like a thief, stealing for his own selfish gratification. He smiled tenderly as he picked up a thick strand of her hair.

"You're as hot as your hair," he told her thickly, and leaned down to capture once more her sinner mouth beneath his own. Pete wasn't disappointed. Her returning kiss was as responsive and hungry as his own. Gradually, he eased from her wet lips and smiled into her eyes.

"You're moonlight, you know that?"

Tess felt weak but good. She languished in his arms, content as never before. "Moonlight?" She laughed softly.

"Mmm, moonlight." Pete held up the lock of hair and studied it. "Red rubies for hair, and pearls of moonlight dancing off the strands."

She stared up at his relaxed features in awe. "There's a poet inside of you."

Flushing, Pete laid the strand on her white shoulder, glistening damply in the room's low light. "Sometimes. You inspire me, Tess." And she did. "Your eyes," he whispered, kissing them in turn, "are like dark pools of wonder. I can see rainbows in them." Sparkles of joy interspersed with satisfaction. He liked what he'd given to Tess. It made him feel strong and potent and protective of her.

"I'm happy," she whispered, and slid her hand up across his arm and broad, powerful shoulder. "*You* made me happy."

"We're good at this," Pete teased. He'd never in his life felt as good as he did now. When Tess's mouth pulled into a tender smile, he felt himself go hard with longing all over again. There was such simplicity to Tess, no games or coyness about her. And then, Pete sobered.

"I heard you scream, honey. It scared the hell out of me. I must have risen two feet off my bed."

Her brow wrinkled. "Oh, the nightmare..."

"Yeah. Do you get them often?" Pete stroked her brow until it smoothed again. He saw the terror banked in her eyes now and mentally chastised himself for bringing up the topic. He wanted to see the joy and fulfillment back in her lovely eyes.

"Sometimes," Tess hedged softly. She felt she never wanted to leave Pete's arms. She saw the undisguised caring in his gaze, felt it in the stroke of his hand along her arm. There was a wonderful sense of protection in his embrace, something she'd never experienced before.

"Sometimes," Pete mimicked, then grinned. He captured her lips, stroked her lower lip and then the corners with his tongue. "Sometimes," he whispered against her lush mouth that blossomed beneath his. "Woman of mine, it don't pay to hedge your bet with me. Now tell me the truth."

Giggling, Tess threw her arms around his neck. "I like you so much. You're so different when you come out from behind those walls."

He growled and pinned her gently beneath him. "Don't try and evade my question by giving me a string of compliments, either."

Breathy laughter escaped Tess as she closed her eyes and absorbed his weight, the power of him against her. "Umm, you feel so good...."

She was right, just the act of pressing their bodies together created another fire from the coals of their desire. Pete fought the need to love Tess once more. He eased off her and brought her into his arms. Her hair fell across his shoulder and chest like living fire.

"I want the truth, Tess," he told her, serious now.

Lost in the intensity of his narrowed gaze, feeling safe at last, Tess admitted in a low voice, "I've been getting them more and more the last couple of months."

"Because things are heating up out there."

She nodded and ran her fingers across his furrowed brow. "Now you're scowling."

"That's because," Pete whispered, framing her face, "I care about you, honey. I worry about you out there alone in those villages at night."

With a shrug, Tess closed her eyes, feeling satiated and suddenly very tired. Resting her head against his shoulder, her hand on his darkly haired chest, she murmured, "I feel safe now. Here. With you..."

Pete knew he should leave, but he didn't have the strength to do it. Overwhelmed by his sensitivity to Tess and what she needed, he maneuvered her around on the bed and brought the covers up around them.

"You are safe with me."

She laughed softly. "Sure, the fox is in the hen-house."

A grin edged his mouth as he lay down, Tess's weight feeling like utter heaven to him. He closed his eyes, happy beyond belief. "I'm the hen and you're the fox."

Tess sighed, contentment flowing through her. She closed her eyes, her arm across his flat, hard belly. "I'm too tired to argue with you, Pete...."

"Go to sleep, honey," he coaxed thickly. "You've got a year's worth of tiredness to sleep off." And before the last of the words were out of his mouth, Pete dropped off to sleep, too—the woman he had wanted forever peacefully in his arms.

Pete jerked awake. Sunlight was spilling like a golden waterfall into Tess's room. His awakening senses shifted quickly to her. She was sleeping deeply in his arms, her head nestled beneath his jaw, her arm across his torso and her legs tangled between his. Releasing a sigh, he dropped his head back on the pillow. He hadn't been dreaming after all....

Savoring the moment, Pete felt her firm skin against him, and heat began to throb through his lower body. The silky strands of her hair were a pillow against his chest, and lazily he stroked her head, utterly contented. This was heaven. Pure, unadulterated heaven. How could he be so damned lucky? What had he done to deserve a woman like Tess?

Pete didn't want to look at any possible answers to that question too closely. He knew he *didn't* deserve Tess. With other women, he'd wake early, climb into his wrinkled clothes and steal out of the room, leaving without so much as a goodbye. But the last thing he wanted to do this morning was get out of bed, much less leave Tess here alone in the room. As he gently ran his fingers idly up and down her smooth arm, Pete closed his eyes. He wasn't tired anymore—he just wanted to absorb the moment, the fragrance of Tess, the sound of her soft, shallow breathing—to luxuriate with her against him.

Worry intruded on his bliss. He'd made love to Tess, and he realized with a sinking feeling that she might take his coming into her room last night the wrong way. Would she accuse him of just waiting for the right opportunity to steal in and take her? Or would she see the honesty in his actions? He'd come into her room out of care and concern, not with any design to make love to her.

His hand stilled against Tess's shoulder. Pete envisioned waking up every morning like this with her in his arms, sleeping soundly, deeply, against him. Sweet heaven, what would that be like? Opening his eyes, he stared intently up at the plastered ceiling where the fan moved lazily around and around. What did he really want? Tess was redefining his options, what he thought he wanted out of life. Dammit, she *was* his life!

Shaken by that discovery, Pete lay a long time feeling his way through that thought. There were so many fine lines to tread with Tess. Would she believe him if he told her that making love with her had been completely unplanned? Would she see their coming together as an act of commitment and not fulfillment of some plan he'd been working on for a month or more? In that moment, Pete cursed himself for his old habits and ways. Tess was honest about her feelings and emotions, and he hadn't been—until last night, until he'd come in to offer solace against her pain. She'd helped him discover something beautiful and good in sharing another's pain—that it was freeing and uplifting, not necessarily the uncomfortable or messy situation he'd feared.

Pete didn't want Tess to awaken just yet. He felt like a thief, wanting to steal a few more moments with her before the real world, the ugliness of the war and what it did to people, intruded upon them once more. Somehow, he had to make Tess believe he had reformed. Vulnerable feelings he'd never experienced shimmered through him, fragile and new. Having no experience with these delicate, budding emotions, Pete was scared.

One day at a time, buddy, he warned himself grimly. *Take things one day at a time with Tess. Then maybe she'll come around and believe you've changed.* He formed a fist with his right hand, symbolizing his determination. First things first, though—he had to get the generator for Tess's village and prove he was good at his word. Maybe that would inspire her further belief in the new Pete Mallory and make the old one fade a little bit more from her mind.

Tess clapped her hands in triumph and laughed as she watched the chugging generator supply the electricity to the village pump. The children, half-naked and barefoot, screeched with delight as water began burbling out of the pipe set up on several blocks of wood. They dashed in and out of the stream of pure water and threw up their hands, scattering droplets over everyone. The villagers had crowded around and watched in silence for several hours while Pete and his helicopter crew rigged up the entire unit.

"Look at them!" Tess said, pleasure in her voice as she stood next to Pete. He wore his flight suit, the sleeves pushed up to his elbows, his hands greasy and muddy.

Pete grinned and wiped a film of sweat off his brow. At least thirty children, aged two to twelve, played in the water. His heart burst with joy as he looked down at Tess, who stood at his shoulder. Making love to her had worked a major miracle of sorts between them. He'd begged Gib for the day off with his crew so they could come to the village and set up the equipment for the pump. Gib had smiled and said nothing, approving the orders.

As Tess looked around at the faces of the adults, all of them awed by what was occurring, she took a deep, shaky breath. Looking up at Pete, she said, "Do you realize what this means for them? No more typhoid, dysentery or so many other killing germs." Tess turned and threw her arms around Pete and kissed him—something she'd been longing to do since their return.

Stunned and pleased, Pete had no time to capitalize on Tess's spontaneous gesture. Her mouth had been warm and lush against his, but just as he tried to capture her in his embrace to kiss her back, she stepped away. Her green eyes shimmered with gratitude.

"You're a very special man, Pete Mallory," Tess whispered unsteadily. "And you've saved a lot of lives. I hope you know that."

He smiled self-consciously as his crew grinned proudly over at him. "I'll settle for being special to you. Okay?"

Tess gripped his hand and squeezed it, not caring how dirty it was. "Okay." Her heart swelled with fierce emotion. Since their intimate moments, first in her hut, then in Saigon, there had been a subtle but powerful change between them. Tess savored the growing feeling in her heart for him. Each day was becoming precious to her as never before—because of Pete.

"Don't you think you ought to come back to the base tonight? Gib's had to carry through with selling Dany Villard's plantation. He was mentioning the VC are getting pretty bold. Intelligence said there's a massing of enemy near the place, and that's not far from here, Tess."

She didn't want to spoil the moment. "I'll think about it, Pete."

"Dinner at the O club tonight? Maybe not as fancy as the Caravelle, but your favorite guy will be there waiting for you."

Her hand tightened around his. "No promises. If I can make it, we'll have dinner together."

Worried, but knowing Tess's stubbornness, Pete nodded. "Okay, honey, I'll look forward to seeing your pretty face."

That night, Tess shared her meal of rice and meat with the family of the village chieftain instead of going back to Da Nang. The old man spoke in low tones after the meal.

"Binh Duc, the local VC leader, is angry at all Americans," he warned Tess. "He plans to attack the Villard plantation. You, Missy Tess, must go to Da Nang, where it is safe. Even though we now have the marine pacification program here, Duc hates all Americans. You are special and we don't want to see you harmed. You must go."

Uneasy, Tess nodded. "Does Dany Villard know about this?"

The old man shook his head. "No...one of my informants, a young boy, brought this information to me just a little while ago." He waved his finger toward the north. "Go to Da Nang for the nights, if just for a little while, until Binh Duc finds something that interests him more."

Tess thanked him for the warning and got up after saying her goodbyes. She walked thoughtfully back to her hut. First thing tomorrow morning, she would catch a marine convoy heading north to Da Nang and talk to Gib about the chieftain's warning. She knew Gib loved Dany and wouldn't want to see anything happen to her.

* * *

Pete was with Gib Ramsey when Tess told her brother of Binh Duc's plans.

"Dammit, Tess, you need to stay at Da Nang each night!" Pete jammed his finger down at the plywood floor of the tent. "No more staying in the village."

"Pete—" Tess protested wearily.

"He's right," Gib said as he rubbed his furrowed brow. "Look, Tess, can you drive down to Dany's plantation? I can't do it because of work responsibilities. And if Duc sees a marine vehicle there, he'll lose it and possibly attack her place. You can use that Citroën I borrow from my Vietnamese officer friend. Tell Dany to start packing. I'm going to call her, but I need you to go down and convince her. Maybe you could help her pack in the next couple of days?"

"Sure, I'd be glad to."

Pete stood aside, angry and concerned. "That's dangerous, too," he growled.

Gib nodded. "There's nothing about this country that isn't dangerous."

Holding on to his worries, Pete waited until Tess was done working out the details with her brother. When she turned to leave, he gripped her by the elbow.

"Come on, you and I have some talking to do," he stated bluntly.

Outside the tent, Pete rounded on her. "Now look, you've got to quit staying in Le My at night, Tess. It's getting too damned hot out there!"

"You're overreacting, Pete."

"Like hell I am!" He gripped her by the shoulders. "What does it take to convince you? I like you. One hell of a lot! I don't want my woman out traipsing around where she can get her stubborn head shot off! You're close to breaking, anyway. As far as I'm concerned, you've got battle fatigue. Does that get to you, Tess? Is that what you wanted to hear from me?''

She stared up at his taut, angry features. His fingers bit deeply into her shoulders without hurting her. Pete's voice was off-key and filled with undisguised emotion, fear mingled with concern in his eyes. For the first time, Tess understood just how much she did mean to him. Shaken, she took a deep, unsteady breath.

''Listen, I'll come in at night, okay? And I don't have battle fatigue. I've just been wrung out lately, that's all. I may be bullheaded, but I'm not stupid. I'll work with Dany over the next three days and help her get moved out of the mansion and over to the base.''

He gave her a little shake. ''And you'll come in every night? To Da Nang to sleep?''

''Yes.''

Relief shattered through Pete. ''Good,'' he said gruffly. ''Tess, you mean a lot to me.''

''I know . . .''

''Be careful at Dany's place. I've heard of this Binh Duc. He's a cobra.''

''He's sneaky,'' Tess agreed. She forced a smile. ''Everything will be fine.''

Pete didn't want to release her. His eyes bore into hers. ''Tess, we've got a lot to talk about . . . and dammit, time's not on our side. I . . . well, you're important to me, okay?''

''Okay.'' She reached out and touched his recently shaved face. ''You be careful, too, Pete.''

Leaning down, he captured her parted lips. The instant his mouth met hers, he felt Tess tremble. It was a good kind of tremble that told him how much he affected her. As he slid his mouth along hers, testing and tasting her, Pete felt his entire body consumed in a raging fire of need. As Tess leaned against him, her body supple against the harder planes of his own, he groaned.

"I want you all over again," he rasped thickly against her wet lips, "I want you so damn much, Tess, I ache. We're right for each other. I know we are...."

As he drowned in her heated offering, the thought of the war lurked in the back of Pete's mind. No matter how tightly he held Tess, how deeply he kissed her, he couldn't escape the fact that the war was beginning to impinge on them in the most highly personal way possible—he feared losing Tess in a firefight. Whatever wall was left around his guarded heart shattered. For the first time in his life, Pete Mallory felt nakedly vulnerable.

He loved Tess. It was that simple. The discovery was frightening—exhilarating. Her goodness, her trust in her own heart and feelings had torn down any last vestiges of self-protection. As he tipped her head back and framed her face with his hands to share his heat, his own unspoken love for her, Pete felt a fear so numbing and terrifying that he could barely breathe. What could he do to combat the terrible sense of helplessness that stalked him?

Chapter Nine

"Captain Mallory! Captain Mallory!"

Pete jerked up, hit his head on the hood of the jeep and cursed. He was working with a marine corporal, repairing one of the motor pool jeeps. If he could fix it, he could have it at his personal disposal because the gunny sergeant had already written off the cantankerous vehicle to the scrap heap. He'd scrounged the parts from the air force—in fact, he'd spent the last two weeks working on the beast.

"Ouch, dammit." He rubbed his scalp as he saw his gunner, Lance Corporal Randy York, galloping toward him, waving his arms above his head.

Running up to Pete, the gunner was sobbing for breath. "Cap'n, you gotta come quick! Major Ramsey's alerting the whole squadron. Miss Villard's plantation is under attack!"

Pete froze, his eyes narrowing on the straw-haired youth of twenty. "What?" The word came out strangled. Tess was over there helping Dany pack on this third and final moving day. His heart slammed against his ribs double time.

"Yes, sir! We gotta wind up! The major says we need all the firepower we can muster. It's a daytime attack by the VC!"

Cursing under his breath, Pete grabbed a cloth and wiped his greasy hands as he sprinted out of the motor pool area, the lance corporal hot on his heels. With every stride he took, he thought of Tess—and Dany. They were women alone, unable to defend themselves.

"What's the VC throwing at them?" Pete shouted over his shoulder to his gunner.

"Dunno, sir!"

It could be mortars—or worse, rockets. And if Binh Duc had heavy machine guns, the helicopters could become targets, too. Ground fire from rifles aimed at them would be bad enough.

"Is ordinance loaded on board our helo?" Pete wanted to know. They ran hard, surrounded by frantic activity at the landing apron.

"Yes, sir! We're fueled, armed and ready to go. Mr. Taylor is revving up the chopper right now. All we need is you!"

Good. Pete was pleased with his new crew. They were not only responsible, but reliable in the heat of a crisis. His mind and heart revolved quickly back to Tess. He knew she was a Texas woman. She could shoot a pistol or rifle as well as any man. But never had Tess had to defend herself against the Vietnamese people she loved. Pete slowed just enough to leap up on the lip of the helicopter deck. That might be the deciding difference between the two women being killed and staying alive, Pete thought grimly—if only they could reach them in time.

The Sikorsky shuddered as Pete manipulated the controls for takeoff power after he'd picked up a squad of marines. Ahead of him, in a line of six choppers, he saw Gib take off first. Then each helicopter in succession lifted into the humid late-morning sky cobbled with white clouds. Pete's aircraft was the last to take off. The line of dark green helos churned steadily toward its target twelve miles southwest of the base.

Pete's mind raced with possibilities, emergency procedures, worry for his crew's safety and, most of all, a frightening realization that Tess was down there under fire. He felt as if a part of him died because, as he craned his neck, squinting through the tinted visor toward the horizon, he could see a telltale column of dark smoke rising lazily into the pale blue sky. It had to be the plantation on fire.

As they arrived on station at the Villard plantation, the groves of rubber trees—hundreds of acres in long, neat rows—were scattered with VC running toward the main house to capture the occupants inside. There was no time to think, only to react. Gib gave orders for the squadron to begin laying down a blanket of fire to force the VC back away from the house, which they now surrounded. It required precision flying. Gripping the controls, sweat running down his body in rivulets, Pete flew as he never had before. If his door gunner was sloppy, if he banked the helicopter a little too steeply, the stream of machine-gun fire would stitch right through the plantation house, perhaps wounding or killing the women inside. *If* they were inside. Pete had no idea where they were hiding.

Time halted and froze to single frames of terrifying clarity for Pete. His helmet headphones were filled with orders, shouts and intercabin communications with his copilot and gunner. Ground fire was a blazing steel curtain thrown up at them, and to Pete's horror, the VC had heavy machine guns to fire at the choppers.

In a clear area a quarter mile away from the main house, the helicopters landed to disgorge the squads of marines. Pete heard his crew chief shout, "They're out! They're out!"

Just as Pete lifted off the helicopter, the crew chief yelled, "I see the women, Mr. Mallory! They're making a run for Mr. Kincaid's chopper!"

Bullets splattered across the nose of Pete's Sikorsky, and he yanked back on the controls to get the bird out of range. He had no time to try and look below. Alive! The women were alive! But could they make it to Kincaid's chopper without getting wounded or killed?

Just as he banked the aircraft, Pete heard his copilot scream.

"Major Ramsey! Oh, God, they just hit Ramsey's bird!"

Out of the corner of his eye, Pete saw fire erupt along the fuselage and envelope the nose of Gib's helicopter. The bird jerked up, the machine-gun fire impacting heavily against the stricken craft. An explosion followed. Gib's helicopter nosed over sickeningly, the blades flailing, reminding Pete of a bird trying to fly with a broken, useless wing.

No! There was no time to cry, scream or feel. Wrenching his aircraft into a sharp, banking turn, Pete shouted, "Protect them when they're down! Randy!"

"Yes, sir!"

For the next ten minutes, hell existed in Pete's world. Ramsey's helicopter crashed. Kincaid lifted off with the women safely aboard. If not for the rest of the marine helicopter squadron laying down a heavy sheet of firepower, the VC would have gotten the only survivor from the Ramsey helicopter as he dragged himself out of the burning bird. A medevac helicopter flew into the fray and rescued the crewman, heading directly back to Da Nang and the nearest MASH unit.

Pete was assigned to remain on station by Captain Gerard, who had assumed command of the situation. The marine ground forces sent the VC scurrying back into the heavy brush, the last place Pete wanted to be.

As they headed back to base an hour later, the pitched battle was won for now. Below, the Villard plantation was a blazing inferno. Pete's mind spun with questions. How was Tess? Dany? And who had survived Ramsey's crash? The questions ate at him, and he wanted to push the helicopter faster than it would go. Luckily, although his bird had taken its share of fire, his crew hadn't been wounded.

It was an hour before Pete landed at Marble Mountain after unloading the marines to their area. Unstrapping his harness, he quickly left the aircraft and ran to the headquarters tent to find out about the women and the survivor of Gib's aircraft. He stood inside the stuffy, humid tent and used the phone on the desk of a sergeant to get hold of the Da Nang MASH unit.

Breathing hard, Pete tried to steady himself. Sweat stung his eyes, and he blinked several times as he waited impatiently for the phone to connect to the MASH unit. The flight suit clung damply to his body, and Pete tried to take several deep breaths to steady his pounding heart. The sergeant at the desk gave him a sympathetic look and reluctantly returned to his stack of paperwork.

Finally, a nurse from the unit came on the line.

"Yeah, this is Captain Mallory from the marine squadron. Who did you just get in from that firefight at the Villard plantation?"

"Major Ramsey, sir."

"What's his condition?"

"Critical."

"What?"

"Yes, sir, he's lost a foot and ankle. We've got him stabilized and he's on his way right now by C-130 to Saigon for extensive surgery."

Shutting his eyes tightly, Pete leaned against the desk for support. "No..."

"I'm sorry, sir."

His voice cracked. "What about Tess Ramsey and Dany Villard? Have you seen them? Are they wounded?" His heart was throbbing painfully at the base of his throat, and he feared the nurse's answer.

"Sir, they've both flown with Major Ramsey down to Saigon."

His eyes narrowed, his heart stopping momentarily. "They're wounded?"

"Miss Villard sustained a cut on her arm from flying glass. Miss Ramsey received many minor cuts from wood splinters, but that's all. They both wanted to

escort her brother down to Saigon. They didn't want
him to be left alone at a time like this.''

"Yes, of course. Thanks, thanks a lot.''

"Yes, sir.''

Pete hung up the phone and stared blackly at it for
several moments. Tess had gone to Saigon to be with
her brother. She was all right. Relief cascaded through
him and he suddenly felt his knees go weak. Forcing
himself to stand upright instead of leaning against the
desk, he locked his trembling knees. His heart, his
soul, wanted to be with Tess right now—and with Gib.
He liked the man immensely, almost like a brother.
The taste in Pete's mouth was bitter as he walked
stiffly out of the tent.

First things first: he had to see the colonel. As he
walked along the path to the next tent, Pete rubbed his
brow. Right now, Tess needed him. She would have to
be strong not only for her brother, but for Dany Villard, who loved Gib. Inwardly, Pete knew Tess wasn't
up to it. She'd been in country too long, seen too
much, and had allowed all of it to impact her emotionally to a high degree.

As he swung up the steps of the tent to talk to the
colonel, Pete knew there was no way in hell he could
leave the squadron right now. He was needed here.
Most of the birds on the firefight had been badly shot
up and needed massive repair work. There were other
flights that would have to be flown almost immediately, and as much as Pete wanted to be with Tess, he
knew it was impossible at the moment.

"Damn war,'' he hissed under his breath as he
jerked the door open. At his earliest opportunity, if he
had to move heaven and hell to do it, he was going to
fly down and see Tess and Gib. How he was going to

perform such a feat, Pete wasn't sure. What he did know was that right now, Tess needed him more than she'd ever needed anyone in her life. And he wasn't going to abandon her in her hour of need. No way...

Tess sat wearily on the plastic lounge chair. She felt grubby and dirty. She'd scarcely left the operations lounge area since Gib had arrived at the naval hospital in Saigon two days earlier. The waiting was the worst part. Her eyes smarted, and she rubbed them, realizing she needed to sleep. But sleep now came only in sporadic snatches. Since Gib had come out of recovery she'd been able to see him, once an hour, for five minutes. And Tess didn't miss one of those opportunities to be with her brother. Thanks to Dr. Gail Froelich, Gib's surgeon, Tess was kept informed. If it weren't for the bubbly, tall naval officer—a human dynamo around the hospital—Tess was sure she'd be more of a wreck than she was. The doctor had a crisp efficiency about her, but compassion was always in her touch.

Empty paper coffee cups sat on a table in front of the plastic couch where Tess tried to get comfortable. The lounge was empty, and she'd never felt more alone. Slowly, Tess moved and lay down, making the couch her bed. She placed her hands beneath her head as a makeshift pillow, confident that the nurses out at the station would come and wake her at the hour so she could see her brother.

As she closed her lashes, Pete's face hovered before her, as it always did. Tess had called Marble Mountain to try and get in touch with him, but he'd been out on another mission. At least she'd heard that he was safe. It was going to have to be enough. With a sigh, she surrendered to the darkness, to a world where she couldn't feel the pain in her heart for her brother, or the anguish Dany had suffered. It seemed her whole world was coming unraveled at the seams right now, and Tess longed to see Pete. But she knew it was impossible. Impossible.

Pete jerked off his garrison cap as he stalked into the naval hospital in Saigon. He went directly to the information desk, discovered which floor Gib was on and took the nearest elevator. His mouth moved into a thin line to fight back all his rampant feelings and needs. He stepped off the elevator and stood outside the doors a moment to orient himself. The nurse's station was to the left, the visitor's lounge to the right. Where was Tess? Dany?

Moving to the desk, Pete tagged the first nurse he found.

"Excuse me, I'm looking for either Tess Ramsey or Dany Villard. Are either of them here?"

The nurse smiled and pointed to the lounge. "Miss Ramsey's here, Captain. Miss Villard has left."

Left? Pete opened his mouth to ask the question and then snapped it shut. "How's Major Ramsey?"

"Critical but stable."

"And his leg?"

She shook her head sadly. "He lost his foot and ankle."

Dammit! Tears pricked Pete's eyes and he blinked them away as he spun around on the heel of his flight boot. Tess was here.

"Thanks," he called over his shoulder to the nurse as he hurried toward the visitor's lounge. Tess... God, how he loved her!

At the door, Pete halted. He saw Tess lying on a couch, asleep, and his heart thudded powerfully in his chest. Her copper freckles were dark against her pale skin, her form almost in a fetal position of protection. His gaze moved rapidly across her face. Taking a shaky breath, Pete quietly moved forward. He saw many cuts on her forearms and several on her cheek and brow. What kind of hell had she endured in that firefight at the plantation? As he drew closer, he saw the darkness beneath her eyes, and her glorious red hair limp and in need of a brushing. The clothes Tess wore, a pair of dark green cotton slacks and a white blouse, dirtied and bloodied, testified eloquently to the trauma she'd experienced. Tess had had no one to hold her during that hellish time, and Pete knew she'd probably expended every bit of care on Gib and Dany, not herself.

Crouching down, Pete gently caressed her mussed hair. Her lips were parted, and Pete knew she was in a deep sleep. One part of him knew he should allow her the badly needed rest. The other part, the part that loved her fiercely and with a blindness that frightened him, wanted to awaken her, hold her and let her know she was safe and hadn't been abandoned after all.

He continued to stroke her hair, and as he removed one thick strand from her cheek, he saw a large cut, sewn together with at least ten stitches. Shutting his eyes, Pete let his hand hover over her wound. He allowed the pain he felt to rush through him instead of ignoring it. Tess's beautiful skin would be marred for life with this scar, this reminder of Vietnam and what the country did to people who stayed too long, who cared too much. It sapped good, caring people of their lifeblood without apology.

The cut was swollen, but not infected. Leaning down, Pete gently pressed a kiss to her temple. Tess stirred, her lashes fluttering open. A soft smile pulled at the corners of his mouth as she slowly awakened. Her lashes barely lifted. Drowsy green eyes studied him dully for several moments before realization occurred.

"Pete!" Tess whispered, and struggled into a sitting position. ·

He straightened and brought Tess to her feet and into his arms. "Come here," he rasped, his voice rough with emotion, "just let me hold you, Tess."

A broken cry escaped Tess as she stood and leaned heavily against Pete's strong, tall frame. She felt his arms go around her and press her hard against him. Burying her face in the folds of his flight suit, she placed her arms around his waist.

"Oh, Pete..."

"Shh, I know, I know. It's okay, Tess. Everything's gonna be okay. Just lean on me. You're tired...."

Exhaustion lapped at Tess as never before. Tears slipped from beneath her lashes. "You came," she croaked, holding him as tightly as she could.

"I wanted to be here," he murmured, pressing small kisses on her hair. The words *I love you* wanted to be torn from him, but he was afraid to say them, even now. Pete felt Tess tremble, a fine shudder at first, and then he felt her convulse, a sob escaping. He held her tighter.

"Go ahead, cry, honey. Cry for your brother. Cry for yourself." He kept stroking her hair, whispering words of comfort. How long Pete stood holding Tess in the glare of the fluorescent lights, he didn't know.

He didn't care. The woman he loved was in his arms, and that was as far as his world extended right now.

Finally Tess grew quiet. Pete pulled away just enough to look down at her damp, ravaged features.

"Look, you need some rest. Let me get you a hotel room and—"

"I've got one at the Caravelle," Tess said, her voice hoarse. She lifted her chin and drowned in the warmth of Pete's blue gaze. He was so strong when she felt so weak. "Dany's gone. She left last night. I tried to get her to stay, to understand that Gib wasn't yelling at her... that he was in pain and coming out of anesthesia...."

"Whoa, slow down, honey, you're not making a whole lot of sense." Pete sat down and pulled Tess into his arms. She lay against him, her head nestled in the crook of his shoulder. "Dany left?"

"Y-yes. She went in to see Gib right after he came out of recovery, and he started yelling at her to leave."

Frowning, Pete rested his jaw against her hair. He gently stroked Tess's shoulder and arm. "He was out of his head, then. Gib loves her."

"I know. Oh, it's so frustrating, Pete. The firefight at her house... it was awful. Dany was in shock from it, and she had an awful injury on her arm. I—I tried to tell her Gib didn't mean what he said, but she wouldn't listen." Wiping her eyes, Tess whispered, "She returned to Da Nang. She's staying at a hotel until she can retrieve what's left from her house."

Grimly, Pete blinked back his own tears. "Does Gib know about Dany leaving?"

"Not yet." A shudder worked through Tess. "I'm trying to wait until he's a little further into recovery."

"How's Gib?"

"Stabilized, thank God. His surgeon says he's going to make it."

"That's the best news yet," Pete declared, and gave her a gentle hug. "Dany's gone and you're still here." Pete looked down at Tess. "The crisis is past, honey. Let me take you over to the Caravelle."

"But, Gib—"

"I'll stand the watch here at the hospital with him, Tess. You need a hot shower, sleep and food, in that order."

Never had it felt so good to be held. Tess nodded. "I know.... It's just that Gib shouldn't be left alone at a time like this."

"Does he know he lost his foot?"

"Y-yes."

"How's he taking that news?"

Tess sat up and pushed the hair out of her eyes. "As well as he can. Right now Gib's on a lot of painkillers and he's floating in and out."

"I understand." Pete stood up, bringing Tess to her feet again. "Come on, let's get you out of here for a while."

Wearily, Tess picked up her small white leather purse from the lounge coffee table. "I'm so tired, I'm rummy."

Keeping a grip on her waist, Pete led her out of the lounge. "I know that. Let's go."

Tess woke slowly, sunlight streaming in through the double balcony doors. The beige drapes had been pulled aside. What time was it? She lifted her wrist and stared at her watch. It was three in the afternoon! Sitting up, her cotton nightgown wrinkled around her, Tess groaned. Gib! How was Gib?

As she turned and reached for the phone on the nightstand, she saw a note:

Dear Sleeping Beauty:
Your brother is doing fine. He was rallying strongly when I left at 0800 this morning. The doc says to tell you to stay here at the hotel, that Gib's been given sleeping medication and won't wake up until later this evening. Her prescription for you is plenty of food and rest. I've got a room on the next floor—301. When you feel up to it, give me a ring and wake me up. Pete

Tess called the hospital first and talked to the nurses' station. Gib was sleeping soundly, they reported, getting better by the hour. Relieved, she called Pete.

"...Yeah..."

"Pete? It's Tess."

"Tess? Everything okay? Is something wrong?"

She smiled and cradled the phone. "No, everything's fine." His voice was sleep-filled. "I just woke up, and I'm going to take a shower."

"Sounds great. Can I join you?"

She smiled softly. A huge part of her wanted to say yes. "You never give up, do you?"

He chuckled. "No. Hungry?"

Tess was hungry for Pete. "I'm starving."

"For the same thing I am?"

It was her turn to laugh.

"You sound so beautiful when you laugh. You know, you hardly ever laugh. But then, Vietnam isn't a very funny place, is it? How about I meet you down at the restaurant in half an hour?"

"I'd like that," Tess whispered, a catch in her voice.

Pete waited restlessly at the table in the restaurant. When Tess appeared, the change in her was telling. The shadows were gone from under her eyes; her hair, damp from her recent shower, was caught up into a single braid down the back of her clean pink blouse. The khaki slacks and sandals she wore gave her the look of a young American woman, not someone stuck in Vietnam. The picture she presented reminded Pete of home, of a saner place, of normalcy. And right now, he desperately needed those reminders.

Standing as Tess approached, Pete pulled out a chair for her. As he seated her, he inhaled her scent, a spicy fragrance. He sat down opposite her, and the waiter came over and took their order for hot coffee. When the waiter had left, Pete captured Tess's hand.

"You look a hundred percent better."

"I feel all of that," Tess admitted, her heart starting a slow, jagged pounding. Pete was dressed in a clean flight suit. "Why aren't you in civilian clothes?"

"Because I'm here on orders from our command." Pete grimaced. "I've got to fly back tonight to Marble Mountain, Tess. I don't want to, but twenty-four hours was all I could wrangle out of the colonel."

Warmth flooded Tess. She squeezed his fingers. "I was so surprised to see you."

"I hope you were glad."

She smiled. "I was."

Pete frowned and cradled her hand in his, looking at the puckered pink scratches garnered from the VC attack. "Do you feel like telling me what happened at Dany's place? What went wrong?"

For the next fifteen minutes, over a fortifying cup of hot coffee, Tess told him everything. By the time she was done, she had broken out in a cold sweat.

"Look at me! I'm shaking and I'm freezing, Pete. What is it? What's wrong with me?"

His heart wrenched with pain. Tess's pain. "Honey, that's called a combat reaction. It's adrenaline."

"Just from talking about it?" she whispered in confusion, wiping her sweaty, cool hands on the linen napkin.

"I'm afraid so." He leaned forward and gripped Tess's hands. "Listen to me for once, will you? You've got that ten-thousand-yard stare, Tess. It's combat stress. You've got to get away from this place and go home. Do you understand me?" Never had he wanted Tess to listen to him more than now.

Tiredness swept through Tess as she studied his tortured eyes. "Pete...I can't. I have another ten months on my contract."

"Then break the damned thing!"

His anger slammed against her, and she knew she couldn't take any more emotion from anyone. "Please," Tess begged, "I don't want to get into an argument with you, Pete."

His hands closed protectively around hers. "I care about you, Tess. I'm worried about you. You've had it here in Nam. You need to get out, get Stateside. Why don't you fly back with Gib? The doc said they'd fly him out of here shortly. Go with him. He needs you now more than ever."

Tears stung Tess's eyes. She pulled out of Pete's grip. "Don't do this to me!" she cried softly.

"Do what? Help you?" he demanded hotly. Pete lowered his voice, realizing other dining-room patrons were watching them. "Dammit, Vietnam has you by the jugular and you don't even know it, Tess! Well, I do. I'm a hell of a lot more objective about this stinking place than you are right now. Go home with Gib. Help him. Help yourself."

Blinded by tears, Tess stood up, pushing her chair back. "It's not that easy, Pete! There are no simple answers. I'm under contract and I *want* to stay. I love these people. They're human beings just like us! And they deserve all the help we can give them, because we're the ones coming into their country and screwing it up!" She backed away from the table. "You'd better go. Thanks for coming, but I don't need this lecture. Not now."

"But—" Pete rose, his hand extended toward her.

Tess gave a little cry, whirled and ran from the dining room.

Pete stood helplessly, anger combined with frustration deluging him. What could he do? He loved Tess, dammit, and she was being bullheaded as hell about the situation. Couldn't she see she was burned out? Gib could genuinely use her help, but she was entrenching. Pain jogging through him, Pete made a decision. Whether Tess loved him or not, he would get her out of Vietnam. His stomach growled, but he'd lost his appetite. Just what the hell was he going to do when Tess got back from Saigon? Had he just destroyed their relationship?

Grimly Pete placed his hands around the cup of coffee. No answers were forthcoming. Tess had once accused him of running every time the chips were down—and rightly so. But this time he wasn't going to. Because he loved her.

Did Tess love him? Pete wasn't at all sure. And moreover, it didn't matter—because he loved her enough to get her out of this stinking place before it killed her.

Chapter Ten

"Well, looks like you're leaving Nam, Tess."

Tess looked up from where she was sitting on her cot in Da Nang. The day was at an end and she'd just gotten back to base. It had been three weeks since Gib had been flown Stateside, and her life finally was returning to a more comforting pattern of normalcy—except that she hadn't seen Pete since their fight. The man standing before her now, Bob Pond, her Saigon supervisor, smiled and handed her a set of crisp, recently typed orders.

"What? Bob! What are you doing here?" Tess put aside her work—the quarterly report she prepared for Bob on Le My. His appearance was totally unexpected.

Still smiling, Bob, a fiftyish man in khaki coveralls, sauntered into her small tent. "Thought I'd drop by and see you personally about this, Tess. Sorry there was no warning, but you know how it is over here." He handed her a set of neatly folded papers. "Hope you like the idea of going back to the States. We need you there for the next nine months of your second-contract tour. Looks like you're getting a promotion to a desk and lots of paperwork back in D.C. Congratulations."

Shocked speechless, Tess looked up at him for a long moment, then hesitantly reached out for the orders. "The States?" she managed to croak. This was impossible! Pulling the folding metal chair away from the small desk near her cot, Bob sat down. "I wanted to give these orders to you personally, in case you had questions."

Despair flooded Tess as she rapidly read the papers he'd handed her. The orders were real. "B-but," she stammered, "I don't want to leave! I mean, I've been here—"

"Tess," Bob interrupted gently, "orders are orders."

"Who cut these? You?" She looked more closely at the orders, trying to ferret out the responsible party.

"No, these came direct from Washington. Someone must have read your reports, recognized your good work here in Vietnam and decided that your talents and skills would be of even better use back home. I understand Phil Adams, your new supervisor, has some great plans in store. It's quite a challenging assignment he's given you. I'm jealous."

Her heart pounding, Tess tore through the entire set of orders. Sure enough, they had come from the States. "But," she began lamely, "I don't understand. My work's been good here, and the villages are coming along...."

Bob scratched his balding head and sat back in the chair. "No complaints from me. I hate to lose you, Tess." He shrugged unhappily. "I'm sorry if you aren't glad about this transfer."

She stood suddenly. "Can't you make a call? Get them changed?"

Bob shook his head sadly. "Your replacement's already arrived, Tess. He flew into Saigon on a C-130 two days ago carrying these orders with him."

Tess stood. Her heart felt as if it were breaking. "No..." she cried softly. "No!" Blindly, she dove past Bob and out of the tent. Since the attack on Dany Villard's plantation, Tess had watched her life turn into a quagmire of unhappiness. The worst had been the fight with Pete in Saigon. Then the VC had stepped up their activity in the area, making it impossible for her to remain at night in any of her three villages. The marines' twenty-man occupation teams had already provoked several firefights, and a number of Vietnamese civilians had died in the crossfire.

Her hands shaking badly, Tess read the orders again, more slowly. Who had done this to her? She didn't want to go back to the States! Tears blurred her vision and she angrily dashed them away. The past three weeks had been a living hell of worrying about Gib, helping Dany Villard and sleeping poorly at night, her dreams haunted by Pete. The memory of their relationship was like an open, festering sore. She hadn't had the courage to face Pete and talk it out with him. She wasn't sure she was ready for the consequences. Mostly she feared that Pete would run again—permanently, this time. Or that, like Eric, he'd leave her without reason.

Bob came up and placed his hand on her shoulder. "Tess, there's a C-130 scheduled out of here two days from now. I've got you listed as one of the passengers. Pack your belongings. You're going home."

More tears came, but Tess forced them back. She clenched her fist, the orders crinkling in her fingers. "Okay," she replied hoarsely, "I'll be on it."

"You've done a hell of a job out here for us, Tess, and I'm writing you a glowing recommendation." He patted her shoulder. "Any door you want opened will be open after they read it. Who knows? When your contract's up with us, you may decide to quit being an AID advisor and hire your services out to the highest bidder. There certainly won't be any lack of takers. Your background, reputation and skills make a terrific résumé."

Still traumatized by the shock of the orders, Tess stood there unable to say anything. Bob murmured goodbye and moved past her, disappearing down the long row of tents. How long Tess stood there she didn't know. She was awash in an overload of grief, anger and sorrow. Finally, she forced herself to move. She had to be alone to think, to feel.

Pete saw Tess head for the Da Nang beach. He stayed out of her sight, waiting until Bob Pond joined him.

"You delivered the orders?" Pete demanded.

Bob frowned. "I did, Captain." He gave Pete a sharp look. "I don't know who you are, but it's obvious you've got connections in high places."

"I don't like cashing chips owed me," Pete said grimly, watching as Tess moved away from them, "but this is one time I'm glad I had them to play."

"You're right," Bob said heavily. "Tess is in need of some rest. She was very upset and on the verge of tears. That's not like her."

Pete held on to his anger. If Bob had been a more alert supervisor, he'd have gotten her out of the field well before this. "The States are safe," Pete ground out. "That's all I care about."

"Well, it's done. Tess said she'll be on that C-130 forty-eight hours from now. I'll see you around, Captain."

"Yeah . . . thanks."

As Bob disappeared around the corner of the tent, Pete remained. He tried to justify what he'd done. In his heart, he knew it was the right thing to do. But if Tess ever found out that he'd convinced a government official who owed him a favor to get her contract changed from Vietnam to Stateside, she would never forgive him. Still, what else could he have done? She had battle fatigue, and no one seemed to recognize it except him. He was going to haul her out of here to protect her from herself.

Although she was going to a physically safe place—if Washington, D.C. could be considered a noncombat zone, Pete thought wryly—he worried about her mental state. He wondered if Tess would have trouble fitting back into society. Would she have what it took to buckle down to a job in the States despite the overwhelming urge to come back here? He was counting on the fact that Tess would honor her contract with the government, no matter what.

With a shake of his head, Pete closed his eyes, assimilating a barrage of guilt and anxiety. In her own way, Tess was going to want to run. He knew of one advisor who, upon returning to the States, had taken off for the Cascade Mountains of Oregon to hide because he couldn't readjust to the "real" world. What would Tess do without support, help or understanding? He wasn't going to be able to be there for her the way he wanted. He had another four months of combat duty to fulfill before they'd rotate him Stateside—if he survived it. And by that time, it could be too late....

A bitter taste filled Pete's mouth as he reopened his eyes and slowly moved out of the shadows of the tents to follow Tess, who had disappeared below the white dunes in the distance. The bottom line was he loved her, and he'd do anything to see her safe. Anything— even resort to this kind of trickery. As he lengthened his stride, Pete wondered if Tess loved him as much as he loved her. Would the months of separation stretching ahead of them change her mind about him?

Settling the utility cap back on his head, Pete laughed at himself. He was acting like a love-blind fool. Instead of looking out for himself and his interests, he'd spent the last three weeks focusing on caring for Tess, getting her to safety and a period of rest. He'd ignored his own selfish needs, setting them aside to help her. His heart began a slow pounding as he crossed the dunes and saw her sitting down by the shore, only a few feet from where the ocean lapped up on the sand. She looked so alone. Abandoned...

Swallowing hard, Pete circled so that Tess could see him coming. She held the orders in her hands, her head bowed. When he was about ten feet away, her head snapped up, her eyes wide.

"Pete!"

He halted about five feet away and smiled uncertainly. "Hi. I was going over to your tent to see you. I heard you'd come in early from the village. I saw you take off for the beach and thought I'd follow. Everything all right?''

The sweet joy of seeing Pete warred with Tess's grief over having to leave Vietnam. His vulnerable smile sent warmth cascading through Tess, thawing some of the freezing cold inhabiting her knotted stomach. Finally, she whispered, ''I thought you'd left me.'' And then with a painful shrug of her shoulders, Tess murmured, ''I'm sorry, you didn't have that coming. I've been hiding, too, in my own way. It's good to see you again.''

''Leave you? Nah,'' Pete teased lightly, his heart pounding so hard in his chest he could feel its reverberations. What if Tess told him to get lost? Never to see her again? His vulnerability at his life being in her hands hit him starkly. His throat constricted with fierce emotion, but he fought past the reaction and offered thickly, ''Maybe we were both scared, Tess. Maybe we both ran for just a little bit. But look at us. We're here together, aren't we?''

Tess closed her eyes and felt her world cartwheeling out of control. ''I—I'm glad you came, Pete. I'm as much at fault as you are for not trying to see you after our fight.''

''I'll take the fall. A man should always come after his woman.''

Tess tried to smile, but it was wobbly. ''You and your caveman ideas, Mallory.''

He grinned slightly, his knotted gut easing slightly. ''Whether I'm macho or not, you're more important than my pride, Tess.'' He took a couple steps closer, suddenly hopeful that their relationship was still intact. ''What's in your hand there?''

She waved the orders toward him. "You'll be happy about this."

"Oh?" Pete came close enough to reach out and take the orders, not sure if she wanted him to sit down next to her.

Glumly, Tess handed him the papers. "Orders for the States. I've got two days to pack and catch a C-130 for Manila."

Pete pretended to read the orders—but didn't have to pretend how he felt about them. "Mind if I sit down?"

The terrible realization that she'd not see Pete for a long time after she got Stateside ripped through Tess. Patting the sand next to where she sat, she whispered, "I won't bite you, I promise."

With a slight grin, Pete sat down cross-legged opposite her, their knees nearly touching. Handing back her orders, Pete reached out and caressed her pale cheek. The evening sun's hot rays hit his back, and the reflection of light off the water bathed Tess's strained features. He was genuinely worried about her emotional state.

"I've been in hell since our fight in Saigon," he admitted huskily. "At first, I was so damned frustrated I didn't want to see you. Then, later—after I cooled down—I missed the hell out of you, Tess. I came over today to see if I couldn't mend some fences." His voice lowered with pain and indecision. "This is all new to me, this intimacy instead of running. You tell me if we have anything left to work with after that fight."

Touched, Tess closed her eyes and drew in a ragged breath. She opened them and melted beneath Pete's velvet gaze. "Just because we fight doesn't mean it's the end, Pete."

"Whew, that's good. It had me scared."

Tess reached out and gripped his strong, warm hands. It was on the tip of her tongue to whisper just how much she'd come to love him over the past few months. "At least you ran toward me, not away from me this time."

"So, we got nowhere to go but up? Is that it, honey?" His heart was pounding so hard it felt like a drum caught in the middle of his ribcage. His fingers tightened around Tess's cool, damp hands.

She bowed her head, unable to meet his warm, hopeful eyes filled with so much of how he felt about her. "Right now," Tess whispered unsteadily, "I feel like I'm in eight or ten disconnected pieces floating around, Pete. One piece of me feels this, another that. It's a weird, uncomfortable state."

His hands tightened around hers. Pete had to literally stop himself from begging Tess to seek counseling. What good would it do anyway? The medical world didn't recognize what Vietnam was doing to so many who had to stay in this country. "Listen to me," he whispered fiercely, catching and holding her tear-filled eyes.

"What?"

"When you get Stateside, you've got some R and R coming?"

"Yes. Thirty days."

"Take it, Tess. Go home to the ranch, stay with Gib and get yourself stabilized." He lifted his head and glared toward the green ribbon of jungle behind her. "This damn place has squeezed every good emotion you've ever owned out of you. It's been all give and no take for you, Tess. You need to rest in a place where you feel safe ... loved."

His intensity rattled her. "I don't even know if the homestead is where I feel safe, Pete. I—I just feel as if I've become completely disjointed—pulled apart."

Anguish soared through Pete as he held her confused green gaze. Fear paralleled it, and he swallowed hard. "Look," he began hoarsely, "these feelings you've got aren't unusual, Tess. Plenty of guys who have been in the bush too long experience the same things. I've got a friend, an advisor, who went back Stateside, couldn't handle society, and has disappeared into the mountains. I don't know what the hell's happened to him, or where he's at. He didn't have family, so he hid, I guess."

Home. The word didn't hold the magic it once had as Tess tested it against her muddle of confused emotions. Right now, Pete gave her stability. "Being with you helps me feel better," Tess admitted.

"What we've got," Pete told her, his voice cracking, "is good and real, Tess. Nam was the wrong place to meet—the wrong time—but I'm not sorry about it, and I hope you aren't, either."

She shook her head and held his narrowed gaze. "I'm not sorry, either. Isn't it silly? I feel like a scared little girl inside. I feel safe around you, and now I'm going to lose you, too. I feel like I'm about to shatter, and if I do, I don't think I'll ever be able to pick up the pieces again."

Alarmed Pete reached out and framed her face. "Listen to me, Tess. No matter how you feel, no matter how bad it gets at times, you just cling to the fact that you're mine. When I get back to the real world in four months, I'm going to come hunting you down in earnest, honey. You're mine. I'm yours. We just need time to explore what we've got under less dangerous circumstances. You hear me?'' His heart twinged at the sight of tears streaming down Tess's taut, washed-out features. How badly he wanted to tell her he loved her, but he knew it wasn't the right time. It wouldn't help matters; it probably would confuse Tess even more.

''Y-yes, I hear you....''

''Good. You need someone to help you pack? I don't think it's a good idea for you to be alone right now.''

Tess agreed. As Pete helped her to her feet, she moved into his arms. He tightened his embrace, and she moaned softly, her arms going around his waist. She leaned heavily against his strong frame. In Pete's arms, she felt safe, she felt as if she were going to make it.

''I'm so scared, Pete ... so scared....''

He kissed her hair, her cheek, and finally her tear-bathed lips with all the tenderness he could find within himself. Her lips parted, and he tasted the salt of her tears. Her sweetness made him tremble, not with longing so much as an incredible realization that he loved her. For the first time in his life Pete understood what it meant to open up his heart, to become vulnerable and share unselfishly with another human being. As he gradually broke contact with her soft, pliant mouth and stared deeply into her dazed, frightened green eyes, he whispered, ''I know you are, honey, and together we'll get you through this. I promise.''

As Pete placed his arm around Tess's shoulders and slowly walked her back toward her tent in the distance, a black fear snaked through him. How would Tess cope by herself? Had he helped or hurt her by getting her orders home? *No,* he warned himself savagely, *Tess had to leave Nam, or it would end up killing her.* Right now she was injured emotionally, not dead.

Tess needed a place to heal. If only she would go home to Texas and stay with Gib, it would be the ideal solution. Pete knew Tess would have only thirty days of leave before she had to move to Washington, but it was better than nothing. Mostly, he didn't want to look closely at their having to say goodbye to each other less than forty-eight hours from now. His gut wrenched in agony.

Tess shivered, the cool predawn dampness chilling her as she stood with Pete in the cavernous confines of the C-130. The air force crew was just about ready to begin the preflight checklist that would take them first to the Philippines, then on to Hawaii, and, at last, to Travis Air Force Base north of San Francisco, their final destination.

"Look, get a lot of sleep on this flight," Pete urged Tess, his arm around her slumped shoulders. Yesterday, she'd said goodbye to all the people of the three villages. Pete had gotten the time off to be with her, to help her through the wrenching rounds of tears and hugs. He'd given up the idea that the Vietnamese were primitive human beings at best. Tess had changed his mind over the months, and the farewell for Tess had been touching. The exchange of honest emotion hadn't left Pete dry-eyed, either. His arm tightened around Tess.

"I will," she whispered, and leaned her head tiredly against Pete's shoulder. "I'm going to miss you."

He groaned. "Honey, I'm going to pine away without you." Kissing her hair, he added, "But I'm glad you're going, Tess. You need to get out of here and reorient to the real world. I've got your ranch address and the address of your new office in D.C., so I'll be writing."

Tess nodded, feeling more tired than she could ever remember. "I didn't think my heart could feel any more shredded than it did yesterday when I was telling everyone goodbye," she admitted softly, looking up into his shadowed face, "but it does now." Placing her hands on his broad, capable shoulders, Tess forced back a deluge of tears. "Saying goodbye to you is the hardest thing of all, Pete."

He forced a smile he didn't feel, and leaned down to capture her mouth. Their kiss was hot, passionate and filled with such promise. He felt Tess tremble and lean against him. Breaking the kiss, he whispered hoarsely, "I'll be with you in dreams, Tess, you just remember that. I'll write to you. And don't look so worried—I'll make it out of Nam in one piece." He blinked back tears that jammed into his eyes. "Hey," he joked weakly, "I'm the luckiest bastard in the world. I've got you to look forward to coming home to."

"Hey, Captain," the loadmaster sergeant called from the front of the aircraft, "we're ready to get this bird off the ground."

Fear clutched at Pete's heart. His embrace tightened for a moment. "I gotta go, honey."

Tess struggled to take in a ragged breath. "I shouldn't feel like this, so torn up...."

"Sure you should. You're leaving your guy behind." Pete smiled uncertainly into her wounded-looking eyes. "Write to me as soon as you get settled. Promise?"

"P-promise...oh, Pete—" Tess threw her arms around him and buried her head against his shoulder.

The words *I love you* barely remained in his mouth. Pete held her hard, squeezing the breath out of her with his embrace. "Take care, honey. I want you well. I want you to rest." Reluctantly he pulled away, his heart feeling as if it were being torn out of his chest. "I want you waiting for me when I get home. Promise?"

Tears blurred Tess's vision as she clung to Pete's strong, steadying arms. "I—I promise...." Why hadn't he told her he loved her? She could sense Pete holding back. Blindly, Tess moved inside the aircraft. She'd been wrong about Pete, about the love she hoped would spring between them. He'd gotten her into bed, and that was all the further he wanted their relationship to go. Pressing her fist against her lips, Tess struggled not to sob as her world splintered around her.

Pete stood alone on the tarmac watching Tess move into the gloomy, cavernous hold of the C-130. He should have told her! But how could Tess love him if she knew he'd deceived her? Miserably, Pete turned away, tears stinging his eyes.

Chapter Eleven

What's wrong with me? Tess blinked and stared down at the report in her hand. The cool air-conditioned comfort of her new office should have relaxed her, but it didn't. She was chilled—as usual. With a frustrated sound, Tess threw the report on the desk. The door to her eighth-floor office was open, and outside it stretched the vast governmental secretarial pool.

Just as Tess reached for her sweater, a loud crash sounded outside her door. Gasping, Tess automatically winced and froze. Her heart pounded erratically, and she broke out into a heavy sweat.

Her mouth dry, Tess turned toward her open door. The mail boy had accidentally dropped a large, flat parcel on the floor. Gulping convulsively, Tess shut the door, then leaned against it, assailed with sudden dizziness.

What's wrong with me? What's going on?

The surge of adrenaline left her slowly, and Tess forced herself to move on wobbly knees to her chair. She sat down before she fell. With trembling hands, she touched her damp brow. Terror raced through her. She shut her eyes, feeling as if the entire world was slowly eroding out of her control. She sat back, opened her eyes and stared at the stack of field reports on her desk, begging to be read. Why did every little sound scare her so much? Why couldn't she concentrate? Headaches plagued her constantly, sometimes forcing her to leave work a half day early or not come in until noon.

Tess thought about Pete, and felt less hysterical. Good, warm feelings flowed through her, easing the terrible fear that continuously held her in its grip. *Pete. Oh God, if only you were here. I could talk to you. I could tell you about all of this....*

Morosely, Tess looked around her neat, clean office. She'd never felt more unhappy. Gib had tried to talk her into coming to the ranch for her thirty-day leave, but she'd refused. Right now, Gib and Dany needed time to sort out their chaotic lives and settle into their marriage, she'd told him. Gib had reluctantly accepted her explanation. Tess hadn't voiced her real reasons. Gib and Dany didn't need her around. Gib was still adjusting to the loss of his foot, and Tess felt emotionally raw and unable to deal with her brother's suffering.

Right now, Tess admitted, as she touched her blouse where her heart pounded, *I can't handle any more pain—my own, Gib's or anyone else's. What's wrong with me?*

* * *

"Haven't you found Tess yet?" Pete couldn't hide his raw emotional state from Gib at the other end of the phone. Three weeks after Tess had left Nam, he still hadn't heard from her and he'd grown worried. Pete had contacted Adams, Tess's supervisor, and had found that she'd been unable to adjust to the office job. One morning she had left a note on Adams's desk, apologizing and saying that she couldn't deal with anything, that she needed time off to rest. That message was the last Pete had heard. Now he was reduced to infrequent contact with Gib to try to find out where Tess had gone. In his heart Pete knew combat stress was making her run.

Wrangling some time off to fly into Saigon, Pete had managed to get an overseas connection to Gib at the ranch. His hand tightened around the phone as he waited for the hollow sound of Gib's voice to answer his question.

"Pete, we haven't been able to locate her."

"Did you check back with Adams, her supervisor? Maybe she's gone back there by now."

"I called him a week ago, and she hadn't shown up." Gib's voice sounded heavy with frustration and worry. "She's just dropped off the face of the earth. We're doing everything in our power to find her."

"Dammit!" Rubbing his face tiredly, Pete said, "Hire a private investigator, Gib. I'll pay half the costs. Tess must have gone somewhere to run and hide. She's got battle fatigue."

"Battle fatigue? But how... never mind, it doesn't matter." Gib's voice was leaden. "Look, Dany and I are at the end of our rope. We've checked out all of Tess's favorite places where she used to like to hike.

Hiring a private investigator is a good idea. I'll get right on it.''

"She needs help, Gib. Lots of help fast."

"If we find her, I'll have the Red Cross give you the message."

"And if you don't?" Pete wanted to cry. Not for himself, but for Tess. She was hiding, just as his other advisor friend had done.

Gib sighed. "Then I don't know. All I can do is try, Pete. Once I recuperate from this injury, I'll go after her myself, but God, she could be anywhere... anywhere in the world."

Pete wouldn't put it past Tess to try to sneak back into Vietnam under false pretenses just to be with her villagers, her old way of life, once again. If she did accomplish that, it would be the worst thing she could do. "I'll wait to hear from you, Gib. I love Tess. Do you understand me? She loves me, too."

"I know you do. No one wants to find her more than we do."

"Okay... thanks. Goodbye." Pete hung up the phone and sank against the chair at the desk. From where he stood, he could see busy, polluted Saigon. A friend of his, an American importer, had loaned him his office to make the call to the States. Tears flooded into Pete's eyes until, with a muffled sound, he forced them back and took a deep, shaky breath of air.

Pete realized a sense of helplessness he'd never before encountered. The past weeks without word from Tess had been hell, but it had helped him grow into a newfound emotional world where love did exist. Never had he loved anyone as he did Tess, and he was damned if he was going to lose her. Instinctively, Pete knew he could help her if he could find her, but he had

almost four more months of duty to serve before he
could leave.

Each day that went by without Gib finding Tess
meant a greater possibility of Pete losing her—permanently. Gib knew Tess's favorite Texas haunts.
Could he find her? And if he didn't, what could Pete
do?

Mexico was going to be a haven of safety for her,
Tess thought. It was the only choice that made logical
sense to her in her upside down, turbulent world. Guilt
and shame plagued her as she rode the bus headed for
the Mexican border outside El Paso. Right across the
Rio Grande sat Ciudad Juárez. Working with the poor
was the only thing she knew that gave her any sense of
safety and stability from the fear that plagued her.

Clenching her fist in her lap, Tess knew she had to
get back to a world she loved. She was no stranger to
the suffering of Mexico's masses, who left their meager farms in hope of finding a better way of life in the
city. But the farmers and their huge, impoverished
families often ended up even worse off as a result of
their move.

Tess stared blindly out the bus window. She knew
she could help people caught in the vise of poverty;
that was what her life had been comprised of for years.
She'd help Mexico's poor, just as she'd helped the villagers of South Vietnam. God, how she missed her
people! The memory of them was the only thing that
gave her solace, that gave her steadiness in her otherwise out-of-control world. She had to help the poor
improve their lot in life.

Anguish gripped Tess. She'd picked up the phone so
many times to call Gib, to ask for help. But he was still

mending and healing himself. She refused to add herself as a burden to Gib's already transformed life. And Pete—Tess gave a little cry and felt the pain in her heart. She loved Pete, and she needed him desperately. But he wasn't here. Tess worried about him—he could be killed. Tears streamed down her cheeks. She was alone. Abandoned. Was this how Pete had felt as a child? Tess didn't know why she felt so confused, so unable to cope with American society. Nothing was right, and the only thing that could make it right was Pete's presence. He gave her hope and strength. But he was in Vietnam....

Perhaps if I go to Mexico, I'll stabilize and I'll be okay. And then I can go home once I'm well. Or could she? Tess was no longer sure, not even about Gib, who had always been there for her.

Why am I feeling so alone? So cut off? I can't stop crying. The nightmares won't leave me alone. I die inside at every little sound.... I'm going crazy.... There's no hope for me....

"You're taking R and R Stateside?" Army Lieutenant Barnard asked Pete as they stood in line to get on the freedom bird, a Continental jet, at Tan Son Nhut air base.

Pete was dressed in his tan uniform, a small leather satchel in hand. "Yeah, that's right."

"Man, you could go to Hong Kong, Japan or Hawaii. Why Stateside? You only got a week, buddy."

"Got some business there," Pete said grimly and turned away, not wanting to discuss his reason any further with the army officer. It had been a month since he'd last seen Tess. Gib hadn't been able to locate her, despite hiring a detective. There had been many false hopes raised. Over time, Pete's love and concern for Tess grew. Instinctively, he knew that if he could find Tess, he could coax her back no matter where or why she was hiding. One week was all he had to find Tess. A lousy seven days. He would rent a car at the Midland airstrip when he landed. Pete prayed Gib and Dany would have good news about Tess.

As Pete took his seat on the huge jet, his nerves jangled. The last month of combat had changed him—forever. He'd already had two birds shot out from under him. His hands shook uncontrollably at times. He'd spilled more than one drink on himself at the O club after a bad mission. Sitting down, Pete strapped himself in and pushed the satchel beneath the seat in front of him. Closing his eyes, he lay back, sleep taking over almost immediately. It was going to be a long flight home. Home to try to find Tess.

Tess felt the potent tequila start to numb her tongue, then her mouth, throat and finally the mass of raw, unstable feelings that kept her gut knotted. She sat alone outside a Mexican cantina late at night, drinking the liquor to try to prevent the terrifying nightmares that so often awakened her when she finally stumbled home. She lifted another shot glass of the clear liquor to her lips and tipped back her head. One more shot, and she knew that she would go to sleep and not relive the dreams.

Tess hated herself for her weakness, but she was unable to fight it any other way. The last month had been quicksand, and she felt like she was drowning more and more every day. The only way she kept her sanity was by helping José and his family of twelve. She cared for the children and washed clothes down at the Rio Grande; they fed her a meager portion of their food in return. Tess was grateful that neither José or Luna, his wife, asked her about her past.

Miserably, Tess looked down at her hands. They were red, rough and callused, the nails chipped and in dire need of care. Her clothes needed to be washed, and so did her hair. Tess knew she should care about herself, but the feeling of shame held her frozen into immobility until even the simple tasks of daily life seemed like overwhelming obstacles to her.

In her fogged brain, Tess thought of Pete. Her heart cried out for him, but her head shouted that she was no longer deserving of him. Look at what she had sunk to. Look at her. A Third-World refugee herself. Besides, if Pete really loved her, he'd come for her, and he hadn't. Time had lost all meaning. Why had she trusted Pete in the first place? Believed that he'd loved her? He was just like Eric—walking away from her after he'd gotten what he wanted....

"This might help you," Gib offered Pete. He passed a piece of paper across the dining-room table to him. "I got this information late last night and couldn't wait to give it to you."

Gib's voice was emotionally charged, hope burning in his eyes. Rubbing his jaw tiredly, Pete focused on the detective's latest report. He'd arrived at the ranch minutes earlier via a rented car. To his right sat Dany, Gib's obviously pregnant wife. He was happy for them, happy that their terrible, individual tragedies had ended in a mutual love that had sustained them through some trying times. They'd both lost so much. Blinking his burning eyes, Pete read the short paragraph, a report from the Hispanic investigator, Man-

uel Ortega, hired to try to track down Tess. His
heartbeat tripled and he gasped.

"He found Tess? She's in Ciudad Juárez, Mexico?"

"Yes," Gib said excitedly, bringing out a map of
Texas and Mexico. With Dany's help, they opened it
on the round maple table. Gib pointed to the area.
"Take a look, Pete. Ciudad Juárez sits on the other
side of the Rio Grande—across from El Paso, Texas."

"What the hell is she doing there?" Pete muttered,
studying the map intently.

"I don't know. I talked to Ortega yesterday afternoon on the phone. He spotted Tess at a cantina as he
went around with her photo asking bartenders if
they'd seen or heard of her. Later, he followed her,
and she ended up at a cardboard hut. Apparently she's
living there with a Mexican family. He doesn't know
much more. He only found her late yesterday and
hasn't had time to investigate further. My guess is that
she's helping the poor the way she did in Nam. Maybe
she feels safe doing that. I don't know." Gib handed
him a small manila envelope. "This arrived earlier this
morning by special courier. Ortega got pictures of
Tess. You'd better prepare yourself, Pete...."

Pete quickly opened the folder. There were three
black-and-white photos of Tess. "My God—" His
heart slammed against his ribs. The photos had been
taken from quite a distance, but Pete recognized Tess.
She was gaunt, almost like a skeleton, her eyes sunken
and lifeless. In one photo, she was sitting outside a
cardboard shack with a poor Mexican family, a little
baby on her lap. Tess was wearing old, cast-off
clothes. At the second photo, Pete winced.

"She's drinking?" He glanced up sharply at Gib, who shrugged.

"Tess never drank that I know of." He gestured unhappily to the photo. "But the proof's pretty conclusive."

The photo showed Tess sitting outside a bar at a wooden table, with a quart of liquor and a glass in front of her.

Gib's voice grew raspy. "That isn't like Tess. None of this is like her."

"She's running," Pete whispered. The last picture showed Tess down at the Rio Grande washing clothes with the children, who obviously had made her a part of their family.

Gib sat back and glanced over at Dany, then Pete. "I don't understand her behavior. Tess was so solid, so stable before she went to Vietnam."

Jerking his gaze up from the photos, Pete asked, "When is this world gonna wake up to the fact that she and people in a wartime situation get battle fatigue?"

Wearily, Gib gave him a confused look. "You've mentioned that phrase before. What the hell are you talking about?"

"There are a lot of symptoms, Gib. I'm no doctor, but I can tell that Tess has combat fatigue. It messes with a person's mind and emotions. You've seen it in our guys: they get anxious, irritable and depressed. They go through a roller coaster of emotions. You can't tell me you haven't had some nightmares after coming home," Pete added. "Or that you jump when a car backfires. Those are all symptoms."

"Sure, I have those reactions." Gib rubbed his chin in thought. "And I've seen those things in the men."

He looked up at Pete, his face drawn with sadness. "Tess was in a form of combat over there, too. God, why didn't I realize that until just now?"

Pete hurt for Gib, who had always prided himself on his sensitivity to the people he managed as a squadron leader. "I wouldn't have recognized it either if I hadn't seen Tess under stress in those villages of hers, Gib. I saw her swing like a pendulum, and that made me aware there was something going wrong in her." He opened his hands. "Maybe Tess didn't experience combat directly, but she was in situations just as dangerous as those we were in. Tess could have been kidnapped at any second, and she knew that. Or she could've been hit by a sniper's round in those damned rice paddies she insisted on traipsing around in," he said with disgust. Pete shook his head and dropped the photos on the table. His mouth compressed. "I'm going after her."

Dany reached out and gripped his arm. "May we come with you?"

He rose, feeling the fatigue of the seemingly endless two-day flight. Struggling to be diplomatic, Pete said, "I think the condition Tess is in tells us how bad off she is." When Gib met and held his stare, Pete knew Tess's brother understood what he was trying to say. "No, if it's all right with both of you, I'll go alone."

Dany got to her feet. "Let me at least have our maid draw you a bath and get some clean clothes for you to wear."

Pete was grateful for Dany's wise counsel. "Sounds good, Dany. If you'll contact Ortega and tell him I'll meet him at the motel, he can led me to where Tess is staying in Juárez." Not one moment of his time was going to be spent without Tess if he could help it. It was one o'clock in the afternoon now. With any luck, Pete figured he could be in the border town of El Paso by early evening. Perhaps he could intercept Tess by nightfall. Perhaps.

"There she is," the Mexican investigator, Manuel Ortega, said in a low voice. They stood at the corner of the cantina in the darkness so that Tess couldn't see them. "This is where she comes sometimes, to the El Toro Bar. I talked to the bartender earlier today, and he said that table is hers. She likes to be alone. If anyone comes over and tries to talk to her, she ignores them and they go away."

His mouth dry, Pete nodded. "Thanks, Manuel. I'll take over from here." He'd rented a car at the airport and followed the investigator across the border. The cantina was in the seedy, poor section of Ciudad Juárez. From the corner of the adobe building, Pete knew Tess couldn't see them. His heart hurt, his eyes burned with fatigue and he felt like crying.

"You sure, *señor?* She might not want to come back."

"I'm sure. Just get us a room over at that motel where you're staying in El Paso, okay?"

"*Si, señor.*"

Pete waited until the investigator had left. There were a couple of bare electric bulbs inside the bar, shedding dim light outside the establishment. The bar had no door, and brassy Mexican music blared from inside. Pete watched as poorly clothed farmers in bare feet walked in and out of the establishment. No one seemed to pay any attention to Tess, who sat at the wooden picnic table farthest away from the door, against the building. She was covered in shadow, and his mouth quirked. He remembered talking to Tess about shadows once.

Taking a deep, shaky breath, Pete forced himself to move forward. Tess had her brow pressed against her left hand, a drink in the other. She was staring blankly down at the rough-hewn tabletop. Her red hair was in dire need of a brushing and combing. Pete poignantly recalled when he'd brushed Tess's hair in her hut in Nam—how much it had meant to him, helping to open his walled heart.

Tess's clothes were of thin, faded cotton, the blouse oversized and the pants rolled up to her ankles. She wore a pair of leather thongs on her feet. The odor of cigarettes mingling with alcohol assailed his nostrils as he passed the entrance of the cantina. As Pete quietly approached, his heart pounded erratically in his chest. What would she do? Would she run? Scream? Hate him? God, he'd never felt as vulnerable as he did right now. He slowed to a halt opposite her.

"Tess?" Her name came out in a bare whisper. At first, Pete didn't think she'd heard him, but then she slowly raised her head from her hand. Her once sparkling emerald eyes looked dark and dull.

Unconsciously, Pete tensed and held his breath as she gazed up at him. Did she remember him at all?

Tess frowned and shook her head, as if she were seeing things. "...Pete?" And then she slowly sat up. "Am I dreaming?" she whispered in disbelief, her eyes widening.

He released his jammed breath. "It's me, Tess. And this is no nightmare. This is real. I'm real." Pete moved slowly. He didn't want to frighten her. She appeared shaken and highly unstable. As he sat down opposite her, he realized she was drunker than hell. Pete glanced at the bottle of tequila and then back at her. He ached for Tess, understanding all too well why she was drinking.

Blinking, Tess sat up. Her mind moved in a fog of confusion. Surely she was dreaming. One of those crazy, unreal dreams where Pete came to visit her when she needed him most. And each time, Tess woke herself up screaming, drenched in sweat, trying to forget the screams from the firefight at the Villard plantation. Pete slowly extended his hand toward Tess. She stared at the proffered hand, recalling its strength, its gentleness.

"Go on, touch me. I'm real, Tess."

His voice was low, off-key. Tess's heart picked up in beat, and she fought against the hope blossoming in her heart. His shadowed face was grim, but his eyes were soft with invitation. "No," she protested weakly. "This is just another dream.... You aren't real. You can't be."

Pete's fingers closed around her hand on the glass. Tension vibrated through every particle of his being in that instant. "I'm real," he rasped. "And I'm here to take you home, Tess."

His touch galvanized her spinning senses. Tess felt the warmth and strength of his hand around hers, felt the vibrating care in his voice and saw the undisguised concern in his azure eyes. She sat very still and closed her eyes. Just his touch stabilized her careening world. "You are real...."

Pete forced himself to sit very still. He watched a flood of emotions cross her pale features, and felt her fingers tentatively begin to move across his, as if to convince herself she was awake. "We've all been worried for you, Tess. Gib and Dany hired an investigator to find you." His fingers gripped hers, and she opened her eyes, awash with tears. "They want you to come home and live with them at the ranch. So do I."

"You . . . they want me back? After what I did?"

His smile was tender. "Honey, when you love someone, it doesn't stop no matter what happens." Pete released her hand and stood up. He walked around the table. "We want you back, Tess. Will you come home with me?"

A shudder worked through Tess. She pushed the glass away and eased off the bench. Dizziness swept through her, and she automatically put her hand out to grab Pete's, afraid she was going to fall. Instead, he whispered her name, opened his arms and swept her into a tight, hard embrace.

Pete heard Tess give a little cry as she sagged against him. The odor of alcohol mixed with those of her unwashed body and unkempt clothes. "Don't run," he appealed as he eased his grip. "I love you, Tess. God, I love you. I'm going to take you home. I'm going to take care of you, honey, I promise."

Tess sobbed once, her face buried against the folds of Pete's crisp cotton shirt. He was real. This was real. Pete was really here. Her dreams, always crushed by the weight of her devastating nightmares, had been answered. Somehow, Pete and her family had found her. Somehow, he knew she was in trouble. Tess could smell the masculine scent of him, the spicy shaving lotion and the cleanliness of the clothes he wore. Too drunk to talk coherently, she stopped fighting and sank heavily against him, semiconscious.

"Hold on, honey," Pete quavered as he felt Tess go limp in his arms, surrendering to his superior strength.

As he looked down at her ravaged features, tears leaked into his eyes. Tess had run as far as she could and hidden as best she could from the stress of Nam. As he gently gathered her up, he was alarmed by her loss of weight. A few of the Mexicans drinking at the bar looked out from the door with curiosity written on their faces, but they said nothing as he carried Tess to the car.

Sunlight poured through the partially opened motel drapes, waking Tess. She groaned and turned over on her back to escape the bright, blinding light, lifting her arm to shade her closed eyes. A man's hand caught and gently held her fingers. Tess sucked in a breath and jerked her eyes open. The act cost her dearly, and she winced, the pain pounding unrelentingly through her head.

"Take it easy," Pete advised quietly, holding her soiled hand in his. He sat on the edge of the double bed facing Tess. Earlier, he'd gotten up, taken a quick shower and changed into clean clothes, a short-sleeved white shirt and jeans. The night before, he'd brought Tess across the border and to the motel room reserved by Manuel Ortega. After calling Gib to reassure him that his sister was safe, Pete had slept off and on through the night in a chair beside her bed. Tess had woken up several times last night, screamed and then drifted back to sleep. Did she remember him holding and quieting her during those times? Whenever he'd held Tess, she had stopped whimpering and flailing around, had grown still, and had rested against him as she spiraled back into that hell she slept in. Looking into her eyes now, Pete's hope grew. He could see life there again, no longer clouded by alcohol.

"I—I didn't dream you," Tess croaked. She felt the strength of Pete's hand around her own tighten in response.

He managed a slight, self-deprecating smile, the corners of his mouth barely turning upward. "I'm no dream, honey. Maybe someone's idea of a nightmare, but I'm sure as hell not a dream. I'm here in the flesh."

Tess's mind refused to work and she struggled to sit up. Pete released her hand. She looked around as she slowly eased over to sit on the edge of the bed, confused. "Where?"

"El Paso. Remember? I drove you across the border last night after finding you in Juárez at that cantina."

"Oh..." Tess buried her face in her hands. Disgrace mingled with a sense of utter hopelessness. For the first time in a long time, Tess was aware of her disheveled appearance. She hadn't cared about herself—until now. "I feel so ashamed of myself, Pete...."

Gently, he touched the crown of her once-glorious red hair, now desperately in need of washing. "I told you before, Tess, you're mine and I'm yours. I don't care if we are half a world away, I won't let you keep doing this to yourself."

Tears tracked through the grime on her cheeks as she slowly raised her head. Tess drowned in the warmth of Pete's gaze, his voice bringing more tears to the surface. "I—I'm no good, Pete. Not for you...not for myself. Y-you don't deserve this.... Please, just go away. Let me be...."

He caressed Tess's cheek and brushed the tears away. "I don't want anyone but you," he whispered unsteadily. "You're going home, honey. Gib and Dany love you. They need you." He sighed. "Look, I've got some breakfast ordered, hot coffee and some eggs. I want you to take a shower, Tess." He pointed to a set of clothes laid out on the other bed. "Dany got these clothes out of your bedroom at the ranch. They're clean. Come on, I want you to get washed up and into some decent clothes, and then we'll talk some more."

The scaldingly hot water washed away the last of Tess's drunken state. When she emerged from the shower, she found a cup of hot coffee waiting for her on the bathroom counter. Pete must have left it there. Her hair hung in burnished sheets around her slumped shoulders, and every movement made her head ache. She was clean. How long had it been since she had been really clean? Tess couldn't remember. She finished off the coffee and wrapped the thick pink towel around herself.

Stepping out into the motel room, she saw Pete sitting at the small table with two breakfast trays. He got up, retrieved the clothes and handed them to her.

"You look a lot better," he offered quietly.

Tess couldn't meet his eyes. Mortification plagued her. She gripped the blue blouse and white cotton slacks. Without a word, she turned and escaped back into the bathroom. Utter degradation flooded Tess as she slowly got dressed. How could she face Pete again? How? Folding the damp towel, Tess took an unsteady breath. She was such a coward. A coward.

"Tess?"

Her eyes widened and her heart banged at the base of her throat as Pete called her through the bathroom door. "Yes?"

"You okay?"

"Y-yes."

"Coming out?"

"I—yes..." Tess hesitantly opened the door.

Pete gave Tess a cajoling smile as she stood uncertainly before him. Her hair, damp and in need of a brushing, hung around her slumped shoulders. Still, she looked a hundred percent better. "Come on," Pete coaxed in a whisper, and took her hand. "You need some food in that shrunken stomach of yours." He slowly extended his hand, slid his fingers around hers and led her toward the table.

Tess felt bereft as he let go of her hand and pulled out the chair for her to sit down. Her stomach turned as she looked at the large amount of food in front of her. Pete sat opposite her, looking collegiate in his white shirt and Levi's.

"I can't eat...."

"Just some toast then," Pete urged, buttering it and handing her half a slice. "Come on, honey..."

The husky tone of his voice overcame Tess's shame, and she took the toast. She didn't taste it, though. She was too wildly aware of Pete's powerful presence. After she'd had a third cup of coffee, he eased two aspirins in front of her.

Tess looked up.

"You've probably got a headache the size of Texas," he said, baiting her.

A slight, trembly smile stretched the corners of her mouth as she picked up the aspirins. "Make that twice the size of Texas."

Hope spiraled with joy in Pete when she rallied and tried to smile for him. He saw a glimmer of light in Tess's shadowed green eyes, and he wanted so badly to hold her, protecting her against the world that threatened her very existence.

"Alcohol helps anesthetize the pain we feel," he told her as she took the aspirins with a gulp of water. "I know I was starting to drink heavily after every flight." He showed her his shaking hands. "Thanks to Nam and combat," he joked.

Tess stared at his long, well-shaped fingers. It hurt her to think how much pain combat had caused Pete. "I—yes, drinking helped—sometimes." And then she stared down at the table. "I hate the taste of the stuff—and it didn't always help...."

Pete reached over and gripped Tess's hands in his. "You started drinking to drown out the nightmares?"

She nodded, refusing to look up at him. Just the quiet strength of his hands around hers stabilized her out-of-kilter world. "I don't know what happened, Pete."

"Tell me about it, honey."

Tess took in a ragged breath and fought the tears that surged to her eyes. "I'm so ashamed. I ran. And I know I've hurt a lot of people."

"It's okay, Tess," he sympathized. "We all run sometime. Look at me. I ran all my life until I found you."

She sniffed and raised her head. "Some find."

He grinned. "I'm not complaining."

"You've got to be sorry you ever met me."

"I'm the luckiest guy in the world, Tess." Pete raised one of her hands and kissed the back of it. "I'm here, doesn't that prove something?"

With a nod, Tess closed her eyes. "Yes, it does. After I left you at Da Nang, my world fell apart. I became scared—confused. I—I just couldn't handle the job in D.C....all of this...society. I got terrible looks from people when I told them I'd been in Vietnam. The capital's torn apart over the war. A lot of people say we shouldn't be over there at all. I was caught in a crossfire between the hawks and the doves. A hippie couple started calling me names, and I couldn't believe it."

Tess raised her head and she saw Pete's grim features. "No one understands, Pete. No one wants to know why I was there. They saw me as part of the war effort, and I wasn't! If I tried to explain it to them, they didn't want to listen!"

Pete's heart hurt for Tess. He gently released her hands, stood and came around the table. "Come on, let's go over to the couch, and I'll hold you, Tess. I want to hear the rest of your story."

It was the easiest thing in the world to find herself in Pete's embrace again. Tess stopped believing that Pete wasn't really here, or that he wasn't genuine in wanting her back. She eased into his arms, lay her head on his shoulder and felt safe as never before. This time, it was easier to talk.

"I couldn't handle Washington, or the politics. I was lousy at my job. I couldn't keep my mind on what I was doing. I was always daydreaming about my villages. Those people were like my family—not a damned set of numbers on some stupid report. Then I'd get flashbacks of upsetting things I'd seen in Vietnam. I started getting really bad headaches and taking off half a day at a time. I couldn't sleep at night, reliving Vietnam and the things that had happened there."

Tess sighed. "One morning I woke up and felt this terror working through me, like I had to escape. I felt as if I were literally suffocating, Pete. I couldn't control it, no matter what I did. I went to a doctor, and he put me on tranquilizers, but that only made my anxiety worse. I quit taking them. The terror overwhelmed me. I hopped the first flight I could and headed west. I felt like a trapped animal. I went to El Paso and tried to get a job—any job. I didn't want to go home to Gib in that state of mind. I knew he was still recovering from his leg injury, and he didn't need to deal with me in this crazy condition.

"In El Paso I'd hold a job for a few days, and then I'd get fired. It was like my mind was shorting out or something. I couldn't remember things; I couldn't keep track of time. And if someone came up behind me, I jumped six feet off the ground and screamed." She felt his embrace tighten. She dropped her voice to a whisper. "I got fired from three jobs in a row. I was ashamed. I couldn't understand what was happening to me, and neither did anyone else. They didn't want to.... I went to two doctors, and all they wanted to do was give me more tranquilizers. They tried to tell me it was all in my head or had something to do with my menstrual cycle. That made me angry. I ditched them and the prescriptions. The nightmares got worse. I kept dreaming about children I'd lost in the villages, or about them being kidnapped or—" Tess sobbed "—the ones that were killed stepping on those awful mines! I saw their faces floating in front of my closed eyes day and night. No one understood what was happening to me, and I didn't, either. I still don't."

"Shh," Pete soothed, kissing her damp hair and stroking her shoulder and arm, "it's going to be okay, honey. It's going to be okay. There's nothing wrong with you, nothing at all. You needed some special help and there was nothing out there. I'm sorry you've had to go through this hell alone. God, Tess, I love you so much it hurts. I hurt for you."

Pete's words, soothing balm to her shattered world, sent wave after wave of strength through her. Tess clung to Pete for nearly an hour, content just to be held, protected and loved. Words were no longer necessary. His presence, his nearness, were all she needed. Gradually, the words *I love you* impinged upon her and Tess opened her eyes. Slowly, she disengaged from Pete's embrace. There was anguish in his azure eyes, and tears, too. With a shaking hand, Tess touched his damp cheek.

"H-how can you love someone like me? Look what I've become."

Pete caressed her flushed cheek and held her wounded gaze. "Honey, in my heart, you've never changed. Yeah, you've got some problems, but so do I. You never gave up on me, did you?"

Tess shook her head.

He smiled tenderly and cupped her cheek. "I love the hell out of you, Tess Ramsey. These months apart haven't dimmed how I felt about you—they've strengthened my feelings. You didn't run from me when I was in trouble, and I'm not running from you now. We're in this together for the long haul."

"I'm a shadow, a blight on your life," Tess protested unsteadily, absorbing each shaky touch of his fingers against her cheek.

"You're wrong," Pete said hoarsely, "you're not the shadow on the sun for me, Tess. You're my sunlight. My life..."

Chapter Twelve

Tess tried to prepare herself emotionally for her big brother's reaction as she stepped out of the rental car that Pete had parked in front of the Ramsey ranch house. She felt cold and wrapped her arms around herself even though the temperature was in the nineties, with the hot Texas sun beating down on them. Her heart beat faster, like a snared rabbit, when she saw Gib come limping out the back door, braced by a pair of crutches. She saw Dany emerge and move to his side, her eyes warm with welcome.

"Ready?" Pete whispered as he slid his arm around Tess's tense shoulders. He saw how distraught and pale she'd become as they neared the ranch. It had taken every last vestige of Tess's courage to agree to come home. Pete knew she was afraid Gib would be angry at her, but he'd told her that only love and care awaited her here at the ranch—the things she would need in order to heal. Tess trusted his evaluation of the situation, and Pete loved her fiercely for her trust in him and her decision to come home.

Mutely, Tess nodded, her gaze never leaving her brother's haggard, drawn features. Tears swam in her eyes as she approached Gib, and she ached for the pain she saw etched in his face as he limped forward. At his side, with tears shining in her eyes, was Dany. More than anything, Tess was overjoyed that they had married. Love, in her opinion, was the most healing emotion of all, and her brother and Dany deserved nothing but, in Tess's opinion.

"Hi, baby sis," Gib rasped unsteadily, and he stopped and opened his arms to Tess. "Welcome home...."

Staggered by a deluge of hope clashing with fear, Tess left Pete's protective embrace and threw her arms around her brother. They clung to each other for long, silent moments. As Gib squeezed her, Tess realized that Pete had been right: coming home had been the right thing to do. Oh, why hadn't she realized that in the first place? As Gib held her fiercely, Tess began to understand how mixed up she was inside. No one in her right mind would run away from her brother's obvious love and devotion.

"God, am I ever glad you're home," Gib said thickly as he eased away from Tess and gripped her shoulders.

"We were so worried for you," Dany added, coming over and kissing both Tess's cheeks. Wiping tears from her eyes, she said, "Welcome home. Come on, we've got your room ready for you. Pete, would you like to take Tess to it?''

There were no dry eyes among them as Pete slipped his arm around Tess's waist and gave her a tender smile filled with love. Without any further words, they all went into the house—together.

Tess looked around her room. It was papered with a floral design, the wood trim painted in pale pink. White, frilly curtains framed the open window. She heard Pete put down her one piece of luggage and felt him approach.

As he came up behind her and placed his hands on her shoulders, Tess leaned back against him. A ragged sigh broke from her lips.

"Looking around, this seems like some strange dream, as if this room belongs in some storybook world, not mine."

He kissed her hair, haphazardly braided into one long, thick strand down the middle of her back. "It's still your world, Tess. You've got to rebuild emotionally before you'll know that. It'll take time, honey. Give yourself that time. One of these days you'll remember this room and you won't feel like a stranger in it. It will be a part of you again."

Turning around, Tess found her way into Pete's embrace. "I feel so tired, so old...."

Pete understood what Tess meant. He felt that way on a daily basis. Although he hadn't known whether to attribute it to the stress of combat or not knowing where Tess was. "Vietnam ages everyone," he agreed softly. He caressed her pale cheek. "Why don't you get a nap? The flight from El Paso, and the anxiety of coming home have drained you." He curbed his worry, trying to keep his voice light for Tess's benefit. She nodded wearily and walked over to her single bed. A colorful pink, red and purple afghan her mother had made for her years before lay over the top of it. Tess remembered that when she'd been frightened as a child, she'd always curled up in that afghan and somehow felt safer—as if her mother's arms were around her, protecting her.

"Sleep as long as you want," Pete urged.

Tess sat down and pushed off her sandals. "I'll probably wake up screaming and scare everyone to death if I do."

"We'll handle it," Pete assured her. "Gib gets his share of nightmares, too."

"He does?"

Pete heard the hope in Tess's voice—that she wasn't alone in what she was experiencing. "That's right. So do I." He managed a teasing smile to buoy her flagging spirits. "And if you do have a nightmare, I'll come in and hold you for as long as you want. Deal?"

Tess hung her head. How could she tell Pete how much his nearness meant to her newly won stability? "Y-yes, I'd like that."

How badly he wanted to hold Tess. Pete fought the urge, realizing she was on emotional overload. Right now, she had enough to absorb without him adding his own selfish need of her. "I won't be far away, honey." He forced himself to step away and move to the door. As he went out into the hall he said, "I'm leaving the door open—just in case."

With a nod, Tess stretched out on the bed. Moments after she closed her eyes, she had spiraled into a deep, healing sleep.

Pete found Gib and Dany waiting anxiously for him in the den. Their grave features spoke of their worry. Dany poured Pete a glass of iced tea and they all sat down.

"How is she?" Gib asked hoarsely.

"She's going to take a nap," Pete reassured them. "I know she's glad to be home."

Gib shook his head. "She looks terrible, Pete. The weight she's lost—and her eyes . . ."

Dany gripped her husband's hand. "Darling, Tess is weary in the way we were after first coming out of Vietnam. Remember?"

Rubbing his face, Gib nodded. His lips were compressed, as if to stop from bursting into tears.

Pete swallowed hard. "With a lot of care, good food and—most importantly—a lot of love, I think Tess will work through all this, just as you are doing. She has nightmares and wakes up screaming at night, so be prepared."

Dany nodded. "I still have bad dreams." She slanted a warm glance toward Gib. "There are nights when one of us wakes up screaming."

"Yeah," Gib confided in a rasp.

"The nice thing about our situation," Dany said reflectively, "is that the one who isn't having the nightmare can simply roll over and hold the other one." She squeezed Gib's large hand. "At least we have each other to help us through this phase of adjustment, Pete."

Gib mustered a slight smile filled with emotion. "Thank God we've got each other, and we understand what's going on."

"That's the difference," Pete said. "Tess came back to the States and went straight to Washington. She walked unprepared and ignorant into a world that neither understood what she had survived nor wanted to try...." Pete launched into an explanation of Tess's journey to Washington, and how she'd ended up first in El Paso, and finally in Mexico.

Gib looked distraught when Pete finished the story. "There isn't a day that goes by that I don't feel the same things she does." Gib glanced over at Dany. "Except that here on the ranch, it's easier. No one calls me names or looks at me with a blank stare when I want to talk about Vietnam."

"And," Dany pointed out gently, "you've got work that you love, Gib."

"True," he confessed.

"Tess was pigeonholed in D.C. with a job that was alien to what she loved to do," Dany said. "She's a fresh-air person, not an office type. Tess loves the land, and if we can slowly get her reinvolved in the ranching activities, I'm sure it will help her."

Rubbing his hands together worriedly, Pete whispered, "I hope you're right, Dany. God, I hope you're right."

There was hurt in Gib's voice. "She came back because of you," he pointed out, "not because of me." He shook his head. "But that doesn't matter. At least Tess is home, now."

"It doesn't mean Tess doesn't love you," Pete said quietly. "She was afraid you wouldn't understand how she was feeling. Hell, I'm not sure *she's* clear on what she's feeling.''

''If only…if only we'd talked. I tried to talk to Tess when she was in D.C., but she made excuses about being busy and said she would call back. She never did.''

''The wounds we carry,'' Pete offered, ''aren't always visible ones, Gib.'' He held out his hands and watched them tremble. ''There are times I feel like a bomb ready to detonate.'' With a sigh, he stood. ''Maybe I'm partly responsible for Tess's actions.'' He studied them in the silence. ''There's a confession I have to make.''

''Oh?'' Gib asked.

Guilt weighed on Pete as they looked expectantly up at him. He'd told no one about getting the orders cut to have Tess sent home. In essence, he'd triggered all her problems with that decision. It was hell living with that knowledge every agonizing second. Spreading his hands wide, Pete rasped, ''When I get done telling you what I did, I won't blame you if you never want to see me again.…''

Dany was the first to speak after Pete explained his actions. ''What you did for Tess wasn't wrong. You were the only one who saw she was suffering from battle fatigue in the first place.'' She glanced tenderly over at Gib, who was holding his head in his hands, shoulders slumped. ''Gib was too busy running the squadron and had too little contact with Tess to see what was happening to her.'' She gave Pete a look of admiration. ''But you saw it, that's what's important.''

Pete stood uncertainly, waiting for Gib to accuse him of wrongdoing or to become angry. As Gib raised his head and sat back on the couch, he held Pete's gaze.

"You did the right thing, Pete," he said unsteadily. "I blame myself for this. At least you recognized Tess's condition. I didn't."

"Look, Gib, we were in a war situation," Pete said, hearing the culpability in the man's voice. "It was no one's fault. Even Tess didn't realize what was happening to her." He swallowed hard. "You aren't upset I took things into my own hands?"

With a soft snort, Gib shook his head. "How can I be? No, I'm grateful." And then he managed a slight smile. "You're one hell of a scrounger, do you know that? I didn't know you could pull strings clear up to the Capitol."

Pete shrugged painfully. "Maybe I did the wrong thing. I'm still not sure." He glanced down the hall where the bedrooms were located. "One of these days, I have to tell Tess what I did. It's eating me up inside. If I hadn't wrangled that transfer to D.C.—"

"Tess could be worse off than she is now," Gib interrupted heavily. "I've seen American advisors who have been over there for two or three tours. They're shot emotionally."

"I think you got Tess out just in the nick of time," Dany added softly. "You saved her life, Pete."

Pete wasn't sure, but he didn't say anything. "Look, I'll get a motel in Midland and come out and visit Tess tomorrow morning if it's okay with you," he began in a strained voice. What Pete really wanted was to be with Tess twenty-four hours a day, but he didn't have the right to make that kind of decision. He saw Gib glance up sharply.

"You're staying here, with us. For Tess," Gib said. "You love her, don't you?"

"With my life," Pete whispered huskily.

Gib nodded. "Then it's settled. You take the guest bedroom opposite Tess's room. If she needs you, you'll be close at hand."

Grateful beyond words, Pete stood awkwardly. "This kind of situation is different for me, you know."

Dany tilted her head. "What is, Pete?"

"Well," he hedged softly, "family and all. I never had one, a real one, that is." Pete managed a bashful, one-cornered smile and lifted his shoulders. "I don't know much about how a family operates in circumstances like this. I'm afraid I'll screw it up."

Dany rose and walked over to Pete. She placed her hand on his shoulder. "For the next few days, you're going to find out what real family means, for Tess and for yourself. As for making mistakes . . . well, we all make them. In this family there's no recrimination if you do—only support. We'll all try to figure out the best way to undo the error." She smiled gently. "We're so glad you came, Pete. And more than anything, we know you love Tess."

Pete hung his head and stared at the hardwood floor. "Yeah," he whispered, "I love her." What bothered Pete most was the knowledge that he'd be leaving Tess soon. The hours were slipping away, and he felt a panic deep inside.

"I just don't want to lose her," he admitted hoarsely, glancing at both of them.

Dany nodded understandingly. "You won't, Pete. Despite how Tess is feeling right now, she'll never forget you came to her rescue. Your love for her is that strong. No, she'll see your commitment regardless of what's happened."

"I hope you're right," Pete said softly. Regardless of the consequences, in three short days he had to leave. It would be the most painful separation he'd endured in his entire life.

Tess stood at the pipe rail fence with one booted foot up on the first rung. A small herd of Hereford mothers and their new calves were kept within the confines. She looked over at Pete, who stood at her elbow, his hands stuffed in the pockets of his jeans. It was their last day together. Tomorrow morning, he would leave for Vietnam to finish his tour of duty. Dany was going to drive Pete to Midland to catch the flight that would eventually take him halfway around the world away from Texas.

The sun's long evening rays bathed her back, and Tess felt a peace that always came with Pete's presence. A fierce love for him welled through her, and she fought back the tears. Pete didn't need to see her tears now. He was as miserable over leaving as she was to see him go.

Resting her chin on her hands, Tess admitted quietly, "I'm really going to miss you, Pete."

"It's mutual, you know." He barely twisted his head in her direction. Tess wore a long-sleeved plaid cowboy shirt to protect her arms from the sun, and a pair of jeans. Her hair, woven into a thick braid, rested across her shoulder. In the past few days, Tess had steadied emotionally. She had chosen a woman therapist, Dr. Sandy Lawton, in Midland, and had started therapy.

Turning around, his back resting against the fence, Pete gathered Tess into his arms. He ached to make love with her, to seal how he felt, but now wasn't the right time. Tess was too raw, too vulnerable to every emotion. Insisting on physical union might tip her fragile new balance. As she smiled up at him, leaning into the safe haven of his arms, Pete groaned.

"Your weight always feels good against me," he whispered and pressed a kiss to her hair as she rested her head beneath his jaw, her arms going around his waist. "I'm gonna miss this, you know."

"What?" Tess whispered back, aching to love Pete.

"Holding you, squeezing you, kissing you. Small things—important things."

She managed a soft laugh. "Pete, you're a glutton for punishment, then. You've got dark circles under your eyes from getting up at night with my nightmares." Tess sobered. "But I'm so glad you're there to hold me."

He grinned and squeezed her. "You gotta admit, it's one hell of an excuse to be in the bedroom with you. It's the only excuse the family would find respectable."

Laughing with him, Tess raised her head and drowned in the blue warmth of his gaze. "You never lose your sense of humor, you know that? It's just one more thing I love about you."

Pete felt joy race through him as he drowned in Tess's alert, shining gaze. Since coming back to the ranch, she hadn't touched a drop of alcohol, realizing why she'd drunk it in the first place. This evening, their last evening together, she looked almost like the woman he'd met so many months before in Vietnam. The fixed schedule of ranching was helping give her the necessary stability, a routine around which to begin to refashion her shattered life. And Dany Ramsey was an angel in disguise, Pete decided. She had an intuitiveness about what Tess needed and seemed able to guide both him and Gib in responding to Tess's needs.

"The past few days have been heaven on earth," Pete murmured as he pressed a kiss to her brow.

"More hell than heaven," Tess joked weakly. Worriedly, she touched his shaven cheek. "You haven't gotten the rest you need for going back to Vietnam, Pete."

"Now, now," he chided, "I'll catch Z's on the flight to Nam, don't worry." Framing Tess's face, he whispered, "What I don't want to hear while I'm over there is that you aren't getting better daily. Understand? I want you to go to Sandy every week. She's a pretty savvy therapist, in my opinion. I think she can help you a lot, Tess." He kissed the tip of her nose. "And help around the ranch here as much as you want. Gib can use the extra pair of hands even if he's too damned proud to admit it."

"Yes, sir," Tess breathed, smiling. How badly she wanted to love Pete, but she was afraid to ask, afraid that the love he spoke about wasn't forever.... Would Pete walk out of her life permanently now that she was recovering? Had he remained with her out of guilt instead of love? Half her nightmares had been about that, but she'd been afraid to confide in Pete about them.

"I've got something for you, honey," Pete said, and released her for a moment while he dug into his jeans pocket. "Something," he said with a tender look, "that I hope you like." He held up his Marine Corps aviator's ring, suspended on a gold chain.

"What's this?" Tess asked, intrigued.

"Well," Pete began hesitantly, "how'd you like to go steady with me?" He saw her eyes flare with surprise, and grew suddenly afraid that Tess might turn him down. A lump formed in his throat, but he blindly pushed on. "Remember in high school, how if you went steady with a guy, you always wore his ring on your finger or on a chain around your neck? The girls used to wrap the rings in white angora yarn to make them fit their fingers. Most of the time you'd see this chunk of fuzzy white hair on the girl's hand before you ever saw the ring."

Tess laughed with him and cupped the ring and chain in her palm. "Yes, I remember."

"Did you ever do that?"

"Go steady in high school?"

"Yeah." He watched her lips part as she gently stroked the ring. It was as if she were invisibly stroking him, and he bit back a groan of need.

"Just once...Bobby Tyler gave me his ring to wear." Tess shook her head. "I gave it back the next day."

"That was a fast steady," Pete joked.

"Sure was. Bobby beat up on one of my friends the same day. When I found out about it, I caught him at his locker after school and threw the ring back at him, in tears. No boy who professed to like me was going to beat up on one of my friends."

Pete smiled and rested his arms lightly against Tess's shoulders. "If you accept my ring, you can't throw it back at me twenty-four hours later, you know. I'll be gone."

Lifting her chin, Tess drew in a ragged breath, the ring heavy in her hand. She was bathed in the tender blue of his gaze, and her heart lurched in her breast. "Wh-what does it mean if I wear your ring?"

He felt her tremble and caressed her flaming cheek. "It means we're serious about each other, that we love each other." Glancing down at the gold ring, its red stone gleaming, he met her lustrous emerald gaze. "It means I want you to wait for me. And when I get back, honey, I'm going to ask you the most important question I've ever asked a woman."

Shaken, Tess's fingers closed around the ring. Tears filled her closed eyes and she leaned her brow against his jaw. "I'll wear it for both of us," she quavered.

"You're my good-luck charm. You know that, don't you?" Pete threaded his fingers through her thick red hair and entertained the thought of unbraiding it and making slow, delicious love to her.

With a nod, Tess bit down hard on her lower lip to stop from sobbing. As if sensing her reeling emotions, Pete drew her against him and they stood in the dusk, holding each other. She could hear the slow, hard beat of his heart beneath her ear, a heart that would stop if he was killed in combat.

"When I was a kid growing up, I always envied these men and women walking hand and hand down the street," Pete said in a low voice. "I always wondered why they looked so happy, why they held hands. I wondered why the people I lived with never did that or gave the special looks to each other that I saw other married couples exchange." Pete gently stroked Tess's shoulders and back with his hand as she rested against him. "Now, I understand. The people I saw on the street from time to time were really in love. They weren't afraid to touch, to look into each other's eyes and smile or show their love. I didn't realize it then, but I was seeing a hundred different ways of saying, I love you." He leaned down and met her lovely gaze. "The time we've shared here has been a miracle for me, Tess. We've said 'I love you' in a hundred different ways. I understand what love means now. You were right—it's more than just the bedroom scene. It's about caring for another person more than yourself sometimes. It's about being sensitive to someone else's needs as well as your own."

Pete brushed an errant strand of red hair from her damp cheek. "You can cry, honey. Tears don't bother me like they used to. I understand now how good it feels to cry." Pete's smile deepened as he touched her flushed cheek. "I love you, Tess Ramsey, with every cell in my body. When I leave tomorrow morning, I'm going to be counting the days until I can see you again. I've never been a great letter writer, but you can count on one a week from me. You're my lifeline, my hope of getting out of there sane and in one piece. All I need to hear from you is that you're getting better in some small way every day. If I know you're getting well, I won't worry, and I'll keep my focus on my job."

Leaning down, he slipped his fingers beneath her chin and guided her lips to his. Gently, as if Tess were some fragile flower that could be easily crushed, he monitored the amount of pressure he brought to bear upon her parting lips. A softened moan rose in Tess's throat as he deepened their mutual kiss, and he felt her returning fire, the quiet passion that burned like living coals just beneath her surface. He lost himself in the lush texture, sweet taste and scent of Tess as his woman—the woman he wanted for his wife, as the mother of his children, for the rest of his life. As he hungrily gave and took the fire of life with Tess, the only fear that hung in the back of his spinning mind was that someday—before he could ask Tess to marry him—he had to tell her the truth about what he'd done to her.

Chapter Thirteen

January, 1966

"Pete! Pete!"

Exhaustion pulled at Pete as he stumbled to a halt just inside the air terminal at the Midland airport. He wore his summer marine uniform, a short-sleeved khaki shirt and matching slacks. His garrison cap sat at a rakish angle on his head. It was early evening, and he smiled tiredly as he spotted Tess among the small crowd, wearing a white, short-sleeved shirt and jeans. She ran toward him. The last three months had been utter hell without Tess's smile, her spontaneous warmth and laughter.

Dropping his leather satchel, Pete opened his arms and grinned as she came running up to him. The change from the last time he'd seen her was heart-stopping. Encouraging. Her red hair was loose and free, a crimson waterfall across her shoulders. The life in her eyes made his heart pound double time. But most of all he cherished the welcoming smile on her lovely mouth—for him alone.

"Tess..." Pete whispered, and he caught her full weight as she pressed herself against him. A groan started deep inside him as she threw her arms around him and kissed him repeatedly, like a wildly happy puppy. Pete couldn't get enough of Tess, meeting, molding his mouth repeatedly to hers, inhaling her wonderful feminine scent—the fresh, clean Texas air, the sunlight—everything.

Moments sheared to a halt as Pete lost himself in the startling, welcoming sensations of Tess against him. Never had he wanted to make love to a woman more. Never had he wanted to love as fully as now.

"Oh, Pete," Tess whispered as she framed his face with her hands and looked deep into his weary blue eyes. "How I've missed you. I love you—I love you so much!" And she kissed him hotly, deeply.

The months melted away beneath her torrid welcome, and Pete wanted nothing more than to stand with Tess in his arms. Finally, both of them breathing raggedly, unwilling to let go of each other, they separated a bit. Tess rested her brow against his cheek and squeezed him.

"You're real," she gasped. "You're really here. You're home."

A lump formed in Pete's throat, and he could only nod silently. His hands wouldn't remain still, touching, smoothing and gliding across Tess's shoulders, back and waist. As she caressed his face and her hands came to rest on his shoulders, Pete managed a crooked smile.

"You're a sight for sore eyes, honey."

Tess grinned and kissed his cheek, nose and, finally, his wonderfully shaped mouth. As she broke the kiss, she whispered against his lips, "I missed you so much, love you so much."

Pete held her tightly against him. "I love you, too," he rasped, the words finally working their way around the constriction in his throat. How could he tell Tess how beautiful, how natural she looked? Inhaling deeply, Pete could swear he smelled the sunlight on Tess. The coarse thickness of her red hair felt wonderful against his cheek. Pete ached to tunnel his hands through that living mass of fire. Dread filled him. Despite Tess's happiness, her love for him, Pete knew he had some things to clear up with her first.

Gently, he pulled her away enough to meet and smile into her happy emerald eyes. "Where's Gib and Dany?"

"At home." Tess smiled back. "They said they'd meet you at the ranch." And then she blushed even more. "I think they wanted us to have some privacy."

Pete looked around, at all the prying eyes in the small airport watching them. He grinned. "We've definitely got an audience."

"Oh, dear."

Pete reveled in Tess's innocence as he leaned down to retrieve his satchel. The first thing he wanted to do was to get out of his uniform. Some of the people staring at them were scowling with obvious dislike for it. Not wanting Tess to be the target of anyone's opinion, he put his arm around her shoulders and she fell in step at his side.

"Let's get my duffel bag and get out of here," he told her.

Tess wasn't unaware of Pete's reasons for wanting to leave the terminal. Vietnam had erupted into a full-fledged war without ever being officially declared, and the country was more divided, more vocal on both sides, than ever before. With a nod, she led him toward the small baggage-claim area.

"You look tired."

"It was all that flight time," Pete said. The duffel bag was there and he released her and picked up the long, bulky piece of military gear, slinging it across his left shoulder. Gripping Tess's hand, he led her out the glass doors into the hot, dry Texas sun. It must have been nearly a hundred degrees in the shade, but Pete didn't care. Anything was better than the humid heat of Vietnam. He could survive this kind of dry heat a hell of a lot easier.

Tess led him to the white Ford pickup, coated with a light film of yellow dust. Pete slung the duffel into the rear of the vehicle and climbed into the cab. He was glad that Tess was going to drive. Exhaustion lapped at his senses.

"Heaven," he sighed, closing his eyes as Tess started the truck and drove out of the parking lot.

"You're heaven," Tess said. She glanced at Pete from time to time as she drove out of Midland toward the ranch. The black strip of asphalt wavered in the rising heat. The surrounding yellow desert was sparsely dotted with hardy dark green sagebrush. The pickup windows were open, and hot wind moved through the cab. Pete's eyes were closed, his head tipped back against the seat.

"The guest bedroom is ready. Once we get home, you can take a bath and hit the bed. I think you need twenty-four hours of uninterrupted sleep," Tess told him.

Pete rolled his head to the left and drank in Tess's profile. "Yeah, I could use some sleep." *With you at my side.* But he didn't say it. He couldn't. Not yet. Maybe never. He reached and captured her hand, which was resting on her long, curved thigh. Her hand was darkly tanned and work-worn. It was obvious she had returned to the land; she radiated health. He squeezed her fingers tenderly. "More important, how are you doing?"

She smiled, dividing her attention between the nearly empty highway and Pete. "I'm doing okay. I think my letters reflected my state. I still have bad days, sometimes a bad week, but not so much any more. Thanks to Sandy's guidance and your letters." Tess's voice dropped. "Your letters—all of them— were wonderful, Pete. I don't think I'd be half as well if you hadn't been there with your support, your love."

It was Pete's turn to blush. "Honey, your letters meant the world to me over there."

"I didn't make you worry too much, did I?"

He shook his head. Tess had written weekly—long, five-or-ten-page handwritten letters, painstakingly honest and unflinchingly realistic about her healing process. God, how he'd look forward to receiving them. Sometimes, because of the war buildup, mail was delayed a couple of weeks, and then Pete would become a miserable son of a bitch to be around. "You were a lifeline," he said seriously. The joy reflected in her eyes at his admission made Pete feel as if he owned the world.

"You were no less mine," Tess said, never wanting to let go of his hand.

His gaze moved to her slender throat, glistening with perspiration from the ovenlike heat that surrounded them. "I see you're still wearing my ring."

"I only take it off when I bathe," Tess confessed, and she touched the ring at the base of her throat with reverence. She frowned, but said nothing. Pete closed every one of his letters with "love," but he'd never mentioned marriage, or even a possible engagement after his return. It bothered Tess, and she wondered privately where she really stood with him. What did he ultimately want from their relationship? Had he been supporting her all this time as a friend, perhaps, instead of wanting to get as serious as she felt about what they shared? Was it out of some kind of guilt? Tess didn't know, and the worry had gnawed repeatedly at her the past months.

"You didn't worry too much about me, did you?" Pete probed.

Tess shrugged. "A little."

"I didn't pick it up in your letters."

"I'm glad." And then she leveled with Pete. "I got so I hated the national news on television, showing film clips of Vietnam every night. Whenever they showed the Da Nang area, I broke out into a heavy sweat. Of course, I hoped to see you on film, but never did. Then I'd be so upset that I couldn't sleep. I'd have recurring nightmares about officers coming to the ranch house to inform me that you were missing in action or dead."

Pete lifted Tess's hand to his lips and gently kissed her palm. The change in her eyes was instantaneous, exciting. Pete stopped himself from going further. "I'm sorry you had to go through that hell," he whispered, cradling her hand between his.

"It was a lot less than you went through." Tess shrugged. "I've never been on such a nonstop roller coaster as the last two and a half years of my life."

"Nam will do it to you," Pete agreed tiredly, and he tipped his head back once more. It felt good to hold Tess's hand. "But I'm home now. For good."

Tears jammed into Tess's eyes and she fought them back. Gripping Pete's hand, she whispered, "I can't believe you're here. It's like a dream. . . . You're here. You're really here."

Pete jerked awake, a scream ready to tear from his lips. He sat up in bed, breathing heavily, his body covered in a sheen of sweat. Shakily he tried to reorient himself. He looked around the shadowy room. Wait. He was in Texas, not Marble Mountain. He listened intently, his body trembling, adrenaline pumping wildly through his bloodstream. No. No, it wasn't a rocket attack. It was only a dream. He was safe. Safe.

Pushing the damp sheet aside, the covers soaked with his sweat, Pete swung his legs across the bed. The cool wood of the floor against his feet helped bring him back to the present. Rubbing his face with trembling hands, he sat for a long time. Slowly, the night sounds of crickets chirping to one another impinged upon his consciousness. Thin streamers of light from a quarter moon glimmered through the transparent white curtains at the open window, filling the room with a grayish glow.

Naked, Pete stood and walked over to the window. A slight breeze shifted the curtains as he looked out on the darkened world of the Ramsey ranch. Below was the lawn, surrounded by a white picket fence. To the right, several pens held Herefords standing around or lying down. Everything was quiet. Peaceful.

Pete's heart still slammed in his chest like a runaway freight train. Turning, he glanced at his watch's luminous dial. It was 3:00 a.m. Rubbing his chest, Pete headed to the shower next to his bedroom. He felt hot and sticky, and wanted to wash away the nightmare that still held him in its insidious grip.

Afterward, Pete dried off and wrapped the white towel around his hips. No one would be up at this hour, and he wanted to make a cup of coffee to calm his jittery nerves. In Nam, no one wore pajamas or a robe. He'd usually been either in his flight suit or naked as hell. Opening the door, Pete looked down the hall both ways before he stepped out. Everyone was asleep.

Across the hall Tess's door was closed. Pete had such a fierce desire to open it and seek the security of her arms. He was trembling badly, and he knew only Tess's strength would help calm him. Halting, he wiped his mouth with the back of his hand. No, he couldn't do that to her. He couldn't take advantage of Tess without her knowing the full truth of his actions.

With a muffled sound, Pete turned and quickly walked down the hall. Memories of Nam haunted him like harpy eagles wheeling around him. Coffee always helped to calm him. When he'd returned to Nam after being home with Tess, he'd quit going to the O club to drink beer or whiskey. Instead, he'd chosen coffee over alcohol, and with good reason. He'd seen what it had done to Tess, and he had no desire to be driven to that limit.

Padding quietly through the living room, Pete headed for the kitchen. He jerked to a halt at the doorway. Tess was sitting at the darkened table with a cup in her hands.

"Tess."

She looked up. Pete stood tensely in the doorway, his face and body deeply etched by moonlight and darkness. "Pete..."

He hesitated, his heart starting to pound unrelentingly. Tess was dressed in a dark jade silk robe, her hair loose and framing her face. She looked excruciatingly beautiful bathed in the moonlight shining through the kitchen windows.

"I...uh—"

"Nightmares?" Tess guessed softly, getting up and coming around the table. Her heart was skittering as she took in his magnificently taut body. The white towel hung low on his hips, barely grazing his knees. Being around Pete dissolved her thinking processes, and Tess reacted out of instinct, from her heart.

Pete's eyes widened as Tess approached. He caught a whiff of her wonderful womanly scent. If she touched him, if she—

Without speaking, Tess lifted her arms and placed them around Pete. The instant she glided against his firm, trembling body, his arms wrapped around her like hard steel bands. The air rushed out of her lungs as he gripped her and buried his face in her thick hair. Whispering his name, Tess held him as strongly as she could. Pete's trembling gradually dissolved as the moments spun to a halt. All Tess was aware of was their mutual, ragged breathing, their hearts pounding in crazy unison, and the smooth, firm warmth of him as a man pressed against her.

"I love you so much," she quavered, closing her eyes and simply holding him.

"I need you. God, I need you so much, Tess," he growled rawly.

"It's going to be all right. The shaking will stop soon, I promise...."

How long Pete stood in the doorway with Tess in his arms, he didn't know. Miraculously, Tess's promise came true, and finally he lifted his head enough to meet her dark, lustrous eyes. He nodded.

"I didn't think I'd have nightmares," he confided.

She smiled sadly. "With time, they won't come as often—or be as potent." Sliding her hand across his shoulder, she felt the dampness of perspiration on his flesh. "Would you like a cup of tea? That's what I was having."

"Coffee?"

"Sure." Tess hated to part from him, and saw the same feeling mirrored in his smoky blue eyes. "I couldn't sleep, either," she confessed with a slight smile.

"You had nightmares, too?" Pete asked, finally releasing Tess. He took the chair next to where she'd been sitting. Like a starving man, he watched as she walked to the counter to make him coffee, her movements economical yet graceful.

Wryly, Tess glanced across her shoulder at him. "I couldn't sleep because you were right across the hall from me. My dreams...thoughts...weren't exactly what I'd term nightmares."

Pete managed a faint smile. "More torrid than bad?" he guessed huskily.

"Very torrid. And all about you—and me."

Heat and longing avalanched through Pete's entire body. Tess turned away, and though there was very little light, he could tell she was blushing. Rubbing his face, Pete knew he couldn't go on this way any longer. "Look," he rasped, "there's something I need to own up to, Tess. Something we've got to clear up between us before...well, before we can plan a future together."

Tess felt her heart twinge with real fear. She plugged in the coffee maker and came and sat down next to Pete. She saw the grimness in his eyes and the set of his mouth. His hair was tousled, and beads of perspiration still dotted his broad forehead. "Whatever it is," she whispered, gripping his folded hands on the table, "we'll take it together. Like we did in the past. One day at a time, Pete. One problem at a time."

A fierce wave of love replaced his fear momentarily. Pete unfolded his hands and captured her long, slender fingers between his, rubbing them against his cheek. "I've never loved a woman like I love you," Pete admitted thickly, "so I'm on quicksand, Tess. I'm scared as hell of telling you this—of what it might do to what we have, to what I want for us." He lifted his head and met her warm, tender gaze.

"Tell me," she urged softly.

Pete couldn't meet the compassion and love in her eyes. He dropped his gaze to their entwined hands on the table. "I saw you going downhill in Nam," he began in a hoarse voice, "and I loved you so damned much I was going crazy with worry. I knew you had to get out of there, that Nam was killing you a little piece at a time." Taking a deep, unsteady breath, Pete dove on. "So I contacted a friend of mine in the government, a buddy. He owed me a big favor from years ago. I told him about you, how I loved you and wanted you out of Nam because of your emotional condition."

Lifting his head, Pete forced himself to meet and hold Tess's shadowy gaze. His hand tightened perceptibly around hers. "My friend promised to wangle a set of orders from the US AID department to get you transferred out of Vietnam to Stateside duty." Pete's mouth went dry as he saw first surprise, then anguish in Tess's eyes. "He owed me, and he gave me what I wanted. That's when your supervisor flew up from Saigon with the set of orders."

"You did that?" Tess cried softly.

Pete's grip tightened on her hand, her cry serrating his heart, triggering the worst of his fears. "Yeah," he said heavily. "I was the one responsible for getting you home. I'm not sorry I did it, Tess. I am sorry for the reactions it triggered. I—I didn't know that would happen. I've felt like hell about it. I didn't mean to hurt you more than you were hurting already."

Tess got up suddenly, pulling her hand free. She moved to the counter, her emotions in violent turmoil. The kitchen was quiet save for her ragged breathing. Gripping the cool counter, she stared blindly out the window into the darkness. Minutes rolled by and the silence deepened.

Pete got up, the chair scraping against the white tile floor, the sound grating against his taut nerves. He moved over to where Tess stood, tense and unmoving. Wanting to touch her shoulder but not daring to, he allowed his arm to drop.

"I did it because I loved you, Tess," he rasped. Her profile was filled with suffering, her mouth pulled into a line of pain. "I knew you had battle fatigue, and I knew that if you didn't get out of there soon, you'd crack up. Honey, I didn't want that to happen."

Tess jerked a look in his direction. To her surprise, she saw agony in Pete's eyes. But it was her pain, not his. Some of her anger dissolved. "Why didn't you give me a choice, Pete? Why didn't you come clean from the start? What you did was sneaky and underhanded!"

Wincing at the truth of her words, Pete hung his head. He stared down at his feet. "Yeah," he admitted roughly, "it was sneaky and underhanded."

"You didn't trust me with the truth."

Pete shook his head. "No, I didn't. You were too committed to your villagers, Tess. I made a command decision based on knowing you, the situation and my gut response to it." Looking up, he held her angry, accusing gaze. "Just try and keep in mind why I did it. I'm sorry I didn't tell you because it's hurt you— and what I want for us." He opened his hands. "Honey, you taught me how to quit running. But in another way, you were running at that time, too."

"How?" Tess demanded scratchily, wiping the tears angrily from her eyes.

"There's such a thing as getting overinvolved in something, Tess," Pete said heavily, "and that's a form of extremism. To me, that's another form of running. You get so enmeshed in what you're doing, you disregard your own emotional and physical needs, driving yourself at breakneck speed toward that wall at the other end. You don't know when to stop, when to rest or when to step away from it. I was running away from commitment. You were running toward commitment to the extent that it was beginning to destroy you. And no commitment, no matter what it is, should do that to a person."

His words fell hard on Tess. Her eyes blurred with tears, and a wealth of new and startling emotions roiled through her as she stared up at Pete in the darkness. Moments jagged by, creating a gulf between them.

Finally, Tess touched her trembling lower lip with her fingers.

Pete groaned and reached out, but Tess backed away from him. His heart plunged with fear. His worst nightmare was coming true. The tears tracking down her cheeks tore at him and he stood there, helpless.

"I'm sorry," he croaked, "I'm sorry I hurt you like this, Tess. My intentions were good, but it backfired on me—on you. God, I love you. Maybe my love, however twisted or screwed up it is, fouled my ability to see things...us...clearly. I never loved before, Tess. I never allowed a woman inside those walls you saw around me. You gave me the faith to begin to trust a woman again, to trust you. I did, all the way. I never knew love could be like this—the euphoria I'd feel sometimes when I'd think of you...or the fear I'd feel knowing I had to tell you the truth and what it might do to our relationship. God, Tess, I'm sorry. I guess I still don't know what real love is all about, because look what I've done to you . . . to what we might have had—'' He whirled around and stalked out of the kitchen, hearing Tess's sobs behind him, each one tearing him apart just a little more.

The first light of dawn stained the east as Pete stood by the corral full of lowing Herefords and their calves. The metal was cool against his damp hands as he gripped the pipe fence, watching dawn blossom from gray to a deep purple, then red, and finally a pale gold high in the cloudless sky. He was immune to the beauty that surrounded him, enmeshed in his own suffering, the web of deceit he'd spun for Tess and himself. He could still hear the way her sobs had sounded as he'd rushed down the hall to his bedroom to get dressed and escape from the house.

Hanging his head, he laughed derisively at himself. This time, he'd run, not Tess. He'd left her when he should have stayed and helped her, or taken the heat he deserved. With a ragged sigh, Pete rested his brow on his arms, a tiredness sweeping through him worse than the one he'd brought back from Nam. Tears crept into his tightly shut lids, and a scream, forming deep down inside his gut, wrenched upward. It took away his breath, jamming high in his chest while his throat constricted. Pete wanted to howl like a wolf that had lost its mate. Never had he felt so alone, so abandoned. And the worst of it was, he'd created the situation. Tess hadn't abandoned him. He'd run from himself.

"Pete?"

Swallowing hard, Pete slowly raised his head. He blinked back the tears, thinking he'd heard Tess call him. *Impossible.* And then he felt her hand tremble as it lightly touched his shoulder. Disbelieving, Pete turned around.

Tess winced at the tears she saw in Pete's narrowed eyes. She allowed her hand to drop back to her side and stood before him, terribly unsure of herself. In the dawn light his face was deeply carved with shadows of grief.

"Forgive me," she whispered, "for everything...."

Pete was afraid to breathe. He stood there, staring down at her. Tess's face was pale, her eyes dark with suffering as she huddled in her silk robe, the coolness of the dawn surrounding them. "What?"

"I've been so blind, Pete," she began unsteadily, and wrapped her arms more tightly around her body. "I'm sorry I yelled at you." Tess shook her head. "War—God, I hate war. It tears us up, skews our perspective and rips the hearts out of us." Taking a huge breath, Tess took a step closer, hoping that the love she held for Pete was enough to see them through this last, terrible test. She wouldn't blame him if he walked out of her life for good.

"The last few hours, I've had time to think...feel, really. That's part of my problem: I think too much, and I keep stuffing down my emotions, which is what got me in trouble in the first place." She gave a small, nervous laugh.

Pete felt first one muscle and then the next begin to ease within his tense body. He attempted to smile.

"Yeah, I got the same problem. At least we have that in common, Tess."

Taking a terrible risk, Tess reached out, her hand settling on his arm. "We share so much more, Pete. Good things. Wonderful things. I—I just got off track when you told me what you'd done. At first," she said, holding his bleak gaze, "I was angry at you for having done it. But then, when I had time to feel my way through what you'd confessed, I realized you'd done it out of love. Maybe even necessity." With a shake of her head, Tess's voice cracked. "How can I be angry at you when you did it out of unselfish love for me?"

Blindly, Pete groped for and found Tess. He hauled her into his arms and crushed her against him. "Jesus, I love you," he whispered brokenly. "I'd never do anything intentionally to hurt you, Tess. *Never.*"

With a small cry, she reached up and framed his suffering face. "I love you. And I'm afraid I may have damaged your love for me because of what I did back there in the kitchen. I'm afraid I'm going to lose you...."

Pete realized the utter, raw courage it took for Tess to admit her deepest, darkest fear to him. With a little laugh, he gripped her by the shoulders. "That's my fear, too."

"C-can we be afraid," Tess choked out, "together, Pete?"

A shudder worked through Pete, and he held her so tightly he was afraid he might crush her to death. "For the rest of our lives, Tess. I want to marry you. I want you to be my wife. Hell, you're my best friend already." He kissed her repeatedly, kissing away the tears from her eyes and her warm, welcoming lips. "Marry me," he pleaded huskily. "Marry me now. Today. This morning. I don't want to spend another night without you in my arms, Tess. I need you, honey. I need you so damn badly I can taste it...."

Epilogue

Pete jerked awake, bathed in sweat. The darkness was complete. He wanted to scream, but he fought the clawing, desperate need. For one split second he felt that terrible aloneness—until he felt Tess stir at his side. Relief swept through him.

He eased back on the double bed and breathed raggedly, his heart slamming against his ribs. *Tess. Tess is here, beside me. Oh, God, I'm safe. Safe.*

"...Pete?"

Tess's sleepy voice sheared through his panic, and the nightmare that lingered behind his tightly shut eyes began to recede. He felt her move, and then sit up in bed. The cool dryness of her hand skimming his sweaty chest took away some of the fear holding him captive.

"It's okay," he heard himself gasp. "I'm okay now...."

"I know, I know," Tess soothed and leaned across him to turn on a small lamp on the nightstand. Pale, soft light flooded their bedroom. The clock on the stand read 3:00 a.m. Pete always got his nightmares around this time. Tess gathered him into her arms and pressed herself along his length. He slept naked, and the silk of her nightgown absorbed the excess perspiration created by the terror he'd experienced in the throes of his nightmare.

"Come here," she urged softly, and she got him to turn onto his side and lean against her. He groaned and buried his face in her shoulder and thick red hair.

"Damn," he rasped, "I'm sorry, Tess. What a lousy way to spend a honeymoon."

She smiled gently and began to stroke his taut shoulders and tense back. Just touching Pete helped ease the anxiety he lived with twenty-four hours a day. "I'm not sorry for anything, darling. Just lie here and let me hold you...."

The combination of light from the nightstand and Tess's touch eased the worst of the fear inhabiting Pete's gut and head. After a few minutes, he heaved a long, unsteady sigh. He inhaled Tess's sweet scent, inhaling life instead of smelling the stench of death that accompanied his nightmares. The strong silk of her hair was a cloudlike cushion for him to bury his face in, reminding him of her gentle, quiet strength. Most of all, her low, contralto voice flowed across his screaming nerves, releasing the rest of the nightmare from within him.

"I thought—" he whispered, "I thought three weeks back in the States would make them go away. Instead, they're worse."

Tess smiled softly. "Darling, when I started therapy with Sandy, my nightmares came boiling through me with a regularity that defied description. I thought they'd never stop. Sandy assured me it was natural—that when we tap directly into whatever we fear the most, those things quickly surface because we're consciously stirring them up." Leaning down, Tess pressed a kiss against Pete's damp hair and tenderly stroked the side of his face. "You trust me enough to allow your fears to surface," she whispered, "and what a wonderful thing that says about us."

"Hell of a team, aren't we?" Pete joked weakly. "A hell of a situation."

Tess nodded. She kissed his cheek and rested her head against his. "We're lucky, darling. There are so many men coming home to wives or families who don't understand. We've both been through it, and we've gotten help, so we're doing better than most of them."

Pete eased his hold on his wife and propped himself up on one elbow. He guided Tess onto her back so that he could absorb her lovely natural beauty. It was the serenity in Tess's eyes that gave him such stability, and the love shining in their depths for him alone. "I wouldn't want to go through this kind of decompression with anyone but you, honey."

She smiled tenderly and responded as he caressed the side of her breast beneath the silk of her gown. The nightmare was receding in Pete's eyes, replaced with banked coals of desire. "You're stuck with me," she whispered.

"Glutton for punishment, aren't you?" Pete teased as he leaned down, sought and found her willing mouth. The way Tess trembled as his lips parted hers sent a fire through his body. Pete had never been happier or more frightened than he had been in the past three weeks. Loving Tess with the newfound fierceness of his open heart had brought him to the heights of heaven. And just as savagely, the nightmares had plunged him into the darkest depths of a living hell each night.

Smiling beneath his questing mouth, Tess gloried in Pete's weight as he covered her. She never ceased to marvel at his fierce, rising passion for her. Time melted beneath his fiery assault, and a part of her understood that Pete needed to bury himself within her not only to escape, but to heal, too. Loving someone was quintessential, a multilayered veil of reasons, needs, passion and desires compressed together in one heated moment. A softened moan rose up through her as he found the straps of her gown. The silk fell away beneath his exquisite assault, and she turned, pressing herself against him.

Her breath coming in ragged gasps, Tess hungrily found his mouth again, wildly exploring him, feeling his strength, his need and longing. As his hand caressed her breast, she tensed, wanting him just as badly as he wanted her. The moment his lips settled on the taut peak of her breast, a little cry issued from her throat. She threw back her head and drowned in the fire created by their contact. Darkness ceased to exist and lights exploded beneath Tess's closed lids as his hand sought and found the juncture of her thighs. As his knee settled between them, Tess shivered with anticipation, his hands reverently gliding across her until he captured her hips and brought her forward.

A cry of pleasure mingled with a ripple of heat as she met and felt him sink deep into her welcoming body. The rocking rhythm reminded her of a primal dance that created heat, fire and scalding pleasure in every nerve ending in her body. She heard him growl, his hands tightening, gripping her by the shoulders, and she arched upward, drawing him as deeply as possible into herself. As they strained together, a powerful explosion rocked through Tess. She clung to Pete, her face pressed against his corded neck, and she felt the steel-cable tension within him snap.

With a groan, Pete relaxed and felt Tess's arms grow tight around his body. He held her against him, breathing raggedly, feeling the darkness turn into blinding, beautiful sunlight as the tidal wave of pleasure spread like soothing balm through him. Whatever fear and anguish had been left from the nightmare was burned up in the heat and desire of their love for each other. As Pete lay there for long moments afterward, sweat running in rivulets down his temple and along his jawline, he quivered. The beauty of Tess, of her loving heart and giving body had once again healed the wounds he still carried within him. Maybe the wounds were psychic, not physical, but it didn't matter.

As Pete weakly raised his head and pressed a kiss to her pouty, glistening lips, he whispered, "I love you, woman."

His words caressed Tess as she lay languidly in his embrace. "I know you do," she whispered raggedly, and lifted her hand to touch Pete's cheek, his beard prickly beneath her fingertips.

Pete reached over and turned out the light, plunging the room back into darkness except for the streetlight outside the hotel. Both of them had wanted to honeymoon in the Rocky Mountains in Colorado. Even in the tiny mountain town of Vail, streetlights reminded them of civilization. Picking up the sheet, Pete pulled it across them, then brought Tess back into his arms.

With a sigh, Tess snuggled against him. She was content to be held, kissed and touched. "I don't want this week to end," she murmured, resting her hand against his damp chest.

"Me neither."

She opened her eyes, allowing them to adjust to the darkness. "Your orders are for El Toro?" It was a Marine Corps air base near Los Angeles, California.

"Yes."

"I just worry they'll send you back to Vietnam if this war keeps escalating."

Pete snorted and kissed her hair. "No one's taking me away from you. I don't want to go back over to that mess."

Relief flowed through Tess. "How much time do you have left on your six-year obligation?"

"One year."

She licked her lips. "Will you sign back over?"

Pete heard the tremor in her voice. "If I do, I'll be sent back to Nam."

Fear jagged through Tess. "What will you do?"

"Find a job as a civilian chopper jockey."

Tess whispered, "Thank God...."

Pete propped himself up on his elbow. Tess's face was drawn with concern; real fear was mirrored in her eyes. "Honey, once is enough for you *and* me." He brushed several errant strands of hair off her wrinkled brow. "I've got an idea. A real off-the-wall idea, but I think it might work."

"What's that?"

"I was thinking of putting a sales pitch together for some of these big hospitals in the metropolitan area—trying to talk them into contracting me and a helicopter that I'll get a loan to buy once I get out of the corps. I can fly to the scenes of accidents and take the victims back for surgery. I got the idea in Nam with the guys who fly the medevac choppers. Time saves lives, Tess. I saw it happen so often."

Hope thrummed through Tess. Although Pete was proud to be a marine, she didn't want him to sign over again. Even though she would lovingly support whatever decision he made.

"That sounds wonderful!"

He shrugged. "I'm not sure, Tess. Maybe it's just a crazy idea." And then he grinned, some of his old cockiness resurfacing. "I gotta have some kind of job to support us. The way we're making love almost every night is gonna guarantee a baby in no time at all." He leaned down and pressed a warm, tender kiss to her lips. Smiling, he whispered, "Besides, you're going to make one hell of a great mother. I've just got that feeling."

Giggling as he captured her in his arms, Tess felt herself being rolled on top of him. Her hair flowed like a crimson waterfall across his chest as she opened her eyes and drowned in his happy gaze. "We've got each other, that's all that counts. And if a baby comes along, I wouldn't mind that, either."

"Gib and Dany can hardly wait until their baby is born." Pete slid his fingers through her hair in a gentle motion and grew sober. "I want that same kind of happiness for us, Tess. I know we can have it."

"We'll have to work for it just as we do now, Pete."

"I know that."

"We believe in each other. That's what really counts."

Whispering her name, Pete drew Tess down to kiss her long and hard. "From now on the only place I'm running is to your arms, honey. No more shadows on our lives. We've got a lot of wartime things to work through...."

"We'll do them—together," Tess whispered, resting her lips against his. "One day, one hour, at a time."

As Pete captured Tess and lost himself in the splendor of her welcoming kiss, he knew their internal wounds, their memory of Vietnam, would wane but never completely die. As he brought her to his side to make love to her once again, he prayed that their children would never have to experience war as they had. What had brought them out of it, what was helping to heal them, was their love for each other—forever.

*   *   *   *   *